Rodeo

Jaketa A. McClure

GIG

GIG Publishing

Benton, AR

For Kyree, James, & Jontae

Philippians 4:13 I can do all things through Christ who strengthens me.

Acknowledgments

First, I'd like to give thanks to God. Without Him, I wouldn't be here. Without Him, I wouldn't have the talents that I have. Without Him, I wouldn't have been able to write this book. Without Him, I am nothing. With Him...all things are possible. Glory to You. Thank You for everything.

To my wonderful children Kyree, James and Jontae. I'd like to thank you all as individuals and as a whole. I truly believe I wouldn't have pushed myself to work as hard if it hadn't been for you guys. You all have brought such great joy to me and so much laughter. You are great inspirations. Mommy loves you! ☺

To my parents, Anthony Zachary and Joann McClure, for having me and keeping me. I know I was made out of love. Mom, thanks for being so understanding throughout my life and for always believing in me. Love you two always.

To my late grandmother, Doris McClure. I don't know where I'd be without you. I thank you for your time, your love, your wisdom and so much more than I can name. I wish you could have seen my accomplishments here on earth, but I know you're still around. Even more, I know you're having fun with God. I love you.

I'd like to give a special thanks to my favorite auntie, Pauline McClure. Thank you for all those long nights of dancing and listening to music, especially our favorite, Sam Cooke. Thank you for you. Love you!

To Mr. and Mrs. Anthony and Barbara Watkins. To say that I am grateful for you is an understatement. You two are the best grandparents a child could ever have. Not to mention, the best people that the world could ever have. Even though, you're not my parents or my grandparents, I am blessed and thankful to know you. In the words of my grandmother, "Treat them good because they always been good to you." The song Thomas is singing with Ms. Rose is dedicated to you guys. Love you!

I'd like to give a special thanks to my spiritual mother, Mrs. Marion Lee Hawkins. I thank God for you from the depths of my soul. I'm so glad that He put you in my path. You have helped shape my life in such a great way and I will never forget you. Thank you for so much. You are wonderful. Love You!

I would like to thank family, friends and everyone who helped in any way throughout the making of this book. Enjoy!

Chapter 1

"*M*omma?"

Out the window, I saw the big moon shinin' bright, like it was before I went to sleep. It was still night time, so I laid back down on the floor. It was a lot of nights I woke up and momma was gone, so it didn't matter to me that she wasn't here now.

Bang! Bang!

That used to scare me a whole lot. I got so used to it, I fell asleep easy some nights. But sometimes, the police cars and gunshots was so loud, it had me and momma up almost all night.

I pulled the cover over my head. It smelled so nasty. I closed it tight, so no roaches could crawl on me. I sucked my thumb, thinkin' bout what it would be like when we moved out of these darn government projects, like momma always said. I never did know when momma would come back, but she was always there when I woke up in the mornin' time, so I went back to sleep.

A loud noise woke me up. I got up and looked out the window. I saw a big, trash truck, dumpin' trash.

Oh no. I'm wet.

I looked down at the pee stain on the big, white t-shirt I had on. Momma's gonna be mad if she see that I pissed on myself again. She always say, "If you piss on yourself, I'm gone beat yo' butt." But she didn't say "butt." She always said a lot of bad words when she talked.

I looked around the livin' room. Nothin' was in there, but the cover we was sleepin' on and a bunch of dirty clothes all over the floor. I started diggin' in the clothes. I found my favorite purple, baby doll dress. It was real dirty. It had food on it and dirt from when I was playin' outside. It was some kind of small, soft, green lookin' spot on it, but I just wiped it off. I looked at it and smiled. I found my purple socks and put them on too. I hated walkin' barefoot on these hard floors. Plus, I didn't wanna step on no nasty stuff either.

Wait a minute. It's mornin' time.

"Momma?"

I walked to the only room in the house. I didn't have to go in to see if she was in there cause it didn't have a door on it. It was just more dirty clothes in there. I looked in the bathroom, and in the kitchen but I still didn't see her.

"Momma?"

I said it louder this time.

Where is she? She always here in the mornin' time.

I went to sit back down on the cover. I didn't know what to do, so I laid down and fell back to sleep.

I don't know how long I was sleep. All I know is, there was still no momma. My stomach was hurtin'. I was so hungry. I went in the kitchen to open the refrigerator. All I saw was the rest of the Cheetos I was eatin' last night, so I ate them. I wish I would have saved more of them.

It was a big, white bucket in the kitchen that momma put water in for us to take a bath. I pulled it to the sink, so I could stand on it, to drink some water. Then, I went to sit back down on the cover. I heard some kids outside, so I looked out the window. There was a yellow school bus.

"The school bus is here. Where's momma?"

Momma always said when the school bus is lettin' the kids off, it's not mornin' time anymore.

"Momma?" I yelled.

"Momma?" I yelled louder.

Then, I started to cry. I couldn't help it. I didn't know where my momma was. I kept callin' her, but she never came. I cried until my head hurt. Then, I laid down and fell back to sleep.

I woke up when I heard somebody at the door. It was still light outside. I rubbed my eyes and smiled.

"Must be momma."

I scratched my head. I was ready for her to do my hair. It was so nappy, like momma always said. She couldn't even get a comb in it sometimes. Momma had some good hair. It was long and pretty, but she still had some crazy lookin' wigs on all the time. She had so many colors.

I sat there, waitin' for her to open the door. Then, I heard somebody talkin', but it wasn't momma. It was some men. It was a closet by me in the livin' room, so I ran in there to hide. I hid under some dirty covers.

I could see the men when they came in cause the door was broke, so it didn't close all the way. One of them was old, but the other one wasn't that old. I had seen the old man a lot of times before. One time, he told me his name was Mr. Ron. He was talkin' to the other man.

"Yep. Say they found her behind the dumpster out back."

"Dang forreal? When this happen Mr. Ron?"

"That was just bout, 3 somethin' this mornin'. Yep...one shot to the head."

"Dang that's messed up."

What happened? Why they in me and momma's house? And who they talkin' bout?

~ 5 ~

I watched them put our clothes in big trash bags. Then, they went in the other room to get the clothes out of there too. Mr. Ron told the other man, "Go get that cover up from over yonder."

When he picked up my cover, some roaches fell off of it. It was funny how he jumped when that happened.

"Roaches and stuff falling off the cover. Man, I don't see how people can live like this."

Mr. Ron walked up to him and said, "Son, when you suck on a pipe for a livin', you don't care how you live."

"Seriously?"

"Yep. She used to be all over the darn place. Been over to mine's a few times too."

Mr. Ron laughed real loud.

What was so funny?

"Yeah but, she got a lil' girl too."

"She do?"

"Yeah. I see her playin' out in the hallway sometimes. Mainly when her mammi done put her out cause she got company over."

"Well, where the little girl at now?"

"I reckon some of her family done come and got her already."

Mr. Ron was kickin' our clothes around while the other man was just standin' there. He looked like he was thinkin' bout somethin'. Then, he said, "You know how old she is?"

"Bout 7."

"Um, Um, Um, that's a shame. You know her name?"

"Hmmm, what-is-her-name? Darn it, I know it cause it was somethin' different. It sound like, Ro-Ro-Rodie or Ro-Rodia…"

"Rodeo? Like the jeep? Mr. Ron please tell me her momma didn't name her that."

"Well, she didn't say it like that. It was kinda fancy like."

"Oooh, Rodeo?"

"Yep that's the one. Rodeya or whatever you just said."

"Like Rodeo Drive? That's a famous street out in California."

That's my name. Why they talkin' bout me?

I was not gonna move cause I didn't know what they might do to me and momma always said men was real nasty and I should not trust them.

"Caliphonia? Hmph. Well son, this here Atlanta, G-A and it ain't nothin' famous bout that woman or the streets she been on. Anyways, let's go grab somethin' to eat. It ain't much in here but stuff that need to be put in the trash. We can get the rest out later."

I saw them leavin', but then, the other man stopped at the door and looked around. He said, "Yeah man, I hope lil' Rodeo be alright. That's messed up her momma got killed like that."

When they closed the door and locked it, I got up.

Killed? Is that what they said? Momma got killed? I hope that was not bout my momma. But my name is Rodeo and I am 7 years old. They was talkin' bout me. If momma was comin' back, why they in here takin' all our stuff? And how come she not back yet?

I started cryin' cause I couldn't help but think bout momma. I kept cryin' and cryin' and callin' for momma. She never came.

Why did somebody wanna kill my momma?

I laid down for a long time. Cryin' so much always made my head hurt real bad. My stomach was hurtin'. I was hungry. I heard somebody in the hallway, but they didn't stop at our door.

What if the men come back? This time they might look in the closet.

I didn't wanna leave, but momma got killed. She wasn't comin' back. I looked all over for my play shoes. I couldn't find them. The men must of took my shoes. I looked down at my socks. They was already dirty, so I didn't care if I had shoes on.

When I looked out the door, I saw some boys in the hallway playin' with some dice. It was always a lot of them with so much money on the floor. I snuck down the hallway, out the other door. I hated that hallway. It always smelled like piss, like momma always said.

I ran fast around to the side of the big, brown buildin'. It was some light outside, but night time was comin'. I sat down on the ground by a big dumpster.

Where can I go?

I didn't know nobody but momma. Every time I thought bout her, I couldn't help but cry. I didn't even get to see her before she left. I felt tears comin' again.

"I want my momma."

I heard somethin' movin' in the dumpster. I knew what that sound was. It was that squeaky noise I heard in me and momma house at night. It was rats. I had to get far away from there. I got up and ran fast away from the place me and momma used to live.

I didn't run long cause my legs got tired, but the place I was at now looked like the place I had just left. It was a lot of trash and stuff on the ground. It was no grass, just dirt and big, brown buildin's. I was standin' in front of a long, dark alley. I didn't wanna go in there, but I knew I could hide somewhere in it. I startin' walkin' real slow. Then, I stopped by a dumpster. It was a lot of boxes, trash and clothes by it. I always saw people by my house sleepin' on stuff like this, so it must not be too bad.

I was bout to sit down, but then, the stuff moved and I heard a noise come from it. Somebody was sleepin' under the stuff. I started to run, but then, I saw a burger. I knew it was one cause it was wrapped up in some Wendy's paper. Sometimes, when one of momma's man friends came over, he brought me a Wendy's burger. I was glad when he did cause sometimes that was all I had to eat all day.

I wanted that burger, but it was between all that stuff and the dumpster. I rubbed my stomach cause it was hurtin' real bad. I know it was bad to steal, but I was hungry. I had to try. I stepped on the stuff real soft. Then, the person under it moved again.

Maybe, I should do it real fast and run. That way, if they wake up, they won't catch me.

I was real scared, but I was real hungry too. I took one more step. Then, I grabbed the burger. I ran so fast I know they didn't see me. I heard somebody yellin', "Hey! Come back here with my darn burger!" It sounded like a old man, but I didn't look back, I just kept runnin'.

I ran for a real long time. I didn't wanna stop cause I didn't know if somebody was gonna come after me. I just wanted to get somewhere else so I could eat the burger. When I did slow down, I didn't know where I was. It was grass everywhere I looked. I couldn't see that much cause it was night time, but I could see some street lights a long way in front of me. So, I walked that way.

I ate the burger while I was walkin'. It was cold, but I didn't care cause it was good to me. I started thinkin' bout momma.

I wonder who killed her? Why they do that? It's not fair. Now what am I gonna do?

"What is that?"

The closer I got to where the street lights was, I could tell it was somethin' big up there. I ran to get closer to it.

"Whoa."

It was a big train, but it wasn't movin'. It was just sittin' there on the train tracks. I walked pass all the train car things. Then, I saw one where the door was open. I saw people on TV jumpin' in trains like this all the time. They always be sleepin' in them, so this is where I was gonna sleep.

It was so high up, I had to run and jump a lot of times just to get on it. I didn't see a lot of stuff on it. Just a bunch of long, wood boxes. Some was sittin' on top of each other. They was all covered up. I looked in one and it was nothin' in it. I looked at the grass and the night time all around me.

"I ain't got nowhere to go."

I climbed in the box and laid down. I fit in it just right, like the three little bears. I'm glad it wasn't that cold cause I didn't have no cover.

I miss my cover. I miss my shoes too. Momma.

Oh, no. Here come the tears. I couldn't help it. I just didn't know why this happened to her. I didn't know why this happened to *me*. I'm the one who don't got a momma no more. I cried and cried until I fell asleep.

Chapter 2

I was dreamin' bout momma. It was nothin' but night time around us. We was runnin' cause some dogs was chasin' us. No matter how fast we ran, they kept gettin' real close. Then, the dog got so close and loud, I thought it was real.

"Aaaarrrgh!"

I screamed so loud when I opened my eyes cause it really was a dog barkin' at me. He was one of them dogs I always seen where me and momma was livin'. Momma always called them kind of dogs Pits. I just laid there screamin'.

"Hey dad, you might wanna come see this."

The dog was so big, black and scary. I didn't even see the man that was standin' by the dog until he said somethin'. I just kept screamin'.

"Get on away from here Rocky! Go on now, git!"

The dog ran and jumped off the train. I was so scared, I was still screamin'. Really cause, now it was two men standin' there lookin' at me and they was white.

"Look what Rocky found."

That's what the man with the bald head said. After a little while, I stopped screamin' cause it was making my head hurt. I was so scared, I was shakin'. Momma always said white people evil cause they did black people wrong. One of them was real old, with some short, white hair. The other one, with the bald head, wasn't that old. They was both dressed like old McDonald who had a farm.

The old man with the white hair said, "Well, hello there sweetie. It's okay, hush now."

He was bout to rub my nappy head, but I moved away from him, so he couldn't touch me. The bald-headed man rolled his eyes and said, "Dad, you take care of this. I'm gone finish loadin' the coal."

He left, but the old man stayed and sat down in front of me. I was still scared, but I wasn't shakin' no more. He was just starin' at me. I was thinkin' he must be crazy and then, he smiled.

"You've got some of the prettiest, big, brown eyes I have ever seen."

Was he talkin' bout me?

I just put my head down.

"And your skin…" He put his hand under my chin and made me look up, "It's so smooth and pretty, like caramel. You're beautiful."

Beautiful? Now I know he was crazy. Momma never said I was beautiful.

"What's your name, pretty girl?"

I didn't say nothin'. I just looked at him. To me, he looked like Wendy's daddy, Dave, but he didn't have no glasses. One time, I told momma I wish I had a daddy who named a burger place after me. I said her daddy must really love her. Momma said, "You was named after somethin', but it was for another reason," whatever that mean.

He sounded nice to me. He didn't sound like that other bald-headed man. That other man talked real country. This white man didn't look mean. He looked nice, just like Dave. So, I told him my name.

"Rodeo."

He smiled and said, "Rodeo. Like Rodeo Drive. That's such a nice name. It's different too. How did you get all the way out here by yourself?"

I just looked down. He put his hand under my chin and made me look up again.

"Where do you live?"

I still didn't say nothin'.

"What's your momma's name, sweetie?"

What's my momma's name?

Nobody never asked me that before. I just told him what I always call her.

"Um, momma?"

He just looked at me. Then, he said, "Where is your momma?"

I didn't say nothin' at first cause I didn't know where she was, but I did know what happened to her. I said, "M-momma...momma got killed."

His eyes got real big. Then, he closed them and put his head down. He didn't say nothin' for a long time. I thought he had went to sleep, but then, he got up. He put his hand out and smiled and said, "Come on, sweetie. Come with me."

I don't know why I wasn't scared of him. He looked like a nice man, so I grabbed his hand and he helped me out of the box. Then, he helped me off the train and carried me in his arms. I looked at the sky. It was turnin' blue, like it was mornin' time, but I still saw the moon too.

I didn't know where we was goin', but when we got around to the front of the train, I saw a big, white house. It had a big yard with some nice grass and flowers. It had two nice cars in a driveway that was made like a big circle around the yard. I thought it was a business place or the house that the president stay in. I asked him, "Is this the president house?"

He laughed and said, "No sweetie, this is my house."

He put me down when we got to the mailbox. He pointed to some red letters on the big, brick mailbox and said, "Look. Do you know what those letters are?"

I looked at the red letters. I know I had seen them on Sesame Street, but I couldn't remember what it was, so I just didn't say nothin'.

"Do you know any of these letters?"

I shook my head.

"How old are you?"

"7."

"Hmph," he said, "We've got a lot of work to do."

He pointed to the letters and said, "This is a D-O-N-O-V-A-N. That spells Donovan."

He put his hand out like people do when they wanna shake yours.

"My name is Thomas Donovan. It's a pleasure to meet you Miss Rodeo…what's your last name?"

Now, I did know that. It was, "Turner."

He smiled and said, "Well, it's a pleasure to meet you Miss Rodeo Turner. He picked me up and carried me in the house. I had seen houses like this before on TV, but I had never been in one. I thought he must be rich or somethin'.

He put me down by the front door. The walls and floor was so white and clean, I didn't wanna move and get nothin' dirty. The old white man, I mean, Thomas Donovan, was walkin' around like he was lookin' for somebody. Then, he yelled, "Rose."

Some old, white lady came out of another room. She had on some of them black and white clothes like the maids wear on TV. Her black and white hair was in a nice, ball lookin' ponytail.

"Oh, Thomas. I went looking for you out by the trains. I wanted to tell you about the…" She stopped talkin' when she saw me and said, "Oh, well, who do we have here?"

Thomas Donovan smiled and came to where I was. He put his hand on my back and we went up to the lady.

"This here, is Miss Rodeo Turner. Rodeo, this is Ms. Rose."

The lady smiled and said, "Well, hello there, Rodeo. Such a pretty name."

She sounded nice. Just like a sweet, old grandma. I know I was supposed to say somethin' back, but I was scared cause I still didn't know what was goin' on. I just waved my hand. She smiled at me. Then, she looked at Thomas Donovan like she didn't know what was goin' on, just like me.

"I'll talk to you about it later," he said. "For now, could you please do me a favor? Get her cleaned up for me. Then, take her to get some things and get her hair done. Would you, please?"

She looked at me, then, back to him and said, "Of course, I will."

He got down on one of his knees, so he could be my size. He looked at me and said, "Rodeo, Ms. Rose is going to take you with her for a little while. You don't have to be afraid because she is a very nice lady. Okay?"

He looked at her and they smiled at each other. He smiled a lot. It made me smile a little bit. He was a nice man. If he said she was nice, she must be. I said, "Okay."

Ms. Rose really was the most nice lady I ever met before. We had been gone for a long time and we had just got back to the house. Ms. Rose took me around the house to show me where stuff was. I saw the nice, big kitchen and some other rooms, but it was so many, I can't remember what they was called.

She told me the other man name Richie, stayed in the basement, but we didn't go to his room. She showed me where Thomas Donovan room was and she showed me where her room was. Now, I was across the hall, from her room, in somethin' called the guest room. It was nice, like it was already somebody room. The covers on the big bed, the dressers and the floor was white. It had a nice, big TV in there and some nice, flower pictures on the yellow wall.

Ms. Rose had got me a bunch of movies. I was watchin' Cinderella. I always liked that movie. The door opened. It was Thomas Donovan. He was lookin' like he had never seen me before. Like he forgot I was at his house or somethin'.

"Wow," he said.

He came over to where I was and sat down on the bed.

"You look amazing, dear."

Deer? I ain't no deer.

I didn't say nothin' cause I still thought he was crazy. Specially cause he got me all this stuff. But I was happy. Ms. Rose got me so many purple clothes, but only cause I asked her to. I got some pretty shoes too and some Barbie dolls to play with.

"Your hair is so pretty and I love that dress on you."

I smiled cause I liked my hair and my dress too. My purple dress was kind a like the dirty one I had at first and I had baby doll curls all over my head. The lady at the hair place did it so good, it wasn't even nappy no more. I know momma would have been happy to see it.

"Did you have fun today?"

I smiled and said, "Yes," cause I really did. But then, I got sad cause I didn't know where he was gonna take me now.

He said, "What's wrong?"

"When I leave, can I take that?"

He looked around and said, "What?"

"I'm talkin' bout the Cinderella movie."

"Sweetie, we definitely have to work on your vocabulary. I apologize," he laughed, "I used to be an English teacher."

He started tellin' me bout some of the words I say. Like words that have a 'ing' on the end of it, but I don't make the 'g' sound.

"But we shall get into more of that later," he said. "And of course, you can take the movie, but may I ask, do you have somewhere to go, Rodeo?"

I just looked around cause I didn't have nowhere to go.

"Do you know where your grandparents or your father lives?"

I didn't say nothin' again cause I didn't even know them.

He said, "Well, I was thinking, maybe you could stay here with me."

Ooohh I would love that.

~ 23 ~

"But, what about in the mornin' time? Where you gonna take me then?"

He smiled and said, "Well, actually, I was asking if you would like to live here with me. I mean, since you don't have anywhere else to go."

Uh oh. Now I know he crazy. He might try to do somethin' bad to me. Why this white man want me to stay with him?

I guess he could tell I thought he was crazy cause he said, "You probably think I'm crazy, huh?" He laughed. "Well, sweetie, this old, white man's not crazy. I just know God and when I know He's telling me to do something, I do it."

God? Who is that? He must be crazy too cause he don't know me either.

He was bout to say somethin', but he stopped. He looked at me and said, "Rodeo? Do you know who God is?"

"Uumm, that's your friend?"

"Well…yes. But He's a different kind of friend. In fact, He's the best friend I have. So, you've never heard of Him?"

I shook my head.

"Hmph. Well, I'll definitely have to tell you all about Him, but first, would you like to live with me, Rodeo?"

I don't know why I was even thinkin' bout it cause I didn't have nowhere to go. Plus, him and Ms. Rose was already actin' so nice to me. They did more than momma ever did, in just a little bit of time. So, I said, "Yes."

He smiled and said, "Good."

I don't know what Ms. Rose had cooked, but it smelled real good. Me and Thomas Donovan was in, what he said was the "dining room." I looked around and saw two of those big glass things that rich people keep nice dishes in. I was tryin' not to stare at Thomas Donovan, but I had never seen a man in pajamas before. They was light blue and nice lookin' too.

I had on my new, Snow White pajamas and we was sittin' at this long, brown table that had 10, nice, brown chairs around it. He was lookin' at some newspapers and I was watchin' Ms. Rose.

She was goin' in and out of the dining room to the kitchen. Every time she came back, she put some different kind of food on the table. It was already some green beans and biscuits on the table. Now, she just put some fried chicken on it and it looked real good. Then, she went back to the kitchen. I was thinkin', what is she gonna bring out next?

I was hungry, but not that much cause I had already ate two times. I was thinkin', do we eat like this every day?

"Thomas Donovan?"

He looked like I surprised him. Then, he laughed. He said, "Sweetie, you don't have to call me that. Although, I'm glad you remembered my name. You can just call me, Tom."

"Okay. Um, Tom? Do we eat like this all the time?"

"What do you mean?"

"Like, how we ate two times already and we bout to eat again. That's three times in one day."

"First things first Rodeo, *bout* is not a word, at least, not the way you're using it. It's *about*, but we will get to all of that later. Now, even though, I know not everyone is able to do it, eating three times a day is something that everyone *should* do. First you eat your breakfast, like you did before you went to get your hair done. Then, you eat lunch, you know, something to keep you from starving while waiting for dinner time. Then, after that, you eat dinner. Did your momma feed you three times a day?"

I shook my head and said, "Uh-uh, never. Sometimes I didn't eat one time a day."

He looked at me for a while. Then, he said, "Hmph."

I wonder why he always make that noise?

I asked him, "Why you always make that noise?"

"What noise?"

"That 'hmph' noise?"

"Oh," he laughed. "Well, I guess it's just a habit. I do that a lot when I'm thinking about something."

"What's a habit?"

"A habit is something that's done repeatedly or on a regular basis. A person can do something so much, they get to the point where they're doing things almost automatically. Even without realizing they are doing it. Just like the noise I make, I've been doing it for so long, I'm usually unaware of when I'm doing it. Unaware, meaning, I don't know I'm doing it. Do you understand what I'm saying?"

"Is it like on Sesame Street how Cookie Monster always eat cookies?"

"Well, that's a good way to look at it. He loves cookies and he's been eating them for so long, that's all he eats without even thinking about it. I knew you were a smart girl."

I just smiled.

"You learned a lot from watching TV, didn't you Rodeo?"

"Yes, but one day momma took it cause she said she didn't have no money, so I couldn't watch it no more."

He was bout, I mean, about to say somethin', but then, Ms. Rose came back. She put a white bowl, with some mashed potatoes in it and a pie, on the table. I didn't know what kind of pie it was, but I couldn't wait to eat it. She must have saw how I was lookin' at the pie cause she said, "Rodeo, do you like peach cobbler?"

I said, "I don't remember if I had that before."

She looked at Tom. He just smiled and said, "I'm pretty sure Rodeo will have a lot of first-time experiences here with us."

She smiled and said, "Well, I guess we could go ahead and eat unless…" She looked around and said, "Do you know if Richie will be joining us for dinner?"

Tom threw his hand like momma used to do when she said, "Child hush."

"No," he said. "Let's go ahead and eat."

Ms. Rose moved all the newspapers Tom was lookin' at. Then, she fixed the plates. When she was finished, she sat in the chair next to Tom, across from me.

"Now," Tom said, "Let's bow our heads and thank God for the food we are about to eat."

I was thinkin', why is he thankin' his friend for this food, cause I thought Ms. Rose made it. I was gonna ask him that, but then, we heard somebody come in the door. It was that bald-headed man, Richie.

He said, "Um, Umm, somethin' smells good. I see y'all done started dinner without…"

He stopped talkin' when he saw me.

It seem like everybody stop talkin' every time they see me.

"Well," he laughed a little bit and then, he went to stand by Tom. "What's goin' on dad?"

I was eatin', but I could see him lookin' at me.

"Nothing's going on. We're eating dinner," Tom said.

He laughed a little bit again. He had his hands in his pockets and he was rockin' on his feet like a rockin' chair.

"Come on dad."

Tom looked at him. Then, Richie looked at me.

"Oh, well, we've added a new edition to the family. This is Rodeo. Rodeo, you remember my son Richie from this morning, right?"

"Yes," I said.

Richie was standin' there lookin' around at everybody.

Tom said, "Have a seat and eat Richie. I'll talk to you later."

Then, Richie shook his head. He fixed his food, then, he went to sit at the other end of the table. Far away from us.

"Dad, we gotta get that coal to Missouri by Wednesday mornin'. They say we gotta be there by 7 am."

"Well, we'll just have to leave a little after dinner tomorrow night. Did you and the others finish loading the trains?"

"Course we did."

I didn't know what they was talkin' bout...about. I just finished eatin' my food. Ms. Rose took me to the guest room I was sleepin' in, after I said goodnight to Tom. I told her I wanted to watch Cinderella again. So, she put that in the DVD player. While I was watchin' it, I started thinkin' bout...about momma. I don't know what we would've been doin' if I was at home right now, but I know momma would've really liked it here.

"Momma."

I don't know how long I was gonna keep thinkin' about her. I wanted to stop cause every time I did, I started cryin'...like now. I guess I just missed her a lot. I laid in the bed cryin', til I fell asleep.

I don't know what time it was when I woke up, but I could see the sun shinin' in the window. I looked around cause I almost forgot where I was.

Uh, oh.

I got up real fast. I looked under the covers and I saw a big pee spot in the bed. I got scared cause I messed up the nice bed and covers. I started lookin' around for some clothes. Then, I heard the door open. It was Tom. He had scared me and made me jump. When he turned on the light he said, "I'm sorry. Did I scare you?"

"I-I pissed on myself. I'm sorry."

He looked at the big pee stain on the bed.

"Oh sweetie."

He started walkin' over to me, but he was laughin'. He got on his knee and said, "It's okay Rodeo. I guess we will just have to make sure you use the bathroom before you go to sleep."

He started laughin' again. Then, said, "I don't mean to laugh, but please, don't say 'pissed'. Young ladies shouldn't say that. Or women, in my opinion. It doesn't sound all that nice. Say, I wet myself. Okay?"

"Okay."

Tom sure was nice. I was so scared at first. I thought he was gonna whoop me cause momma would of tore my butt up.

"Now, you just wait here while I go get Rose for you."

After I got finished takin' a bath, all of us, except Richie, ate breakfast. Then, me and Tom sat on the porch together.

The porch was real big. It had glass all around us. Tom turned some wheel on the wall that made the windows on the ceilin' open up, so the sun could shine in. He was sittin' in a rockin' chair and I was sittin' on the floor playin' with my Barbie dolls.

"Rodeo, tomorrow I am going to start teaching you at home, okay?"

"You mean, like I'm in school, but you gonna teach me here at the house?"

He nodded his head.

"It's called home school. We are going to work on that vocabulary of yours. I'm going to teach you everything you need to know. Have you ever been to school?"

I made sure I talked a little slow, cause I didn't want to mess up my words.

"I went for one day one time, but then, momma forgot to come get me from school and the people had called the police on her, so she never took me back. She was real mad too."

"Did she get mad a lot?"

"Uh huh."

We was on the porch for a long time talkin' about a lot of stuff. Every time I said somethin' wrong, he stopped me and told me the right way to say it. I told him how momma used to have so many men comin', I mean, coming over and how she used to make me sit in the hallway a lot.

I even told him bout…about the time momma beat me so bad cause, I mean, because I threw some white stuff she had laying on a piece of paper away. I told her I was hungry and I thought it was some rice, but when I bit it, it was real hard and nasty.

I told him a lot of stuff and the most he said was, "Hmph." I guess he was thinking. He had told me how Richie was his only son. He said he wanted some more kids, but before he could, his wife died because she was real sick. I liked talking to him and I could tell he liked talking to me too.

❀

We started sitting on the porch almost every day after he taught me my school stuff. We would get up and eat breakfast. Then, I would put on my clothes, just like I was going to school and we would sit in his office and he would teach me stuff. Tom was real smart. He knew everything. I started calling him "My Dave," but I never told him that.

One day, we had went to this business place and My Dave got all my stuff to find out who I was. He said he knew a lot of people and he was going to get my birth certificate. He said he knew it would be easy to find because he had never met anybody with the name Rodeo.

I'm glad he did because I didn't even know when my birthday was. We found out it was September 27th and I was born in 1995. My Dave said it was about to be April, so I have to wait a little while before my birthday comes. Rodeo Julia Turner. That was my whole name. Momma's name...Teresa Turner. Now it make sense why people called her TT all the time. At least now...I know her name.

Chapter 3

Today was my birthday. I didn't know nobody, so it was just me, Ms. Rose, My Dave, Richie and his friend Danny. Ms. Rose had fixed the porch up real nice with balloons and stuff. I had a nice, round Cinderella cake, ice cream and presents. I didn't care if I didn't have no friends. I never even had a birthday that I can remember, so I was real happy. I had turned 8 years old.

I had on some pink pants and a pink shirt with a Barbie doll on it. I had picked it out the other day when me and Ms. Rose went to the store to get me something nice to wear for my birthday. This morning, Ms. Rose took me to get my hair did in my favorite baby doll curls. When we got back home, she gave me some black, furry looking boots for my birthday. I loved them so much, I was going wear them all day.

After everybody had finish singing happy birthday to me, we all ate cake and ice cream together. Now, I was in the family room playing with my new toys. I got a lot of dolls and a new pink car for me to drive them in. I got some other stuff too, like a little computer learning thing, some movies and some clothes. Daddy even got me some little diamond earrings.

Ms. Rose was cleaning up now, like she always do. My Dave was sitting at the kitchen table, looking at the newspaper, like he always do. I started thinking about what me and My Dave was talking about when we was on the porch, after we found out when my birthday was. He said...

"Rodeo?"

"Yes?"

"Do you know what an adoption is?"

"Annadoption?"

"Adoption. Have you ever heard of it?"

"Oh, um, no."

"Well, it's when a person voluntarily accepts a child as their own. It's like, the child has their real birth parents, but someone else wants to take that child and raise them as their child. You have to go through the legal system to make it official, but they make that child a part of their family. Permanently. Forever. Let me put it to you like this. I would love to make you my daughter. My little girl. Forever. Then, you can live with me until you grow into a woman, get your own house, and do great things. Even when you are a grown up, you will still be my daughter. Of course, that's only if you say you want to be my daughter."

I loved everything I got, but the very best part about my birthday, was when My Dave told me that he had adopted me. He said that made me his daughter now and he was my daddy. He even told me I could call him daddy if I wanted to. I forgot he said that. He said he wasn't going to change my last name because he wanted me to keep that part of who I was. All I thought about was how everything would be from now on.

I got up to look out the window because I heard Richie and Danny laughing outside. They was so loud. Danny talked real country just like Richie. They was sitting on the side of the house, on some chairs, drinking beer. Richie was letting Rocky lick on his face. He always let him do that. I liked Rocky, but I didn't like him that much. Maybe because he wasn't my dog.

Danny said, "Aye Richie. Why didn't ya get ya lil' sister something for her birthday?" Then, he laughed real loud.

"That ain't my darn sister."

Richie spit that nasty looking stuff out of his mouth. One time, I asked daddy, "What's that brown stuff Richie be putting in his mouth all the time." He called it dip. I didn't know what he was talking about. I just guessed he called it that because he have to dip his fingers in it, so he can get some out.

"I tell ya, I don't know what's wrong with my dad. He probably gone crazy. What was he thinkin' bout, adoptin' a lil nigger girl like that? I mean, who does stuff like that?"

Danny burped loud and said, "Well, I can tell yo' daddy really loves her. I mean, he got to for him to do somethin' like that."

"Well, I don't like or love her and she ain't none of my darn sister. She just done lucked up and found her a soft, old, white man, that's all."

"I bet your dad gone treat her just like she his real daughter and leave her some money when he gone too."

"Count on it bein' a cold day in hell before I let that happen."

He spit again.

I was listening to everything they was saying. I didn't care if Richie didn't liked me. The only person that mattered to me was my daddy. Plus, I didn't like him either with his ugly, bald-headed self.

One day, me and daddy was sitting on the porch. We had just got back home from church and now we was getting ready to go to the store. Ms. Rose said she had to get some stuff to cook, because Thanksgiving was coming in a few days. Daddy didn't go to church all the time, but he always said he tried to. Plus, every time we stayed home, we would read something out of the bible.

Daddy had got me my own little, pink bible. He said he was going to show me some stuff to remember. The other Sunday, we was reading about the children of Israel. That was so amazing how God made the water move, so they could walk across the sea. Then, he made it go back when the bad men tried to come after them and they drowned in the water. I was thinking, God must really be something amazing to do something like that.

I was glad we didn't go to church all the time because they didn't have no kids and it was boring. Everybody was real old too. But daddy always said God knows your heart. Plus, he was always giving money to somebody and always helping people. I think he was being a good friend to that man he always talk about. He said when I get older, I will understand a lot more about God. But he always telling me God love me. I was about to ask him where his friend was so I can talk to him, but then, Ms. Rose came out the house.

"Okay, I'm ready."

It always seemed like Ms. Rose was always wearing her black and white clothes. I guess that's what she had to wear while she was cleaning and cooking. Daddy got up and started walking and I followed behind him.

I liked riding in daddy cars. He had one that was black, and you can have a roof on it or you can make the roof disappear. We didn't ride in that one that much because only two people could get in it. He said it was called a con...convernible, or something like that. A lot of the time we was in his blue car. It was real nice. I didn't know what kind of car it was, but when I was learning my ABC's, it helped me remember 3 letters real good. They was everywhere. BMW. The car talked too, and it had a little TV that show a whole bunch of stuff. I liked when daddy opened the little window in the top of the car, because then, I could see the sky. That's the one we was in now.

Me and daddy was holding hands when we walked in the grocery store. Ms. Rose was on the other side of daddy. I saw this tall, skinny man looking at us. He had on some black pants and a red shirt. He started walking to where we was.

The man said, "I apologize, Sir. Is she lost? I can call it over the intercom. Sorry for the trouble."

"Oh, no," Daddy laughed. "No, this is my daughter. Thank you."

The man was just standing there looking at us. I don't know if he believed him or not. Daddy didn't say nothing. He just started walking again. It seemed like people was always looking at us. Most of the time, Ms. Rose went to get the groceries by herself, but when we did come together, some people just stared at us. I was thinking, I was going to ask daddy about that.

When we got back, me and daddy was sitting on the porch. He was looking at his newspaper and I was eating my ice cream I had got from the store.

"Daddy?"

"Yes, sweetie?"

"Why do people stare at us sometimes when we in some places together?"

He smiled. Then, he looked kind of sad.

"Rodeo, some people may not like you if you don't look like them. Not everyone is like that. Still, some people just don't have the spirit of God in them. Try not to worry about that, okay? You are you for a reason and you are here for a reason."

"Do you worry about it?"

"Rodeo, as you get older, you are going to see and hear a lot of things. Don't worry about the bad things a person has to say about you. Know who you are. Know that Jesus loves you and you can do all things with Him."

We was on the porch for a long time talking. I could tell he had so much to say, but he kept saying he didn't want to tell me too much right now. He just kept saying, when I'm older I will understand things better. I didn't know what he was saying about God living in me. I was gonna ask him, but I waited because I was ready to go watch the movie Ms. Rose had bought me called *Beauty and The Beast*.

I never even thought Ms. Rose and daddy knew other people. It was Thanksgiving and Ms. Betty was there visiting

Ms. Rose. They was sisters. Ms. Rose said all her other family was living in a place called Ohio.

Even daddy had some people over. One man almost looked just like daddy, but he had more hair and it was kind of yellow. Another man was there too. He was real skinny. His hair was black and came down to his shoulders. Daddy said both of them was his brothers.

I had forgot he told me he had two brothers. One of them was named Paul and the skinny man was named Richard. Daddy was the oldest. They talked to me and they made me laugh a lot. They was nice.

"Oh, excuse me, sweetie."

Ms. Betty bumped into me a little bit. It seem like she was a nice lady. She was big too and real short. It was funny because she was wobbling every time she walked and her curly, brown hair bounced everywhere. I went to sit down next to daddy, because all of us was getting ready to eat.

Anything Ms. Rose cooked was good. We had so many pies and cookies, I didn't know what I wanted. The turkey and the ham was so good. I like how the dressing tasted and this stuff called cranberry sauce. I had never had none of that before. I had some cornbread and macaroni and cheese too. Everything was good.

After a while, daddy stood up and said, "Hello everyone. I would like to thank you all for coming out to celebrate Thanksgiving with us."

Daddy said I was gonna have to wait a little while before I eat my dessert because he wanted to show me something.

"As you know, we have added a new addition to this family, and I have one more addition I would like to add for Rodeo."

Daddy looked at me. I was smiling so much.

"You got something for me, Daddy?"

"Yes. Follow me into the family room."

We all got up from the table and followed my daddy. When we got in there, he went in this big closet that he always hang coats in. When he came out, he was holding some big thing with a white sheet over it. He sat it down and said, "Rodeo, come take the sheet off."

I didn't know what it was, but then, I heard some noises coming from it. I ran over to it and pulled the sheet off. I started jumping up and down because I was so happy.

"Thank you, Daddy. I knew it was a dog, I knew it!"

I ran over to him and I hugged him.

"I love you daddy."

"I love you too, sweetie."

I opened the cage and let the dog come out. It was so small. It almost looked like a toy. It had white fur, with brown spots on it.

He was smiling at me when I looked at him and I asked, "Is it a boy or a girl, Daddy?"

"Oh, it's a girl and it's called a Toy Poodle."

I picked her up and hugged her. I loved the way her fur felt. She was so soft.

"Well," Daddy said, "I guess we can all eat some dessert now."

When everybody got dessert, they came back in the family room to eat. I had to eat mines at the table, but I ate really fast so I could play with Fancy. That's what I named my dog. When I went back in the family room, everybody was eating and talking. I was playing with my dog. My daddy had gave me a ball to roll to the dog. Every time I threw the ball, Fancy brought it back to me. The next time I rolled it too far and it went under the sofa. I was laughing at Fancy. She was trying to squeeze under that sofa to get the ball.

I was about to ask daddy to get the ball for me. Then, I saw Richie looking at Fancy. He didn't see me looking at him. He was looking so mean at her. Sitting there, holding his beer in his hand. He looked up at me. I just turned my head. I got my dog and went to play on the porch.

When I laid down to go to bed that night, I was thinking about daddy. I know he wished I had someone else to play with sometimes, because the other day, when we was on the porch, he said, "I wish you had someone else to play with sometimes." It didn't matter to me, though. I had fun with Fancy and everybody who was around me.

I sat up in the bed to make sure she was still laying at the bottom of it. She looked like she was sleep. I was glad to have her. I laid back down and closed my eyes. After that night, Fancy stayed in my bed every night.

Chapter 4

"**R**odeo, I've got good news."

When daddy came in my room, he had on some of those blue things he wear when he works called overalls. I called them his Old McDonalds clothes. I was already up, playing with Fancy. He walked to where I was and sat down on my bed. Daddy rubbed on Fancy and said, "You like her, huh?"

"Yes, I do."

He smiled at me. Then, he said, "Rodeo, I have to leave for a little while, so I'll be gone almost all day. Richie and I have to travel to Chicago. There was a mix up in some scheduling, so…"

I started thinking about how he was always telling me about his work stuff, but I never understood what he was talking about. I always just smiled and said, "Ok, Daddy."

"You always understand. You're so smart. Oh yes, speaking of smart," he stood up, "The main reason I came in here was to tell you that you will not have school today. If you need anything, Ms. Rose will be here. You two take care of each other."

I like the stuff daddy was teaching me, but I was glad I didn't have school today.

"We will daddy. And Fancy can protect us too."

He smiled and said, "You hear that Fancy? You've got a job to do. Don't let anything happen to my two, favorite girls."

I laughed. He kissed me on my head and told me he loved me. Before he went out, he said, "Oh, yes. What should we always remember?"

I knew what he wanted me to say, because he made me say the scripture every morning.

I smiled and said, "I can do all things through Christ who strengthens me. Philippians 4:13."

Daddy winked at me. Then, he left.

I liked Ms. Rose. We didn't talk a lot, but I guess we talked enough. She was always so nice to me. After daddy left, me and Ms. Rose ate some breakfast. She told me we was going to get dressed and do a little shopping. We had to go to the market because Ms. Rose said she was going to fix a special dinner for daddy. I was thinking, what could be so special? She always fixed good stuff for dinner.

Ms. Rose didn't have on her black and white today. She had on a pretty yellow dress, but nobody could see it because she had on a long, black coat. Both of us had on our black boots. My coat was purple, but my sweater and pants was black. I was glad she put that on me because it was cold outside.

We went in this store that had so many rings and watches and necklaces everywhere. Everything was shining. When Ms. Rose was looking at one of the watches, a white lady came over to where we was and said, "Hello, how may I help you today?"

She looked just like one of those ladies I see on TV, who always smiling and giving people they food and stuff on the airplanes.

"Oh, hello. I was looking for a particular Rolex that you all carry. It's called a Yatch-Master."

"Ah, yes. Nice," the lady said. "We have that one right over here. Please, follow me."

We all went to another part in the store and looked at some watches. The lady took out a watch and gave it to Ms. Rose. She looked at it and smiled.

"Yes. This is the one. I'll take it."

"Yes ma'am. Would you like that as a gift? I could put it in a gift box for you, if you'd like?"

"I would like that," Ms. Rose said.

"Yes ma'am. I'll be right back."

The lady went somewhere in the back of the store. When she came back, she had the watch in a nice gold and red box. We walked to the cash register and Ms. Rose said, "How much will that be?"

"That will be $12,052."

Ms. Rose gave the lady a card and she swiped it. I said, "Whoa. That's a lot."

Ms. Rose smiled and said, "Hey, it's a special gift for a special person."

I don't know who was that special. I just thought she was buying it for somebody for Christmas. I asked her, "Who you talking about, Ms. Rose?"

She looked at me and said, "Oh. You know it's Thomas' birthday today, don't you?"

Today is daddy's birthday? I didn't know that.

"You didn't know?"

I just shook my head. I knew what the date was because daddy made me tell him every morning. It was December 22. Today was daddy's birthday.

"Hmmm, well, if you'd like, you can pick him out something too."

I smiled because I really did want to get daddy something. After I looked around, I picked out a nice, gold ring with some diamonds in it. Ms. Rose got the lady to put that in a box just like the one for the watch, but it was smaller. I heard the lady say that one was $620. I said, "Ms. Rose, you want to pay all that money?"

"Well, it's not too much. Not when it comes to Thomas, anyway."

I smiled and said, "Now I see why he love you so much."

She looked at me kind of strange and said, "Why do you say that, Rodeo?"

"Well, when he was leaving, he said we was his favorite girls, so I thought it was because he love us so much. Plus, we the only girls there."

Ms. Rose didn't say nothing, she just smiled. It seem like that made her happy because every time I looked at her, she was smiling.

That night, after daddy got back, we was all sitting at the table, including Richie. He really liked the gifts we got for him. We had just ate our food and now we was eating this pie Ms. Rose made. She called it a sweet potato pie. I was thinking, why momma never made some of the stuff Ms. Rose made. Momma would have liked all this food. Sometimes I wish she was here with me. But then, sometimes I'm glad she wasn't because I know she wouldn't let me stay with daddy. He wouldn't even be my daddy.

We all heard Rocky and Fancy barking at each other. They ran in the dining room and Fancy jumped in my lap. I started screaming when Rocky ran up to me, because he was still barking at Fancy. It looked like he was going to bite her.

"Get out of here, Rocky," Daddy yelled at him. "Darn it Richie, get him out of here!"

"What you fussin' with me for? That darn mutt must of been messin' with him."

Richie was pointing his finger at Fancy.

"Richie, I told you to make sure that dog stays outside."

Richie got up. I could tell he was real mad.

"I don't know why my dog gotta be outside and that lil' mutt get to stay in the house, anyway. Come on, Rocky."

Daddy said, "Rocky is not a house dog, Richie. You know that."

Richie didn't say nothing. He just pulled Rocky by the red collar around his neck. He looked at me, daddy and even Fancy, with a mean look.

When he left out of the house, Daddy said, "Sometimes I don't know what I'm going to do with him."

He just shook his head. Ms. Rose put her hand on his hand and rubbed it. He looked at her and smiled a little bit.

I think they like each other.

I didn't want to mess with them while they was smiling at each other, but I had to ask daddy something before I forgot.

"Um, daddy, how old did you turn today?"

"70 years old."

Whoa...that's a lot of numbers to count.

Some days ago, I couldn't find Fancy. So, we put up some missing dog papers around where we lived. We thought she ran away, but when I was playing outside with my ball, it rolled in the bushes on the side of the house and that's when I saw her.

"Fancy!"

I cried and screamed her name real loud. Then, I saw daddy and Ms. Rose running to where I was.

"Rodeo," Daddy said, "What's wrong?"

I pointed to where Fancy was laying and said, "I knew she didn't run away."

"Oh, no," Ms. Rose said. "I'll go get something to get her up."

My daddy hugged me and I kept crying. He said, "Don't worry sweetheart. We'll take her to the vet to see if they can tell us what happened."

I didn't care what happened. I just wanted my Fancy back.

"Uh huh. I see."

Me, Daddy and Ms. Rose was all sitting in the family room watching TV, when daddy got a call from the dog doctor. We had to wait until the next day to find out something because the doctor said they had to do some tests.

"Okay. Thank you, Dr. Riley."

He hung up the phone and came to sit back down on the sofa, next to me. Me and Ms. Rose was looking at him.

"Rat poison."

Ms. Rose asked Daddy, "What does rat poison have to do with anything?"

"Dr. Riley says it was rat poison that killed the dog."

I know what rat poison is. Momma used to put some on the floor so the rats could eat it. So they could die. I started thinking about momma and Fancy. It made me start crying. Daddy hugged me and said, "Hush now, Rodeo. I know this makes you very sad. I promise I am going to make it up to you."

Ms. Rose came to sit by me and said, "Poor child. Rodeo, how about I run you a nice bubble bath. Would you like that, sweetie? I bet it'll help you feel a little better."

I said, "Okay."

Daddy rubbed her arm and said, "Thanks Rose."

"You're welcome, Thomas."

Ms. Rose got up to leave and daddy said, "Hey, Rose?"

"Yes, Thomas?"

"Have you bought any rat poison lately?"

"No, I haven't."

"Hmph… Neither have I. Don't you find it awfully strange that…"

Daddy stopped talking when he heard the door open. It was Richie, talking on the phone.

"Richie, could you come here for a second?"

When Richie came in, daddy said, "Richie, have you put down any rat poison lately?"

"Nope."

Daddy looked at Richie like he was waiting for him to say something else. Richie just stood there looking crazy, like he always does.

"Oh, okay. Thank you."

When Richie left, daddy and Ms. Rose looked at each other and shook they head. They didn't say nothing. Then, Ms. Rose left to go run me some bath water.

I said, "Daddy, why God let Fancy get killed like that?"

"Sweetie, just because bad things happen, it doesn't mean God is the cause of it. That's why a lot of people get so mad at God sometimes, because they think everything happened because it's His will. Sometimes the devil uses people to do bad things, because he is bad. Still, God will always make things work together for the good of those that love him and are called according to His purpose, because He *is* good. Don't ever forget that."

"But how she eat rat poison and we don't even have rats?"

Daddy said, "You're a very, very, smart girl, Rodeo. I was thinking the same thing, but you know, the devil is always busy. Don't worry. I'll make it up to you."

Daddy wasn't playing when he said he was going to make it up to me. The next day, me and him went to eat at the Waffle House. Then, we played games at the arcade. That was fun. I was beating him in everything. But I think he let me win sometimes because that stuff was easy.

Daddy said we was going to go see a movie, but first, we went to this office place because daddy said he had to talk to his lawyer about some things. He told me to sit in the waiting room while he talked to his lawyer in the office. I was looking at some magazines, when this white lady came out.

She didn't look old at all. Her hair was in a long ponytail and it bounced around every time she moved. She was asking this old, white man a lot of questions I didn't understand. Then, she took him through the same door daddy was coming out of. Daddy smiled at me and said, "You ready?"

"Yep."

I put my hand in his and we left.

The movie we saw was so funny. It was called Finding Nemo. After the movie, we went to get ice cream and did a little shopping. Before we left to go home, we took pictures in one of those booths where people make silly faces and little pictures come out. I was having so much fun with daddy, I never wanted it to end.

I was beat when we got home. That's what people always said on T.V. shows when they been doing stuff all day. After we ate some of Ms. Rose good cooking, I took a bath and laid down. I tried not to fall asleep until daddy came in to kiss me, but this night, I fell asleep real fast.

Chapter 5

"Wolves in sheep's clothing. That was something,
huh?"

That's what Ms. Rose said while she was walking in
the house. Me and daddy was sitting on the porch.

"Yep," Daddy said. "That was a good sermon."

We had just got back from church. Somebody else was
talking today. He was funny and he wasn't that boring like the
other man, who was always preaching.

"You have to watch out for those kinds of people,
Rodeo."

I stopped playing with my Barbie toys and looked up.
"What kind of people, Daddy?"

He looked at me over his newspaper and said,
"Wolves in sheep's clothing."

I nodded my head slow, but I didn't know what he was talking about. I think he could tell because he said, "Do you know what I'm talking about?"

"No."

He put the paper down on his lap and said, "A lot of people come in many disguises. You know, a disguise is something people hide behind. Think about Scooby Doo. You know how they always find out who the bad guy is when they take the mask off of him?"

I nodded quick and smiled because I knew what he was talking about.

"They try to act like a harmless, gentle and innocent sheep, but they are really wolves. Wolves, which are not considered harmless creatures."

He tapped one foot on the floor and said in a slow voice, "They are dangerous people pretending to be harmless."

That sounded scary to me. The door opened and Richie walked out. He had on some dirty jeans with no shirt. He always looked like that when he working on the trains. Sometimes he looked like that when he wasn't working.

He looked at me, then, daddy. I think he rolled his eyes at me a little. Momma would always get me if it looked like I rolled my eyes at her.

"Rose needs your help in the kitchen. She can't reach some bowl in the cabinet."

"Well, why didn't you help..." Daddy stopped talking when Richie put his hands up. They was all covered in black stuff.

Daddy jumped up and went in the house. When Richie walked past me, he stepped on the back of my Barbie doll car and it got dragged under his feet, across the floor.

"Aww," I said.

That was one of my birthday gifts from my daddy. Now the back is crushed. All because of those big, ugly boots he have on.

He said, "Sorry your stuff was in the way," and walked out the door.

Sorry my stuff was in the way?

I really did not like him.

I was still mad until Daddy came back out and said, "Rodeo, I feel like listening to some music. How about that?"

"Okay."

I never turned daddy down when it came to us listening to music. I followed him to the family room and watched him put the needle on the record that was already on the record player. He grabbed my hand and said, "Come on. I want to dance with my favorite girl."

I smiled big. Daddy always said that to me. Especially, when he played the song he said was our song. "What a Wonderful World" by Sam Cooke. I knew how it was going to go. He would sing his part and then, he'll put his fake microphone up to my mouth when it was my turn.

He sang, "Don't know much about…"

Then, I sang, "History."

"Don't know much…"

"Biology."

We'd go back and forth until it was time to sing together.

"But I do know that I love you…And I know that if you love me too…What a wonderful world this would be."

I loved to hear daddy do the parts where he hums the song. He called it harmonizing. Ms. Rose always said daddy had some soul in him. She would just smile at us. Richie would roll his eyes. I didn't care. Anytime I was with daddy was the best times of my life.

Chapter 6

As time went on, daddy eventually hired someone to do the work he used to do, but he still kept a close watch on things. This gave him more time to spend at home, instead of on the railroad tracks. I'd finally come to understand what daddy's job was about. He transported coal to different states. I understood it even more after he explained how important coal is in the world.

Over time, we'd done things here and there. We went to Disney World when I was 10 and I'd a blast. We even went to Ohio with Ms. Rose so she could visit her family. I'd loved every minute of it.

When I was 12 years old, we spent Christmas in New York and I got to climb the Statue of Liberty. Daddy and Ms. Rose didn't climb it with me. I wasn't upset at all because I knew neither of them could or should do it. Instead, he'd hired a tour guide to show us around and he said he'd climbed it with me. He was a young guy and very nice.

Of course, Richie didn't come with us. Not that he would have come with us either way, but at that time, he wasn't living in the house anymore. He'd met some woman and claimed to have fallen in love, so they got a place of their own.

It had been two years since I'd seen Richie. I didn't care that he'd moved back home just last night, but from the ugly looks he kept giving me, I could tell that his feelings toward me hadn't changed.

Daddy, Ms. Rose, Richie and I were all sitting at the table eating breakfast. I'd gotten up very early this morning because it was a special day for me. Daddy always said, when I'm 13 years old, he'd let me go to a real school. I always thought he'd probably change his mind when the time finally came, but here I am, up and ready for my first day of 8th grade…in a real school.

Don't get me wrong, I loved being home schooled, especially by my daddy. I mean, he'd taught me so much, but I wanted to go to school and see what it was like to be around other students. If my birthday didn't come so late in the year, I would've started last school year. I tried to reason with him because school started in August and my birthday only came a month later, but he wouldn't give way. Honestly, I secretly think he was glad I wasn't able to go to school at that time. He said the only downfall about my birthday being so late, is that I'd graduate when I was 18. Still, I didn't care because it was time now.

After I finished eating, I ran upstairs to grab my black, book bag. Before I left, I stopped to look at myself in the long mirror on the back of my door. I was kind of skinny, but not to the point where it seemed like I wasn't eating. Daddy said I was really growing into myself. He said boys are going to try to talk to me, but I have to be careful because they can get me into a lot of trouble and my education is more important. I don't know how many times he said, "Remember the 7 B's, Rodeo. Books Before Boys Because Boys Bring Babies."

I played with my hair that went past my shoulders now. Of course, it was in baby doll curls, just like I liked them. Last night, I laid out the new blue jeans daddy bought for me, along with my pink, long sleeved Guess shirt. I stared at myself for a quick moment and smiled. I used to think I was ugly. I don't know why. Maybe because, before daddy, I was never told otherwise. Now, I actually thought I was pretty.

I was getting excited. I could feel butterflies forming in my stomach. I was so happy. With everything. I glanced around my room. It had changed over the years. No more, little girl covers and characters all around the room. Even though, it was mostly equipped with different shades of purple…purple covers, purple throw rugs, and curtains… it was done with style and fashion to fit my personality. I opened the door. Before I left out, I said, "Thank you, God," always trying to keep in mind what daddy said about it being God who gives you the things you have.

On my way to school, I was thinking about momma. I wonder what she would've said if she saw me now. As time went on, I didn't think about her as much as I used to. It was usually at night anyway, when all I had was time to think. I eventually accepted the fact that she really must have been dead. I mean…she never came to look for me.

This had to be the biggest school I'd ever seen. There was freshly cut grass and beautiful flower beds with the hedges all trimmed and neat. It looked like a nice, big, college campus. As daddy and I walked up, what seemed like 20 concrete steps, I read aloud the big, white words plastered on the front of the brick building: **WINTHORP ACADEMY**.

Daddy smiled and said, "You excited?"

"Very."

As we waited for someone to buzz us into the double glass doors, I straightened out my hair and clothes, picking any visible lent away from them.

Daddy said I could come in and sit with him while he talked to the principal, but I decided to wait around in the lobby area instead. I wanted to look at the things displayed on the wall in the hallway.

I looked in a glass case where a lot of trophies were displayed. Some were for football, basketball, lacrosse, swimming and even, tennis. There were a lot of pictures everywhere. I studied more than half of the pictures on the wall.

I wonder if there are any black...

"Rodeo."

I turned around to see daddy standing next to some Italian looking man, in a black, business suit.

"Come over and meet the principal, Mr. Demagio."

Mr. Demagio? Yep, he's Italian.

He looked like the type of person who played in mob movies. As I walked up to him, I couldn't help but notice how young he looked for a principal. His hair was slicked back, down to his neck, where it curled up at the ends. It was just as black and shiny as his polished shoes.

"Hello, Rodeo."

Although, he was smiling, I'm guessing daddy didn't inform him that I was adopted because of the, oh-she's-black look written all over his face. I smiled and said, "Hello."

"Your fatha told me you're a great student and a great learna. I have no doubt you'll love it here. Not to mention, this is rated one of the best private schools in the state. Welcome."

I almost laughed from thoughts of me practicing that Italian accent that he carried so well. I just liked how it sounded.

Mr. Demagio took daddy and me on a tour around the school. It was huge. The grades went from Pre-K through 12th. It was split in three big sections, separating a number of grades by floors. Kindergarten through 4th grade was on the main floor, 5th through 8th was on the bottom and 9th through 12th grade was on the top floor. The preschoolers actually had a building all to themselves, located on the east side of the school.

After both daddy and I were pretty much out of breath, Mr. Demagio stopped in front of a brown, wooden door. The black letters on it read: **HISTORY**.

"Well, Rodeo," Mr. Demagio said as he clasped his hands together, "This is your first stop."

He knocked before opening the door. As he peeked in, he said, "Mr. Brown, you have a new student."

A tall, thin, casual dressed man appeared at the door. I could tell he was sort of old by his thinning, gray hair which was slicked back to his neck. His pale skin was still somewhat in place, but I was sure the worry lines all over his face came with years of teaching.

Those teeth. They were just too perfect to be real.

As Mr. Demagio talked with Mr. Brown, I sighed heavily and looked at daddy. He was smiling, which made me smile. I'm sure he could tell I was nervous. He hugged me and said, "Don't worry, my sweetie. You'll do great. I love you and I'll be waiting for you when you get home."

"I love you too, daddy."

He was always the only person who could ever make me feel better about anything.

"Mr. Donovan," Mr. Demagio cut into our sentimental moment, "We have more papers to sign."

With that, daddy left, looking back only once to wink his eye at me.

By lunch time, I'd had 3 classes where I'd been the only one like me there. Simply put...I hadn't seen a black person yet. That was until I heard a very loud, "Hey girl!"

I turned to see some black girl staring at me, like she'd never seen another black person here before. She was about my size, but a couple of inches shorter than me. She pulled out a chair and sat down next to me at the round table.

She was smiling, but then, she turned her nose up and said, "Please tell me you not stuck up too? It's only 4 black girls here, including me, and I can't stand none of them stuck up chicks."

I guess I stared at her too long. I laughed and said, "Oh, no. I'm apologize. Hi. You surprised me, that's all."

She was a pretty girl, just loud. I liked how her black, wavy hair fell around her shoulders. Even though, she was brown-skinned, I could tell she was mixed with Indian or something.

"I was just makin' sure. Well, my name Katina."

"Nice to meet you Katina. My name's Rodeo."

"Rodeo? You from Cali?"

For a long time, I never knew why people asked me if I was from California or why they always made such comments as, "Oh…like Rodeo Drive," or "Like in California?" I didn't know why momma named me that or if she'd even been there before, but one day, I asked Daddy about it and he explained it to me.

"No, I'm not from there. I guess my mom just liked that name."

"Oh, ok. You ever been?"

"No, not yet, but my daddy says that's where we're going the next time we go on vacation."

"Girl, you gonna love it! You see this outfit I got on?"

She stood up to show off her white, Juicy Couture, sweat suit with the matching sneakers. I nodded as I noticed how busty she was, on the top and the bottom. My shape hadn't even begun to come in as much as hers already had.

"I got this when I went there last year with my mom. Anyway, I'm ready to eat. You hungry?"

"What do they have?"

"Well, sometimes the food that the cafeteria ladies make be okay, but they sell real pizza too, so I usually get that."

We both got a pizza and salad from the salad bar. I didn't mind that she invited herself to sit with me. I was kind of glad to have someone to talk to. While we ate, I tried my best to keep up with how fast she talked, as she told me about some of the teachers, as well as, some of the students. She let me know there were only 18 black people in the whole school, with only 8 black boys.

"But now it's 19 blacks since you here. Heeeey, we on our way," she said while throwing her hands up in the air.

I couldn't help but laugh. I didn't care that there were more whites than blacks. In fact, it made me more appreciative of being able to attend such a school.

Katina had been going there since she was in 7th grade. Now, she was 15 in the 10th grade. She said she started going there after her mom married her step-dad, Mr. David. He was some big, time preacher, who had a lot of money. She didn't have any sisters or brothers and from the way she put it, she didn't want any because then she wouldn't get as much as she does.

"Did you see the principal?"

"Yes," I answered.

Katina smiled and said, "He cute ain't he?"

I shrugged my shoulders and replied, "Well, yes. He is kind of cute."

"Kind of?" She smacked her lips and said, "That man is fine. I don't know what you talkin' bout."

"He looks young," I said, right before stuffing a fork full of salad in my mouth.

"Girl, he ain't nothing but 36. When he first got here, a bunch of the parents wanted him gone. It was really most of the dads. See, even they know he fine. They was scared of what he might do with the girls."

"Well, he *is* the principal. I hope he wouldn't do anything like that. He knows he can get fired and possibly go to jail."

"Girl, he do *not* care," she replied with a little bit of attitude, as she picked food from her fake, French tip nails.

"His daddy some fat man with a whole bunch of money. Don't nobody know what his daddy do but he own this school. I heard some things about his daddy being one of those Italian, mob type dudes. With all the power he got, he made his son the principal of the school. Trust me…you definitely gone hear some stories about Mr. Demagio."

"Oh," was all I could say.

I didn't know what stories I'd hear and to be honest, I really didn't care. I was happy to be at school today and I didn't plan on letting anything mess up my experience. As Katina continued to gossip, I got the feeling that I'd hear most of the stories about my new principal from her. I listened, for the most part, as we finished eating our lunch. Then, we went to our classes.

Of all the classes I'd taken that day, the one I liked most was my 6th and last one. French class. I'd chosen this one as an elective because I always wanted to learn it. Also, because I wanted to go to Paris one day.

"Bonjour! Comment ca va?"

We all exchanged glances, wondering what was just said. Our teacher stood in front of the class. Her hands were clasped in front of her, resting on her long, mint green dress. She slightly leaned forward, looking at everyone over the brim of her small, red glasses. As she did, her short bang fell over the right side of her rosy, pink face.

"I said, good morning. How are you?"

I watched how gracefully she strolled around the classroom, speaking in her thick, French accent.

"My name," she pointed to the name she'd written on the whiteboard, "Which is spelled S-A-N-G-E-R, is not pronounced Sanger, but it sounds like Sonjay. Feel free to call me Madame or Ms. Sanger, whichever works best for you."

"I know that you all will not learn everything there is to know about this language, but by the end of this class, in the next year of 2009, I expect you to have learned more than you know right now."

She went on to talk about what she expected from us in this class. I became more excited by the minute, as I thought about what I expected from myself. I really wanted to learn French and do the best I could in all my classes. I believed all in all, it was going to be a good school year.

Chapter 7

*I*t didn't take long for Katina and me to get close.

Over the next few weeks, we ate lunch together every day. I don't know if she took to me so quickly because I was black, but she was pretty cool, even though, she did most of the talking when we were together. I liked listening to the stories she told because they were very interesting. She knew a lot, but that was because she did a lot. Especially, when it came to boys.

One day at lunch, she asked, "Hey, you wanna come over to my house after school?"

"I'll have to go home first and ask my daddy."

"That's cool. Where you live? Maybe I can go with you?"

"I live in the Harrington Club subdivision. It's not too far from the school."

"Ok. I know exactly where you stay. I'm not too far from there. Dang girl, y'all must have money like us. Them some nice houses over there."

I just shrugged my shoulders and smiled. Even though, I knew daddy was rich, he always told me not to brag and boast about things. He said God has a way of humbling you and you have a greater chance of losing much more if you do that.

"Well," she continued, "We can go to my house another time. I'll just come to your house today so we can chill over there."

That would be nice. She could walk home with me. Not too long after the school year began, daddy started letting me walk home from school, being that we lived only three blocks away.

After school, I sat on a bench in the front yard of the school, waiting for Katina. While I sat there, I read this book we were assigned to read in my English class. It was called *To Kill a Mockingbird*. It was very interesting, and I was more than half-way finished with it. It was about this black man who'd been accused of raping this white girl. I believe everybody knew he didn't do it, but because it was set in a time where blacks didn't have many rights, he'd been charged with it anyway.

"Hey."

I jumped when I saw Katina standing behind me.

"Whoa, you scared me. I didn't even hear you walking up."

"Sorry it took so long."

I gathered my book bag and asked, "What were you doing?"

"I had to stop by Mr. Demagio's office for a minute."

"Oh, ok."

She looked like she didn't care to talk about why she was there, so I didn't ask any questions. We just proceeded to walk to my house.

❀

"Dang girl," Katina exclaimed as we approached my home. "Y'all livin' large forreal. This house bigger than mines."

When we entered the house, we were greeted by Ms. Rose as she came out of the kitchen, wearing nothing other than her maid outfit.

"How was school, sweetie?"

"It was great, Ms. Rose. This is my friend, Katina. Katina, this is Ms. Rose."

Ms. Rose held out her hand and shook Katina's.

"Nice to meet you, Katina."

"Nice to meet you too," Katina replied.

I smelled a sweet aroma in the air.

"Mmmm. Something smells good."

"Oh, yes. It's your favorite. Now, let me get back to it. We don't want it to burn, now do we?"

"Oh, we definitely don't," I replied smiling.

I could never mistake her homemade apple pie for anything else.

"It was nice to meet you, Katina."

"Nice to meet you too."

As Ms. Rose hurried off to the kitchen, Katina turned to me and said, "It do smell good in here. What she cookin'?"

"Apple pie. She makes the best..."

Katina cut me off saying, "Dang, y'all got a butler too?"

"Huh?"

I was confused until I followed her gaze towards the staircase. Daddy was walking down the stairs.

"Oh," I laughed. "That's my daddy."

She looked completely caught off guard.

"What? Your daddy? But, he white?"

Once again, I had to laugh a little as I quickly said, "I'm adopted."

"Oooh," she said.

"Hello, dear," Daddy said as he hugged me.

Of course, I'd found out long ago that he wasn't actually calling me a deer.

"Hi Daddy. This is my friend I told you about, Katina. Katina, this is my daddy, Mr. Donovan."

"Well, it's very nice to meet you, Katina."

Of course, he held out his hand to shake hers.

"It's nice to meet you too, Mr. Donovan."

"Will you be staying for dinner Katina?"

I stood there grinning with my arm around his waist. I always felt like the luckiest girl in the world to have such a loving daddy.

"You should stay," I added. "Ms. Rose is the best cook ever."

Katina shrugged and said, "Okay."

"Good then," daddy said. "Do you need to call your parents to let them know where you are?"

"Um, sure."

Katina replied as if calling her parents was not in her original plan.

"Rodeo, please show her where the phone is. Rose will let you know when dinner is ready."

After daddy went in the family room, I told Katina she could use the phone in my room. That's where we stayed, talking about almost anything and everything, until it was time to eat dinner. I could tell she felt really comfortable here.

❁

"Katina, it was nice having you here. I hope you'll come back to visit us again?"

That's what daddy said as I walked Katina to the front door.

"Yes sir, I will," Katina replied smiling. "And I loved the food Ms. Rose. It was nice to meet you both."

When we got on the porch, Katina said, "Girl, Ms. Rose know she can cook! That food was delicious. She got some soul in her."

We laughed.

I asked, "Are you going to be okay walking home?"

Not that I would've walked with her, but I wanted to make sure she didn't want the ride daddy had already offered to her.

"I'll be okay. This ain't the first time I've walked home by myself at night."

I did find that statement easy to believe. We said our goodbyes and then, she left.

❀

I'd already let daddy know that I'd be going over to Katina's house after school. When we finally got there, we were greeted by two, black Pit Bulls. They were in a fenced in yard, next to Katina's house. I hated when dogs came out of nowhere. I was never prepared for all the barking they did, but I'm glad they were a few yards away from us because those were not my kind of dogs.

"Girl," Katina sighed from agitation. "I can't stand them darn dogs. They always barkin'."

She told me they belonged to her neighbors which consisted of three, young, black guys. She said they'd inherited the house, along with a lot of money, from their father, who'd died two years earlier in a car accident.

"They all brothers," she added. "But only the youngest one tryin' to do somethin' with his life. Anyway, let's go in through the side door."

Even though, our house was bigger than theirs, I liked how homely it looked. It was one of those Victorian style houses with rose colored shutters attached to every window.

I approached the side door of her house, with caution, from fear of the Pit Bulls. Before I'd fully stepped in the house, a female voice called into the kitchen saying, "Tina, is that you?"

"Yeah Mom, it's me."

"What's your mom's name," I whispered quickly.

"Michelle," she replied, while removing her red, Gucci jacket.

I smacked my teeth and said, "Katina, I'm not going to call your mother by her first name. What's her last name?"

"Girl, she don't care."

I looked at her side ways. My daddy always told me to mind my manners when it came to calling grownups by their first name. He said it was alright only if they said so. Even then, I didn't like to do it.

She sighed heavily and said, "Daniels."

Just then, a heavy-set woman, wearing a long, silky, black dress, walked into the kitchen. Katina said, "I brought my friend Rodeo with me. Remember I told you about her?"

She'd just put on a red apron and was now tying it around her waist. I'm guessing the Indian traits ran on her mother's side of the family. Katina looked like a spitting image of her mother. The only difference was, Mrs. Daniels was a lot lighter and her wavy, black hair was cut into a short bob.

She smiled and said, "Oh, yes. Hello, Rodeo."

I smiled and said, "Hello, Mrs. Daniels."

She walked over to a wooden, rolling island which sat in the middle of the kitchen. There, she began cutting some onions she had on a cutting board. I liked the way the kitchen was decked out in black cabinets and stainless, steel appliances.

"Katina, make sure you're ready at 5:45."

"Momma, I know," Katina replied in an agitated voice. Then, she turned to me and said, "Come on."

As we made our way up the wooden staircase, I heard Katina's mom say, "Your friend can come too if she wants."

Katina didn't say anything. She just did one of those irritated huffs as we reached the top of the staircase. I could tell Mrs. Daniels loved floral. The long hallway was decorated from top to bottom in a rose, flower print wallpaper. When we stopped at the last room on the left, I was staring at a black and yellow caution sign which read: **KEEP OUT.**

This must be Katina's room.

As we went in, I was greeted by scents of perfumes and colors of pink and green. From the curtains to the covers, these were the only colors I saw. The only thing different was the carpeting on the floor which was a cream color. I suppose she knew I was wondering about the colors. As if reading my mind, she said, "I'm going to join the AKA sorority when I go to college."

I looked over towards her. She was pointing to a license plate she had on her wall. It had the pink and green letters: **AKA** on it.

"My mom was an AKA. This is one of her old license plates. I heard a lot about that sorority. Plus, they the pretty girls, so I gots to be in that one. I know they get all the fine boys too."

I smirked as Katina smacked her teeth and did her "pretty girl" stance, as if saying, "I know I'm cute."

She's a mess.

"Anyway, you can sit down if you want to."

I went to sit down on a hot pink loveseat, located against the wall, directly across from her daybed. Although, her bed was white, she'd tied pink and green ribbons around the whole thing.

As she stood in her bathroom, brushing her hair, I asked, "What was your mom talking about? What's happening at 5:45?"

"Oh, yeah. Wednesday is bible study night. We gotta go to church."

"Oh. Well, I'm sure my daddy wouldn't mind if I came."

She turned and looked at me questioningly.

"I ain't never met nobody that actually *wanted* to go to bible study."

Then, she turned back towards the mirror and continued brushing her hair, saying, "I mean, it's alright. Maybe I don't care too much for it cause it's my step-dad who's preachin'. I can't stand him sometimes."

"Is he here," I asked.

"Nope. He probably already at the church. But hey, if you wanna go, it'll be nice to have somebody there to keep me from fallin' asleep."

I laughed, but she didn't. I called my daddy to ask if I could go. Of course, he didn't say no to church.

The ride to church wasn't long at all. Ten minutes tops. When we got there, Mrs. Daniels pulled through a steel, black gate that opened automatically. She parked her beige, Lexus Jeep next to a shiny, black Hummer. I assumed the Hummer must have been Mr. David's after seeing the license plate on the front that read: **#1PASTOR**.

We walked up the steps of a huge, brick church. Katina was telling the truth when she said he was a big, time preacher. When we walked through the double, glass doors, I was surprised to see how big the inside of the church was. As we walked pass the reception desk, I admired how the big chandeliers, hanging from the high ceiling, was draped in purple and gold cloth.

Every wooden door we passed by, had been engraved with the word: **Sanctuary**, in gold letters. Even though, the hallway stretched even further, we stopped at the next set of double doors we came to and entered into the Sanctuary.

I'm pretty sure this place would have been packed from top to bottom if it were Sunday. Still, even on this Wednesday, almost all of the burgundy covered pews, on the first level, was full of church goers. The second level on the balcony was dimmed out because no one was sitting there. I'm positive this church could hold at least five thousand, if not more.

As we walked down the center aisle, Katina and I stopped short and found a seat on one of the center pews, close to the back of the church. Mrs. Daniels kept walking towards the front of the church and sat on the front pew, directly in front of, who I'm sure was, Mr. David.

He stood behind a dark, wooden pew, wearing a purple robe. He was a short man with really dark skin. He was one of those men who were sort of slim but had a big belly. I could tell he didn't miss any meals. He wiped the sweat from his forehead with a white handkerchief, as he spoke.

"How many of y'all know the Lord is good," he asked.

"Amen," the congregation said.

"I said, how many of y'all know the Lord is good?"

"Yes," some shouted.

"Y'all know I pride myself on my name bein' David. Sometimes I feel just like David. Goin' through some of the same emotions and struggles he went through in the bible. But just like God was good to him, he still good to me."

"Yes," the congregation yelled.

"Ugh, he talk too much," Katina said.

I looked at her, wondering who she was talking about. When I saw her looking at Mr. David with disgust, I snickered, and she did too.

"I keep tellin' my momma he need to cut that stupid, pimp ponytail off his head."

I couldn't help but laugh again, seeing that she was referring to the way he had his hair slicked back into a short ponytail. We were both giggling as quietly as we could, when an older lady, sitting next to Katina, looked at us with one of those mean, church lady looks and told us to be quiet and pay attention. Even though, I was sort of confused about his message, we both sat up straight and listened until it was time to leave.

Today was Saturday, the perfect day for my 14th birthday to fall on. Katina and I had been out since this afternoon, walking along the mall strip. Daddy let us walk there since it was so close to my house. Before we left, he'd given me a golden locket. In it, was one of the pictures we'd taken in the photo booth, a few years ago. I knew I'd cherish it forever.

We'd decided to go to Brewster's to get some ice cream. While we ate our ice cream, I listened to Katina talk about the boy she'd just met at the music store.

"That boy was kind of cute, huh?"

I nodded my head and said, "He was alright."

"Yeah, he wasn't all that. I still might call 'em, though. He look like he got some money."

Katina was very experienced when it came to boys. If my daddy knew all the stuff she did, he probably wouldn't have let me hang around her. I liked hanging out with her, though. Besides, it didn't matter what she did because I wasn't thinking about any of the stuff she was into.

I listened to her as I ate my cookies and cream ice cream. Then, she said, "Hey, ain't that your ugly step-brother?"

We both laughed.

"Where," I asked.

"Over there."

She pointed to a building across the lot.

I leaned in to get a better look and said, "Yep, that's him. Hmm. That's where daddy goes when he needs to talk to his lawyer."

"Anyway," Katina said as she continued talking.

I was listening, but not really. I couldn't help but wonder why Richie was standing outside, in front of that building.

Maybe he did his business there too. I don't know.

Just a few seconds later, a tall, skinny lady came outside and stopped to talk to Richie. I could tell she was young. Her blonde hair was pulled back into a ponytail. She had on a yellow, flower print sundress with some black sandals. It was a little breezy outside, but still, the weather was nice. Which made me wonder why she had on a long, black coat that came all the way to her knees.

After all the talking and giggling she'd done, she finally pulled out a big, orange envelop, from the inside of her coat. She said a few words before Richie snatched it out of her hands and stuffed it inside his own brown jacket. He looked around as if trying to make sure no one saw him.

Hmm, I wonder what he's up...

"Hello? Earth to Rodeo?"

"Oh," I snapped out of my trance. "I'm so sorry girl, I was just wondering what Richie was up to. He looks real suspect over there, talking to that lady."

Katina looked towards them as the lady bounced back in the building. Richie just strolled away like nothing had happened.

"Girl, ain't no tellin' what they got goin' on. He probably do his business over there, too. Or, he might be gettin' some from her."

She burst out laughing.

"Getting some what?"

"For real, Rodeo?"

Katina looked at me like I was joking. When she saw that I wasn't, she said, "Girl, you know. Gettin' some of what she got between her legs."

I burst out laughing and so did she. Now, I understood what Katina was saying. That could have been a possibility, especially from the way it seemed like she was flirting with him. Still, I couldn't help but think there was something more to it. Not long after, I just let it go.

I laughed to myself just thinking about how much I really didn't know about the streets. One would think, with the momma I had, I would've known a lot. Truth is, momma was never there enough. When she was, she was sleeping most of the time. I sighed and let my spoon play with my ice cream. I hated when I had those types of random thoughts. I quickly focused in on listening to Katina.

After we finished eating our ice cream, we did a little more shopping. Then, we decided to go catch a movie. I could have had a party for my birthday, but I told daddy I didn't want one. I was glad he trusted me enough to let me do my own thing. Knowing that alone made this birthday a great one.

Chapter 8

Daddy always said time moves fast when Christmas was approaching. Maybe it was adults who felt that way because they're the ones who had to buy things, but it did seem like we'd just had Thanksgiving the other day. Now, here it was, already about to be Christmas.

It was the day before Christmas Eve, and I was extremely tired. Daddy and I had gone to do some last, minute shopping earlier that day. His brothers, as well as, Ms. Rose's sister, would be in town by tomorrow morning.

I'd taken a bath and wrapped my hair up in my purple, silk bonnet. Now, I was lying in bed, watching my favorite TV show, *The Fresh prince of Bel Air*. I didn't mind that they were reruns. I just liked Will Smith. He was so funny.

Daddy wasn't at home at the moment. He had to go out for a last, minute trip to Chicago with Richie, because the other guy who worked for him had some type of family emergency. He said he'd be back early in the morning before I woke up.

I was getting sleepier, so I got out of the bed to pray. I always tried to remember to do it before going to bed, even though, I sometimes forgot. After I finished, I lay in bed thinking about the life God had blessed me with. Daddy always said I should thank God because if it wasn't for Him, things would have never happened the way they did and then, I wouldn't be here with him. He always said, even when bad things happen, God makes them all work together for good.

Before I fell asleep, I set the sleep timer on my TV. For some reason, I had a bad habit of falling asleep with the TV on. Daddy showed me how to set the sleep timer, so it would turn off automatically. One minute, I was watching TV and before I knew it, I had fallen asleep.

I felt like I was dreaming. At least, I thought I was dreaming, but I couldn't tell. It felt like I was riding in a car, on a dirt road or something. I couldn't move my hands or my feet. I thought I opened my eyes, but it was still pitch black. Suddenly, I bumped up against something really hard. It seemed like I'd hit a bump in the road.

A bump in the road? Why would I be on the road? Maybe, I am dreaming.

I blinked a few times. That's when I realized, I was awake, but I still couldn't see anything. Again, I tried to move my hands and feet. They were tied up with some type of stringy rope.

That's why I couldn't move.

My hands were tied in front of me, so I raised them up to my face. I could feel some kind of cloth over my head. There was rope tied around my neck, holding the sack in place.

"Oh, my goodness. What's going on?"

I felt around for anything that I could get my hands on.

"Oh, no. I'm in the trunk of a car."

Why would I be tied up, in the trunk of a car?

Instantly, I began to panic and that made my eyes tear up. I had never felt so afraid in my life. Not knowing where I was or who I was with, scared me. But, not knowing what was going to happen to me, terrified me the most.

"Daddy, help me," I whispered as I began to cry.

Well, duh Rodeo. If he were around, you wouldn't be tied up in the trunk of a car, would you?

I tried my best to wiggle out of the rope, but it was tied too tight. I started to kick at the door, but that wouldn't do anything. Besides, I didn't want whoever put me here to hear me. That might make them mad.

I wish I knew what they were going to do to me.

Just thinking about that made me cry even more. I figured, if something bad wasn't going to happen to me, I wouldn't be here like this. I just laid there. Struggling to get free from the ropes wasn't going to help because I couldn't get out of the trunk anyway. It was so cold.

They could have at least wrapped me up in some cover. They wouldn't want to be tied up, in the back of a trunk, freezing.

I was glad I put my thick, pink socks on before I put on my pink, fleece, Cinderella onesie.

I thought about daddy, but he wasn't there to help me, so I did the only thing I could think to do. Daddy always said, God said He will never leave us nor forsake us, so I prayed to Him. I prayed that He would protect me, so that I wouldn't get killed. I prayed that He would let me see my daddy again. I prayed that He would let me live, so I could finish school. I liked school. I kept praying for so many things the whole time the car was moving. Finally, the car started to slow down. I stopped myself from crying.

The car stopped and someone turned it off. It seemed as if all the noise around me had stopped, including my breathing. I couldn't hear anything, except my own heartbeat. I heard the car door open. I finally began breathing again. When the door slammed shut, I heard someone cough. It sounded like a man's cough, but I couldn't really tell.

As the person walked, I could hear the sound of gravel, crunching under their shoes. They stopped in front of the trunk. Then, the trunk popped open and that's when, I again, stopped breathing. I didn't hear anything, but I knew they must have been looking at me.

Suddenly, they grabbed me and pulled me out of the trunk. I didn't say anything and neither did they. We didn't go very far before they pushed me to the ground. It hurt from being thrown on those rocks, but still, I didn't make a sound. As I lay there wondering what was going to happen next, I heard a sound that I recognized all too well. I'd heard that sound on TV too many times. It was the sound of someone cocking a gun back, right before they were about to pull the trigger.

I balled myself up and lay there praying in my mind, harder than I did the first time.

Is this how I'm going to die?

I thought about Momma. She got killed. Shot, even. I never thought I would get killed too. I remember what that old man said. "One shot to the head." I was going to die just like momma.

I wondered what was taking them so long. Waiting for something to happen only frightened me more.

Wait. Are they running? Yes. I could hear them running.

I heard the car start. Then, it sped away. I was confused.

Did they really leave? Should I move? Maybe they're somewhere watching me. They might be waiting for me to run, so they can shoot me.

It was freezing, but I didn't move. I was too scared.

I don't know how long I waited before I sat up. I tried to wiggle my way out of the ropes. The more I tried to pull free, the more frustrated I got. I started to cry.

"Come on," I yelled.

I did my best to calm down. Daddy always said, "Worrying will not solve anything and neither will it help you think clearly."

I began to drag myself around on the ground. I was trying to see if I could feel around for a rock or a sharp object or something.

"Ouch!"

I didn't find a rock, but I did manage to scrape my hand on a piece of glass, which was even better. I carefully held it between my fingers, while I cut the rope away from my feet and then, my hands. Next, I cut the rope that was around my neck, so I could remove the sack.

"Where in the world am I?"

I slowly stood up, taking in the scene around me. There was nothing but woods and tall trees on both sides of me. The road I was on consisted of nothing but dirt and rocks. The scary part…there were no street lights. The only light I saw came from the moon. I was cold and I didn't know where I was or where I could go, but I knew I didn't want to stay there.

"I can't believe this," I said aloud.

"Here I am. No coat. It's freezing. I have to walk on rocks, and I keep hearing noises in the woods. Really?"

I shook my head. I was really scared. I only saw dark streets like this on scary movies.

"Good thing it's not snowing."

I put my arms in my sleeves and started walking.

It seemed like it was going to take me forever to get to wherever I could. I didn't see any houses or anything that looked like something which held human life. I slowed my pace because the rocks were beginning to hurt my feet. Suddenly, I saw some car lights a little ways up the road.

"Good. Somebody's coming."

I almost got too excited. Then, I thought, *Wait a minute. What if that's the person coming back.* I didn't know what kind of car they were driving and neither could I see anything, except, the bright lights heading my way. If it was the person who'd left me there, I didn't want to take the chance of them seeing me. They probably changed their mind and now they were coming back to kill me. At the last minute, I ran off the road and hid in the woods.

I watched as the car slowly passed by me. I didn't know if it was going to stop or keep going. Whoever was in the car kept driving, but then, it stopped. Nobody got out. They drove up a little more. Then, stopped again. After a few seconds of sitting there, they pulled up a little more. Then, the car drove away really fast. I watched the tail lights dim behind the dirt the tires had kicked up.

After a minute or two, I started walking back up the road again. I didn't feel like I'd been out there long, but I didn't know how much longer I could go. My hands and feet were freezing. I could hardly move them.

"Come on, God. What's going on? Are you going to send some help for me or what?"

I stopped talking out loud. I started to feel stupid, like I was talking to myself. I didn't even know if God was real or not. I just believed it because my daddy said so.

I don't know. Maybe, if He gets me out of this, then I'll believe He's real.

I mean, Yes, He did 'hear my prayers," as daddy always said, and got me out of getting shot, but maybe that person just got scared and changed their minds. Just like they obviously changed their mind again and decided to come back to see if I was still there. I'm sure they were going to kill me. Otherwise, why would they come back?

I tried to continuously think about a scripture daddy made me learn. The Lord will never leave me nor forsake me. I was wondering how it all worked. I mean, this faith thing. Maybe I wasn't believing hard enough because right now, it seemed like my chances of getting some help were not going to happen.

I was getting tired. My muscles seemed like they were getting tighter with every step I took. It was getting harder for me to move. It felt like my whole body was going numb. I had to sit down. Before I knew it, I was balled up, with my head tucked in my onesie. Then, I laid down.

Chapter 9

"Rodeo. Oh God."

I heard someone talking. I even felt someone touching me, but I couldn't comprehend anything at all. All I saw were lights and everything else was a blur. I closed my eyes.

"Rodeo? Sweetie?"

This time, when I opened my eyes, I could tell the person talking was daddy. I looked at him. His face and eyes were almost the same color red. He looked like he'd been crying.

"Daddy," was all I could say before I started crying like a baby.

He sat down next to me on the bed and held me close in his arms. As he rubbed my back, he said, "I was so worried Rodeo. I'm so thankful God answered my prayers."

"Daddy, I was so scared. I didn't think I would ever see you again."

"It's okay, sweetie. You're safe now."

Daddy held me for a long time. I felt so safe in his arms. I never wanted him to let me go. It seemed as if I'd forgotten everything that I'd been through. Then, it all came back to me when I saw a policeman come into my room. I noticed myself hugging daddy even tighter. I'd also just noticed the tubes in my nose and the needles in my arms, as if they hadn't been there the whole time I'd been up.

"Hello again, Mr. Donovan."

The policeman was tall and brown-skinned, with a shiny, bald head.

"I just received word Rodeo was awake. I'd like to ask her a few questions, if that's alright with you?"

Daddy turned to me a said, "Rodeo. This is Officer Wright. He wants to help us find the bad people who did this to you, but he needs to ask you some questions. Do you feel like answering questions right now?"

How thoughtful of Daddy to think about my feelings. That's just the type of man he was.

"Yes."

Daddy smiled.

"Yes, Officer Wright. That would be fine?"

While daddy and Officer Wright were discussing some details about the night I was kidnapped, I couldn't help noticing the obvious fact that some time must have passed since I'd been in the hospital. I mean, Officer Wright had to have been here before because daddy knew who he was. He did say that I was "awake" now. Honestly, I had more questions than answers.

"Daddy," I said before the officer proceeded to ask me questions.

"Yes, sweetie?"

"How long have I been here? At the hospital?"

He took a deep breath and said, "Well, you've been in a coma for a little over a week now."

Even though, I was very weak, I felt my eyes widen as I listened to him give me the quick details of my ordeal. I was found on the side of the road by some people driving by. No one knows how long I'd been out there, but when they brought me to the hospital, my pulse was extremely weak, and I'd been suffering from hypothermia. As a result, I'd slipped into a coma.

Wow. I didn't remember any of that. Well, of course, because I was in a coma. But, wow.

"Rodeo?"

Officer Wright was standing on the side of my bed, with his pen and notepad in hand, ready to take notes.

"I know this is a scary time for you, but I need you to try your best to remember everything you can about the night you were kidnapped."

I nodded my head slowly and took a deep breath, as I relived the events of that night. Daddy was by my side the whole time as I struggled to hold back tears. I revealed every detail I could remember. From the ride in the truck, to the sound of the gun being cocked back. I even told them about hearing the person run away and speed off in the car.

"They came back too," I added. "I know it was them."

I looked up at daddy with tears in my eyes and said, "I know they were coming back to kill me. I know it."

"Did you see what kind of car it was," Officer Wright asked.

"Well, I know it was a truck and it looked like it was sort of light brown, but I really couldn't tell because it was so dark."

"Hmm," Officer Wright said as he tapped his pen on his chin. "So, you saw a truck, but you know for sure you were riding in the trunk of a car? How are you so sure that whoever was driving this truck came back for you?"

"I know it because of the way they did it. They were driving very slowly, and they stopped at least three times, like they were looking for something. After a few minutes, they sped off like they were angry that they couldn't find whatever they were looking for. Besides, I never saw another car on that dark, deserted road. Why would anyone be out there like that?"

Officer Wright nodded slowly saying, "Good point. Well, it looks like we may have more than one person working together in this."

"Did you see anythang at all?"

I know that voice. Richie.

I hadn't noticed him standing in the far corner of the room, with that dirty, blue coverall on, until now. I shook my head slowly, wondering why he was so worried about me. He never cared about me before.

"I mean, can't nobody help if we ain't got no leads," he added.

We?

From the look on daddy's face, I could tell I wasn't the only one who found Richie's sudden interest in my well-being odd. Neither of us replied to him.

"Thank you very much, Rodeo," Officer Wright said, interrupting my thoughts. "You did great. Mr. Donovan," he turned to daddy, "We will definitely keep you posted on this investigation and please, let us know if she remembers anything else."

"I sure will," Daddy replied.

I really wanted to go home, but I couldn't until the next day, which was a Saturday. The nurse said they wanted to run some more tests and observe me overnight. Richie had gone home, so it was just daddy and me now. I looked over towards him. He wasn't fully asleep, but he was almost there. He was laying back in a recliner chair, with a blanket pulled up to his chin. The TV was on some cooking channel, but neither one of us was really watching it.

Daddy had bought some crossword books from the gift shop, so I'd been doing those all night until I got tired of it. As

I laid there, I wondered how daddy must have felt when he couldn't find me. I could tell he must have been worrying so much. I was glad he at least had Ms. Rose to comfort him.

Ms. Rose. Where is she?

I can't believe I hadn't thought about her this whole time. I looked over towards daddy. His eyes were still slowly opening and closing.

"Daddy?"

"Yes?"

He jumped up, alert, like something was wrong.

"I was just wondering where Ms. Rose was."

"Oh, sweetie."

He relaxed after realizing everything was alright.

"Rose accidentally broke her arm the other night. She was standing on the foot ladder, reaching for something in the cabinet and she slipped."

"Oh, no," I said.

"Don't worry, dear. She's alright. She just can't do a lot right now. I went ahead and hired some maids to keep the house up. I should have done that a long time ago. Rose wanted to come, but I told her to get some rest."

Poor Ms. Rose. I know that must have hurt. She does so much for us all. I told myself that I would start helping her more around the house. Not that I hadn't tried to before, but she's just "set in her ways," as daddy would say.

I flipped the TV channels and stopped when I saw the big ball dropping. It was New Year's Eve? What a way to bring in the new year. After a few minutes, I looked over towards daddy. He'd finally fallen asleep. I'm sure he hadn't gotten much sleep lately. With him sleeping by my side, I felt so safe. I closed my eyes to get some rest. Suddenly, I opened them.

Aw man. I missed Christmas!

I was so glad when I'd finally gotten home. All I wanted to do was ball up in the comfort of my bed and stay under the covers forever, with daddy right next to me. In fact, after I'd taken a long, hot bath, that's what I'd done for most of the day. Daddy had been checking in on me from time to time. He'd even surprised me with the Christmas gifts I'd gotten from everyone. I got some jewelry, clothes and even some electronic gadgets to play with. One of them was a small, purple laptop.

Later that day, Katina came over right after school. We sat on my bed, as I listened to her explain the panic everyone was in, the day I was kidnapped.

"Girl, your dad was so worried about you. They came to my house and everythang. They had me scared for you. My momma was so glad when your dad told us they had found you. Even some people from school was worried about you."

"Really?"

"Yep. And then," she continued, smacking her teeth, "Richie dumb butt said somebody from school probably kidnapped you."

"Why would somebody from school kidnap me?"

"That's what your dad said. Then, Richie gonna say, they could be jealous cause a rich white man taking care of a black girl. He was bout to call you the "N" word, but he stopped. I heard him though."

I just shook my head. I didn't know what to think about the whole situation. One thing I did know was, I didn't trust Richie. Since the first time I'd met him. I did not trust him.

Chapter 10

"*A*argh!"

It had been almost a week since I'd returned home from the hospital. Since then, I'd had bad dreams about the kidnapping. Each time, I woke up screaming in the wee hours of the morning. This Friday morning was no different. I opened my door to look out into the hallway. I listened, making sure I hadn't awakened daddy or Ms. Rose. Then, I quietly went downstairs to get a glass of milk.

Before I reached the kitchen, I heard some voices coming from that direction. As I got closer, I realized it was Richie and Danny. They were trying to whisper, but I could tell Richie was fussing about something. I know Richie didn't care for me, but I didn't care. I was just going to get a glass of milk, go back to my room and I didn't have to say a word to him to do that. As I got closer, I heard my name. I couldn't make out everything they were saying, so I tip toed to get closer and hid behind the wall, by the entrance of the kitchen.

"And then, when I go back to finish the job *you* should've took care of, she already done run off somewhere."

"I just thought that maybe if I left her there, it wouldn't of been no way for her to find her way back home."

"I told ya to get rid of her Danny. Not leave her 40 darn minutes away, like she ain't never gone find her way back here."

"Well, man I'm sorry, but I just, I just couldn't shoot her like that."

"Man, I took care of any and everythang that could've stood in your way. I made sure my dad was gone that night. Heck, I even left the door unlocked so you wouldn't have no problem sneakin' in. I don't know why I thought you could handle somethin' that darn simple."

Richie laughed and said, "She even told everybody how she heard ya run back to the car like a lil' girl."

I could hear the frustration in Danny's voice as he replied, "Rich, I ain't never killed nobody before. And on top of that, she a lil' girl. I can't believe you doin' all this over some darn money."

"You darn right I'm doin' it over some money. It would've pissed you off too if you found out your daddy was

~ 119 ~

givin' a nigger more money than he was givin' you when he die. She ain't even his own blood."

"Richie yo' dad is leavin' you money, and the train business y'all got. That's a lot. At least he still givin' ya somethin'. That's more than I can say for my folks."

"Danny, I was gonna give you $100,000. That should've made you feel good about somethin'."

"Well, I guess I just ain't got that kind of heart to do somethin' like that. If you want it done so bad, maybe you should do it yourself."

"Or maybe I should of got somebody that was gone do it right the first darn time."

Richie laughed and said, "I guess it's true what they say, if you want something done right the first time, you gotta do it yourself."

My heart was pounding so hard, I could hear it. I couldn't listen anymore. I went back up to my room as quietly as I could. When I got there, I made sure I locked the door behind me. I got under the covers and started crying. I couldn't believe he hated me that much. I was so scared just knowing I was living in the same house with someone who wanted me dead.

But why? Because of some money? Because I was obviously getting more money than him when daddy died.

Even though, sleep was calling my name, I'd stayed up for the rest of the night. I was afraid that if I'd went to sleep, I wouldn't be able to hear if someone was trying to get into my room. My mind kept wondering back to the night I'd been kidnapped. Richie wanted me dead. And poor Danny. Even though, he served a part in all of it, he was just someone Richie was using to do his dirty work.

I laid in bed with the covers pulled over my head, until I'd heard the very first sound from either Ms. Rose or Daddy, letting me know they were up.

"Good morning, Daddy."

He lowered his newspaper and turned around to see me standing behind him, in the doorway of the dining room.

"Good morning, dear. How are you?"

"I'm fine."

I lied. I wasn't fine.

He smiled, but I could see a hint of concern in his eyes. He probably noticed something was wrong with me. He knew me so well.

"Well," he said hesitantly, "Come have a seat. Rose was just beginning to make breakfast."

I strolled around the table to sit in the seat next to him. I grabbed some of his papers off of the table and opened it. It wasn't that I was interested in the newspaper, I just didn't want to sit there with nothing to do and time to think. I knew it seemed all too obvious to him that something was on my mind. I was looking at the article, but I had no idea what I was looking at because my mind was elsewhere.

"Automobiles?"

Did I hear daddy say something?

"Rodeo?"

"Oh."

I guess I did.

"Sorry, daddy. What did you say?"

"I said automobiles. Are you looking for a car?"

Not realizing what he was talking about, I gave him a strange look as he glanced over the brim of his newspaper.

"Oh," I said after it finally dawned on me that I'd picked up the Auto section of the newspaper. I smirked a little and shook my head.

He lowered his newspaper and leaned towards me.

"Rodeo, is everything alright?"

I took a deep breath and thought for a minute. I really didn't know how to begin to tell him about what had happened. I wondered what he'd think about his own son. I wondered how he'd take it. I wondered what he'd do. I...

"Rodeo?"

I snapped out of my thoughts. Daddy lay his newspaper on the table and took my hand in his.

"Whatever it is, you can tell me."

I could see the love in his eyes. I knew I could trust him. I just didn't know how to tell him. I started to get mad at myself for even thinking about the welfare of Richie and Danny. I mean, they did plot to kill me. It made me think of the devil and how every time something bad happens, daddy says, "The devil is always busy." I never understood why he said that, so I asked, "Daddy, why do you always say, the devil is always busy, when bad things happen?"

He sat up and cocked his head to the side. From the quizzical look he gave me, I knew that was not what he expected me to say. Still, he took a deep breath and looked towards the ceiling.

Finally, he said, "Rodeo," he cleared his throat before continuing, "God is good to us. Always. It is he, the devil, who is in the world, who brings bad things upon us. The bible says the enemy comes to steal, kill and destroy. All of those are bad things, right?"

I nodded my head quickly in agreement.

"Think about all the bad things going on in this world. Every day, it's something new and even crazier than before that's happening. It's obvious he is always busy. Still, even with the bad things that happen, God will give us what we need to get through it."

That makes sense.

"But, why do you think he is always so busy?"

He looked at me and smiled. Then, he took another deep breath and said, "This is what I believe, Rodeo. In the bible, in Revelation 12:12 to be exact, it tells how the devil is filled with such anger because he knows he only has a short time, okay?"

I nodded, listening attentively.

"You see, the devil knows that he only has a short time to win as many souls as he can before Jesus returns. He already knows, that without a doubt, he cannot and will not win against God, but that's not going to stop him from trying to deceive as many people as he can because he wants to be God. He thinks he is God. And, honestly, I can see why he may think that. I mean, look at the world. More than half the people on this earth are worshiping him. Don't worry, though, I have read the bible and God will win. But I'm getting ahead of myself."

He folded his hands, on top of the table and said, "This is why I believe he's so busy, because he knows his time is limited."

Wow. I love the way daddy explained things. I love him so much.

It seemed like so many emotions began to go through me all at once. Suddenly, it was all too much to contain. I began to sob softly. Daddy gently pulled me from my chair. I sat on his lap and laid my head on his chest.

"Rodeo, whatever it is, please tell me. You can trust me. Just tell me what's going on."

"I-I."

I sniffled between words as I tried to get it out.

"Early this morning, I woke up because I had a bad dream. I came to the kitchen to get some milk, but when I got there, I heard Richie and Danny talking."

I stopped to take a breath. Then, I looked up at daddy.

I could see the concern in his eyes as he said, "Go on."

"Oh, daddy," I blurted out, "I heard them talking about the night I'd gotten kidnapped. They did it. Richie wants me dead."

He shook his head. Not because he didn't believe me, but because he was stomped. He didn't know what to say. He didn't know how to respond.

"Wha-what?"

That was all he managed to say. I went on to tell him everything I'd heard them say. I even made sure I showed more favor towards Danny, letting daddy know he was only being used by Richie. I even told him about the money.

"How on earth did Richie know what was in my will," Daddy said to himself.

"I didn't know what to do daddy. I'm sorry. I wish this hadn't happened."

"Rodeo, you have nothing to be sorry about. This is not your fault. Do you hear me?"

I could see the seriousness in his eyes.

I nodded my head. He looked down and said, "Jesus. I just can't believe...wow. I always knew Richie didn't care for you that much, but I didn't know my own son had this kind of hate in him."

He sighed and said, "We're going to deal with this right now."

I got up and followed daddy. He stood in the middle of the foyer and yelled to the top of his lungs, "Richie."

That brought Ms. Rose out of the kitchen.

"Thomas, what's wrong?"

We all heard Richie coming up the steps and turned our attention towards the door. When he came out, he looked around at everyone looking at him.

"What's everybody lookin' at me for?"

Daddy looked down and took a deep breath.

"Richie, I'm going to ask you one time and one time only." He looked up towards him. "What happened the night Rodeo was kidnapped?"

Richie chuckled, uneasily, "What you askin' me for? You know what happened."

Daddy took another deep breath. I could tell he was trying to stay calm.

"No, I don't, but I have a feeling you do? What did you do Richie?"

Even though, she still didn't know exactly what was going on, that question caused Ms. Rose to look at Richie and gasp.

Richie shook his head, "I don't know what you talkin' bout. You know just as much as I know."

"No, I don't," Daddy snapped.

As he spoke, his voice got louder.

"You know exactly what happened because you were the one behind it all!"

"Oh, no," Ms. Rose said, placing her hand over her chest.

She and I both looked from Daddy to Richie, as they exchanged words.

"You might as well confess Richie, because the truth has come out."

Richie smacked his teeth.

"Ain't nothin' true about that."

"Yes, it is. You wanted to get rid of her because you found out about the money and you were going to pay Danny off with some of it."

Richie tried to speak, but he was stumbling over his words. I could tell he was wondering how daddy knew so much, but he was trying not to show it.

"Speaking of which," Daddy said, "How did you even find out about my will?"

Richie shrugged his shoulders, still trying to play dumb. Suddenly, the day I saw Richie standing in front of that law office, talking to that secretary, came back to me.

Before I knew it, I blurted out, "Daddy. The day of my birthday, Katina and I saw him standing outside of that law firm you go to. He was talking to the secretary who works there. She gave him a big envelop. I bet it must have had your information in it"

Richie looked at me like he could kill me. Daddy looked at him and said, "Did she give you my information, Richie?"

"No."

He sure said that quickly.

"Well, why were you there?"

After waiting a few seconds for a reply, Daddy finally said, "You know what, I'm not going to wait for you to tell another lie. Get you stuff and get out."

"Dad, I can't believe you takin' her side over your own son."

"No son of mine would do something this evil! Now you just get out of here! You hear me! Get out!"

I had never heard Daddy yell so loud before. His face had turned red. I knew he was mad.

"Calm down, Thomas," Ms. Rose cut in, still holding her hand over her chest.

I could see the worry all over her face. I'm guessing this is the first time she'd seen him like this too.

Richie shot a rotten look at her and mocked her in a taunting voice.

"Calm down, Thomas. Calm down, Thomas."

He was about to turn and leave. Then, he stopped and looked at Ms. Rose.

"Why you stickin' round so long, huh? I hope you don't think you gone have a chance with my dad cause guess what," he leaned in a little closer and said, "He still loves my momma."

"Richie stop it," daddy demanded.

"And you know what else," he went on, "You ain't nothin' but the help round here. Now go get my stuff together you maid."

Immediately, Daddy said, "Rose you stay right where you are."

Then, he quickly added, in a softer tone, "Please."

My heart smiled, considering all.

So respectful.

Daddy took his fourth deep breath and looked at the floor. He spoke as calmly as he could.

"Richie. I want you to get your things and get out."

"Dad you really…"

"Richie," daddy cut him off. "I know one day I will be able to forgive you for this evil thing you tried to do, but right now, I can't even bring myself to look you in the face."

Then, daddy walked away. He stopped midway up the stairs and said, "I'll give you one hour. Please, leave."

After we heard the door to daddy's room close, Richie gave me the meanest look I'd ever seen from anyone, before he stormed back downstairs.

I looked at Ms. Rose. She still looked shocked. Then, she shook her head and said, "Rodeo, don't feel bad or guilty about anything. You did the right thing."

She then walked back into the kitchen, while I stood there, not knowing how to feel.

Ms. Rose said I'd done the right thing, but had I?

Something felt so weird. So...wrong. Maybe it was just the tension in the air. I really didn't know what to think about how anyone felt, including myself. I just knew that whatever feelings Richie felt towards me before, he felt that way times 1,000.

I didn't stay sleep long. I woke up when I heard thunder from the storm. It was so loud, it made the windows shake. I was trying to go back to sleep, but I couldn't. I got up to go downstairs and get some milk. Ms. Rose knew how much I liked milk. She always made sure we had some in the refrigerator.

When I got downstairs, I heard some music coming from the family room. I looked in, but when I saw daddy, I hid, so he couldn't see me. He was swaying to the music. Listening to that man he likes. Sam Cooke. It was a little dark, but I started smiling when I realized Ms. Rose was standing in front of him.

They were dancing together, and daddy was singing to her.

"If I go...a million miles away, I'd write a letter...each and every day. Cause honey nothin', nothin' can ever change this, love I have for you..."

I was just smiling. Ms. Rose was smiling too.

I knew they liked each other.

I didn't even want to get milk now. I didn't want to bother them. I just went to lay back down and fell asleep, while that song was played in my head.

The next few days seemed much more different than others. Daddy wanted to spend almost every minute with Ms. Rose and me. We all talked, watched movies and danced to music. We even cooked together. Every chance he got, he told me how much he loved me. He even told Ms. Rose he loved her. He'd always told me he loved me, but there was something so different about it all this time.

Things felt especially weird on the following Monday morning, when I got up to get ready for school. My daddy always beat me downstairs first. Either he'd be eating his breakfast or reading his newspaper. Today, when I got ready to leave for school, he was still asleep. I knew he was entitled to be tired sometimes, especially with him being old and all, but it was just so weird. That bothered me the whole day. So, when school was finally over, I hurried home, with Katina following behind me.

"What in the world is goin' on?"

That's what Katina asked once we turned the corner by the bakery. I knew that was a rhetorical question, but I really wished I'd had a good answer for it. I knew something bad had happened. There was an ambulance and two police cars, sitting outside of our house. The closer I got, the more fear took over, especially when I saw Richie talking to the cops and Ms. Rose knelt to the ground crying hysterically.

Where's my daddy?

Before I knew it, my books fell to the ground and I took off running towards them.

In a matter of seconds, I was standing around everyone else. The paramedics were just closing the doors to the ambulance. Out of breath and trembling, I asked one of the white cops, "Who's in there?"

As if he was annoyed, he turned to Richie and asked, "Who's this?"

Irritated by the fact that he'd rudely dismissed me, I said, with authority, "I'm Thomas Donovan's daughter."

Of course, that brought a look of confusion to both the officers faces. Richie rolled his eyes and said nonchalantly, "She's not his daughter, she's..."

Before he could finish his sentence, Ms. Rose yelled, "He's gone Rodeo! Thomas is gone! He's dead!"

A chill went down my spine.

"W-What?"

That was all I could manage to say. I always wondered why people said, "what," when they heard bad news. I see why now. It was like, hoping what you'd just heard, would change if you heard it again. But you already know it won't.

I searched the faces of those around me. I don't know what I was searching for. Maybe reassurance that this was some kind of joke. I don't know. I felt a hand touch my shoulder. It was Katina. Empathy was written over her face. It felt as if my heart had dropped out of my chest. It ached badly. My breathing quickened as the realization of what was said finally began to sink in.

"No, no, no," I said.

Tears instantly streamed down my face as I tried to pry open the doors to the ambulance.

"Open the door," I yelled. "I want to see my daddy! Open the door please! Daddy open the door! Please open the door!"

I banged and pulled on the doors with all my might.

"Ma'am," the officer grabbed my arm, "You'll have to move back."

"Get off me," I demanded, snatching my arm away. "I want to see my daddy!"

The ambulance started, as both officers forcibly held me back. Then, it was driving away. As it left the driveway, I took advantage of knowing the officers believed I'd finally calmed down. I broke loose away from them and chased after the ambulance.

"Wait," I yelled. "Come back! I need to tell him how much I love him! Please, I didn't get to tell him this morning! Please! Come back!"

Out of breath, I fell to my knees, watching the ambulance speed off in the distance. I looked up to the sky and shook my head.

"You know he was the only good thing in my life. Why would you...take...why?"

I burst out crying worse than I had before. Oblivious to the world around me, I sat in the middle of the street, with my face buried in my hands. This hurting feeling was so weird to me because I didn't even feel this way when my momma got killed. I didn't know how to feel. All I knew was, the person who'd ever truly loved me, was gone. He wasn't coming back. Once again...I was left alone.

"What you still doin' here?"

Through a blur of tears, I looked up to see Richie staring at me. Even after the ambulance had left, I continued sitting in the middle of the street. Katina had to practically drag me to the house, where we sat on the porch. Although, I was still crying, I had to force myself to calm down because I'd worked up such a painful headache.

"What do you mean?"

He looked at me dumb-founded and said, "Like I said, what you still doin' here?"

"I live here."

"Well, you *did* live here with my dad, but he gone now. Ain't nobody here to take care of you. Even if you did try to stay, them people from the children services place gone take you, cause you ain't got no guardian."

I looked at Katina. She smacked her teeth and rolled her eyes. She knew Richie didn't like me. Even though, I knew this to be true, I couldn't help but think about what he'd said. I mean, I wasn't dumb enough to believe that he'd said those things because he was trying to sympathize with my current situation, but…he was right.

I didn't have anyone to take care of me. I knew Richie couldn't do it or should I say, he wouldn't do it. He was the last person I'd want to stay with anyway. Ms. Rose. Poor Ms. Rose. She had to be taken away in another ambulance, shortly after the first one left. She was in no shape to take care of anyone. I didn't know what to think or do.

I looked at Richie with, what could only be described as, hate in my eyes. He was rocking back and forth on his heels like he couldn't wait for me to get out of "his" house. I didn't like him, and I definitely didn't know what to think about him. If he was capable of doing something so sinister to me, it made me wonder if he would do something to his own father.

He looked so stupid as he said, "Well, gone and get as much as you can."

He turned to leave. As he opened the glass door to go back outside, I couldn't help the sarcasm in my voice as I said, "You sure seem really sad."

He stopped. Then, he looked back over his shoulder. With those dark, beady eyes glaring at me, he said, "Get your stuff and get out."

That was all he said as he let the door slam behind him.

"I can't stand that punk," Katina blurted out.

I looked at her and burst out crying.

"What am I going to do? I can't believe he's gone Katina. I don't want to believe it."

Katina put her hand on my shoulder and said, "I'm so sorry this happened to you Rodeo. I liked him. He was real nice. But you know what? Don't even worry about Richie. You can just stay with us."

"Really," I asked through sniffles. "You don't think your parents would mind?"

"No, they wouldn't. Especially not after what just happened to you. Plus, you ain't got nowhere else to go. Come on, let's get your stuff."

I didn't know what the next teenage years of my life would be like. Neither did I know how the rest of my life would turn out. But as I walked to Katina's house, on that cold, winter day, there was only one thing that I was sure of. I'd never forget Monday, January the 12th, 2009 for as long as I lived.

Chapter 11

Katina's parents accepted me better than I thought

they would. It seemed like they tried to do everything to make me feel comfortable in their home. They even offered to give me my own room, but Katina wanted me to stay in hers. Plus, I didn't want to sleep alone, so I slept on her pink couch, which was also a sofa bed. It was alright being there. Of course, being able to be at my daddy's house, in my own bed, would have been perfect, but I surely was grateful.

I was even more appreciative because if it weren't for Mrs. Daniels, I wouldn't have found out that my schooling was paid for. After a few days of wondering what I was going to do about school, Mrs. Daniels decided to take me to the school to see what could be done about my situation. It was then, that Mr. Demagio informed us that Daddy had sent a check in the mail, paying off my schooling, until I graduate. When was the check dated? Sunday. The day before he died. I could only thank God and thank God for daddy. He was something special.

It had been a little over three months since my daddy died. Although, I still cried sometimes, I was getting better. I was just so hurt. I didn't even know what happened to him. I mean, how did he die? He was fine the last time I saw him. It seemed like he was just taken away from me. No warning. Nothing. Just...gone. I didn't even get to go to his funeral. I didn't know how to find out any of that, anyway. Neither did I know how to get in touch with anyone he knew. I'm sure that's how Richie wanted it, though.

Mrs. Daniels had offered to take me to a therapist she knew, but I just told her I'd think about it. I really didn't want to talk to anybody about anything. The school offered to let me stay home for as long as I needed to, but I didn't want to do that either. I figured, I'd be better off focusing on my studies rather than being at home with nothing but time to think.

This morning, I'd been laying down for the most part, only getting up once to go to the bathroom. As I lay under the covers, with my knees pulled up to my chest, I stared at the picture of daddy and me, in my locket. I missed him. So much. Yet, in a sense, I did feel like he was still with me.

Suddenly, as if they were out of my control, memories began to flood my mind. Memories of holidays with daddy. Talk times. Even thoughts of Ms. Rose came up a few times. I tried my best to stop thinking about him because I knew what would soon follow. Too late. I felt my eyes begin to water.

Daddy...why...

"Rodeo."

I snapped out of it when I heard Katina yell my name. I dabbed the moisture away from my eyes, with my purple t-shirt. Then, I got up and opened the door just enough to stick my head out.

"Yes," I answered back.

She stood at the top of the stairs and said, "Come on. It's time to eat breakfast."

I cocked my head to the side, giving her the same look I usually did to let her know I really didn't want to be bothered. Then, she gave me the same look she usually did, letting me know her mom would be the person who'd be coming to get me next. I finally let out a long, "Okaaay," knowing that trying to skip breakfast would be a lost cause.

I stood with my back up against the door after I'd closed it. I was hungry, but I didn't have an appetite. I would have stayed in bed on this Saturday morning, like I usually tried to do, if it weren't for Mrs. Daniels. Honestly, if it weren't for her, gently forcing me to eat, I probably would have lost a lot of weight. And according to Mrs. Daniels, "Baby, you can't afford to lose no weight." I laughed at the thought of her saying that.

I dug through a white tub Mrs. Daniels had given me to put my clothes in, searching for some pants to put on. I settled for a lose pair of gray sweats. Sweat pants seemed to be my usual choice of clothing these days. They were comfortable and easy to coordinate a t-shirt and pair of sneakers with. I hardly cared anymore about putting effort into dressing up. Which is also why a ponytail had become my favorite hairstyle. Like, right now. Maybe I had become sort of depressed. Maybe, Mrs. Daniels had noticed it, that's why she suggested I see a therapist. Maybe. I don't know.

I stood in front of the long, green mirror on the wall, studying at myself. I was kind of skinny, but not in a starving kind of way. I could see my shape beginning to come in. It almost scared me as I noticed my breasts and butt getting bigger. I saw what type of attention body parts like those got, from being around Katina so much. She liked that type of attention, though. Still, Mrs. Daniels was right. I couldn't afford to miss any meals.

❀

"Woman, can I have some mo' tea, please."

Mr. David may have said please, but we all heard the irritation, not to mention, rudeness, in his voice. I sat next to Katina. Mr. David sat across from me, at the black, pub table, that seated eight people. I bit down on my bacon, watching Mrs. Daniels out of the corner of my eye. She took the glass of tea he held from his hand. She poured it down the drain. Then, refilled it with some more. All the while, moving about like the obedient wife she was.

According to him, it was watered down. Before that, he complained about his food not being hot enough. Therefore, she had to reheat it. Not in the microwave. On the stove. Mr. David was alright, but most times, he could be a real butt hole. I mean, was it Mrs. Daniel's fault that he decided to go stink up the bathroom right before it was time to eat?

I glanced at Katina. She was eating, but I noticed the mean glare she was giving him, followed by a roll of the eyes. I'm sure he noticed it, but he was probably used to it by now. The only time Katina seemed to like him is when he was giving her money.

"Tina," Mrs. Daniels said when she finally sat down to eat, even though, we were almost finished.

"Have you thought about what you want to do for your birthday yet?"

Katina's 16th birthday was a month from today, on May 21st. She'd been talking about wanting to have a sweet 16 birthday party for two months now. Although, she'd mentioned it to her mom, Mrs. Daniels told her she didn't think Mr. David would allow it.

"Momma," she whined, "I told you I wanted to have a sweet 16 birthday party."

Before Mrs. Daniels could respond, Mr. David said, "Where? Here?"

The silence let him know that's exactly where she wanted to have it.

"Ain't no darn party goin' on here."

When he said that, syrup dripped from a pancake he put in his mouth, onto his white muscle shirt, minus the muscles. He wiped it off with a napkin as he spoke.

"You ain't bout to be up in here with all them darn horny teenagers, listenin' to all that daggone devil music. Especially, with all that darn dry humpin' goin'on."

"Ain't nobody gone be doin' nothin' crazy, dang," Katina protested while smacking her teeth.

"And what in the world is dry humpin'," she added, annoyed.

"Dry humpin'!" He slammed his fist down on the table. "You dancin' so close it look like you gone make a baby."

"Momma," Katina yelled.

"I said no."

Mr. David glared at Katina. Then, Mrs. Daniels. He dared either of them to go up against what he'd said.

"Tina, honey, just think of something else to do," Mrs. Daniels calmly said.

With a frustrated moan, Katina jumped up from the table and stormed out of the kitchen.

"Tina," she yelled.

Katina continued to stomp up the stairs.

"Naw, let her go," Mr. David said. "She keep actin' like that and she won't get to do a darn thang for her birthday."

I watched Mrs. Daniels as she stared off into space and shook her head. Mr. David continued to stuff his mouth. I, on the other hand, quickly finished eating my pancakes, so I could remove myself from the table. It was too awkward sitting there with them. Afterwards, I returned back to my comfort zone. The bed.

❀

Well, today was Katina's birthday and no matter how much she tried, she couldn't get her mom to change Mr. David's mind about the party. We eventually went to hang out and shop around earlier that Saturday.

Now, we were at the movies and the last place I wanted to be, was sitting next to some guy Katina knew. She begged me to come with her because she didn't want her parents becoming suspicious as to why she was going by herself. So, her mom dropped us off at the mall, where we met, Jontae, her current boyfriend or something of that nature, and his brother. To be honest, it seemed like I was just her excuse to go out with boys.

So, here I was, sitting next to...what's his name, while Katina and Jontae sat all the way in the back of the theater. He was definitely not the type of guy I liked. Plus, I think he was at least 17 years old, which was 4 years too old for me. I'm sure that's what my daddy would've said anyway.

I stared at him. He was cracking up at almost everything that happened in the movie we went to see.

Ugh. He's so annoying.

We were watching a movie called *The Hangover*, which was rated R, but since Katina knew the guy working the ticket booth, we were able to get in. I mean, I have to admit, it was funny, but he was doing too much. I could tell he thought he was every girl's dream. He was light skinned and had good, curly hair. I couldn't deny that he was very handsome, but the last thing I wanted to do, was be with someone whose attitude didn't match their looks.

From what I remember Katina saying, he was one of those popular guys at his school. He had money and he was the captain of the basketball team. I'm guessing he was number 24. At least, that's what the Letterman's jacket he was wearing had on it. I decided to ask, as well as, remember his name, so I'd make sure to tell Katina I never wanted to be paired with him again.

"I'm sorry, what's your name again?"

"Kyree."

"Kyree?"

I repeated it to make sure I'd said it right.

"Yeah, Kyree. K-Y-R-E-E."

He went on to laugh loudly at a scene from the movie. I sighed heavily.

I can't wait until this is over.

After the movie was over, just when I thought my time with him was up, Katina begged me to ride with them for a little while.

"Come on Rodeo, please. It's only 8 o'clock. I told my momma we would be ready at 9."

I couldn't help rolling my eyes because I was irritated. Still, I only agreed because I didn't want to spoil her fun.

We ended up in some park, not too far from the mall. Even though, there were light posts around, he still managed to find the darkest place to park. We sat in the front while Katina and Jontae were in the far back of the jeep. The music from the radio did no justice in drowning out their moans and kisses.

"Dang Jontae. Don't lose yourself back there and forget we got a big game in a few nights."

He responded, "Man, don't hate on me cause I'm gettin' my mack on. Don't worry about me or my game either. I always put up some points."

"Well, you didn't deliver on the last game."

Kyree turned to me and said, "I always make the most points. Plus, I'm always the one doing the most on the team."

Jontae leaned over the back seat to get closer to us. He looked at me and said, "Aye, don't let this dude make you think he the only one on the team. I keep tellin' that fool ain't no *I* in team. He..."

Before he was able to finish, Katina pulled him back to where she was.

"Aye, whatever," Kyree yelled back to him. "Ain't no *I* in team, but it's a *I* in *I*. And *I,* " he points to himself, "Wanna win."

Can we say arrogant...selfish...amongst other things?

"See baby girl, I'm not selfish, I just have to play like Kobe when it comes to basketball. You know, I gotta take charge when I see the team not playin' right, even though, everybody got a job to do. You see, it's like this..."

He started rambling about the different positions on the team and what everyone's job was. I honestly cared less about what he was talking about. I wanted to lay down in bed and get under the covers. I started thinking about daddy.

When am I supposed to get used to not seeing him? If he were alive, I'm sure I wouldn't even be in this car right now. I...

My thoughts were interrupted by Kyree scooting closer towards me.

And no he didn't try to act like he was yawning just to put his arm around my shoulders.

I couldn't help but smack my teeth. He wasn't slick. I remembered seeing Will Smith do that to some girl on *The Fresh Prince of Bel Air.*

"What's up, baby?"

I sighed and said, "Nothing."

"Dang, why you actin' like you got a attitude? You been actin' funny all night."

"I don't have *an* attitude."

He looked at me and shook his head, slowly sliding away from me.

"See, that's why I don't like messin' with girls like you?"

"Girls like me? What is that supposed to mean?"

"Young, stuck up girls who think they better than everybody."

What? No he didn't go there.

"First of all, I'm not stuck up. I just don't want to be here, especially with an arrogant person like you."

"You do realize you in my car right?"

"I could care less if I was in your momma's car. You're just mad because I'm not falling all over you, like you probably expect every girl to do. Don't think just because I came with Katina tonight, that means I'm automatically supposed to be your date and do the things other girls might do."

He smacked his teeth and said, "Man, get outta my car."

Fine.

I didn't say a thing because I was ready to go anyway. I got out and slammed the door behind me.

"Aye, girl," he yelled, "Don't be slammin' my momma car door like that."

I stormed off with my arms folded. I stopped when I heard Katina yell my name for the second time. She straightened out her tight, green halter dress, as she got out of the car. Of course, that's not what she'd had on when we left the house, but it was small enough to fit in her purse.

"Rodeo, what's wrong?"

"I am so ready to go. I can't stand to be around him for another minute."

Katina looked back at the car. I know she was thinking about Jontae. I guess she was trying to decide if a debate was necessary.

"I'm not saying you have to leave, but I'm not staying."

"Come on, Rodeo. You know if you go, I gotta go."

She looked back at the car again. Then, she sighed in a disappointing way and said, "Alright."

"Hey," I stopped her, "I am not riding back in the front seat."

She sighed again, "Okay."

When we got back to the mall, I waited outside the bathroom, while Katina changed back into the shorts and t-shirt she'd originally had on. She finished just as her mother pulled up to take us home, where I showered and went straight to bed.

Chapter 12

The summer went by so fast and 9th grade came even faster. I mean, I wasn't complaining because I really liked school and it was just one step closer to me finishing. The summer had been fun. Katina and I hung out at the mall a lot. We also went to the movies a few times. We even went swimming a number of times at the neighborhood pool.

On my 15th birthday, Mr. David actually let Katina and me go to Six Flags. He dropped us off and even gave us money. I have to say, that was a very fun day for me. Daddy had mentioned Six Flags a few times, but we never got the chance to go.

I didn't hold much against daddy, or anything for that matter, when it came to going to different places. I was smart enough to know that daddy was old, and I mean, I did come along unexpectedly. I am still, to this day, grateful for him and everything we did. I'd take that life back in a heartbeat.

The days came and went, along with Christmas and New Years. During the holidays, we spent a lot of time at the

~ 156 ~

church and helping others. Mrs. Daniels had given me some clothes for Christmas and I really appreciated that, but that time of year always made me think about daddy and the events surrounding it.

January 16, 2010 made a little over a whole year since my daddy had died. It was a Saturday. A rainy day. An even better way to set my mood.

I'd been in bed all morning, reminiscing. I hadn't even gotten up to eat breakfast. Mrs. Daniels didn't badger me about it either. She knew what was going on, but she did check on me to make sure I was alright. She came back around noon to see if I wanted to go get my nails done with her and Katina. I declined.

I couldn't believe it had already been a year since I'd moved in with Katina and her parents. Moreover, it hadn't seemed like a whole year since daddy had died. Even though, this wasn't my permanent home and I didn't know how long I'd be here, I was thankful to have somewhere to stay.

Mrs. Daniels had been very understanding. She'd tried to help with anything she could and up until now, Mr. David had been someone that I had the upmost respect for.

After neglecting my stomach for as long as I could, I finally got up around 1 o'clock, so I could fix something to eat. I only had on my pink, long-sleeved, pajama shirt. I slipped on my black and pink pants to match.

I heard the TV on in the living room, so I knew Mr. David was home. I said, "Hey Mr. David," as I passed by the living room.

"Well, hey there," he said in a chipper voice. "I see somebody decided to get up."

I smiled a little and kept heading towards the kitchen. When I got in there, I opened the refrigerator to take out some mayonnaise, some turkey meat and a slice of cheese, to make a sandwich. As I opened the cabinet to get the bread and a paper plate, I heard Mr. David say, "Rodeo."

I jumped and turned around to face him. He'd scared me. He scared me even more by the way he said my name. It was in a low, drawn out voice. Almost as if he was saying it in an admiring way.

I hadn't even heard him come in. Usually, I could feel someone around me. He was propped up against the frame of the kitchen entryway. He had on some blue pajama pants and a white T-shirt.

He threw up his hands, "Sorry. Didn't mean to scare you."

I laughed nervously.

"That's okay."

I turned back around and continued to prepare my sandwich.

Okay, I thought. *Is he going to say something or just stand there?*

Just then, he asked, "You ever been to California?"

All the questions in the world and he asks that? I get it though. It's the name.

"No," I answered without fully turning around to face him.

I opened the drawer to grab a butter knife.

"You ever wanna go?"

"One day," I said as I spread the mayo over my bread.

"You wanna see what Rodeo Drive like, huh?" He chuckled.

I laughed a little and nodded my head, "Yes."

I mean, I really did want to go one day. I wanted to see what all the fuss was about.

I could hear his slippers slide across the floor.

"You know, the Bible says, "If you give, you will receive.""

He opened the refrigerator and ducked down to look in it. Then, he said, "Wouldn't you like to go to California? Shop? Get you some nice clothes? Whatever you want?"

I glanced at him as he looked up, making eye contact with me.

"Wouldn't you like that?"

Wait a minute...what were we talking about again?

I looked away and said, "I'll get there one day."

"Yeah, but," he closed the refrigerator and leaned against it, facing me, "Money is no problem for me."

Oookaaay.

"Thanks, but I'll get there one day," was all I could say.

Is he implying what I think he is implying?

I think I wanted to believe he wasn't, so I hurried to finish my sandwich. All I needed was some mustard and as I searched through the cabinets, I finally spotted it. It was laying on the second shelf, which was a little far from my reach. I stood on my tip toes and stretched my arm to reach it, when suddenly, Mr. David said, "Let me get that for you."

Before I had time to think, move or anything, he got behind me and reached for the mustard. That meant he was pressed up against me. I gasped and my heart skipped a beat because...I felt *him.*

He lowered the mustard onto the counter and turned to leave. I slowly turned to look at him as he strolled towards the living room. He glanced back once, with a smirk on his face. That let me know, he knew what he'd done, and he'd done it intentionally. He disappeared into the living room.

How dare he? And using the Bible at that.

That was the day I lost all respect for him as a person, but most of all, as a pastor.

For months I avoided Mr. David as much as I could. If I wasn't at school, I was in the room. If I wasn't in the room, I was at the park, the library or hanging around outside with Katina. The only time I was around him is when we were eating at home. Even then, sometimes I'd make excuses as to why I wasn't hungry, just so I could wait to eat after he was finished.

When it came to church, I always rode with Mrs. Daniels because Mr. David always had to leave early anyway. Still, I did have to sit through, what I now saw as, a sermon being preached by a wolf in sheep's clothing. I acted as if I was listening, but I'd really be reading the bible the whole time, closing my ears to any and everything he was saying. There was no way I was going to let him feed me.

There's no real reason as to why I never mentioned it to Mrs. Daniels. To be honest, I was afraid to tell her, more for her sake, than mine, if that makes any sense. There's no denying the fact that Mr. David runs everything in that house.

I thought about telling her a few times, but what will she say to him? What can she say? I mean, if I told her and she didn't say something, would I be mad? Yes. I would. She doesn't even have a voice in her own home. She would probably just try to sweep it under the rug and have me keep quiet about it. You know, make excuses like some parents by saying, "He didn't mean it." So, what's the point?

The funny thing is, my mother did a lot of messed up stuff and by the age of 7, I'd seen and heard things no kid should ever, ever have to witness, but she never played when it came to a man trying to mess with me. I was a witness to that. Yet and still, throughout the few months after the incident, I still showed respect because I had to. I just made sure I stayed out of sight as much as possible.

Chapter 13

One day, after Katina and I had come home from school, we walked in just in time to here Mr. David fussing at Mrs. Daniels, about not picking up his dry cleaning. We didn't bother going upstairs. We just stood in the kitchen because if he saw us, that'd give him something else to pick about. Sad, but true.

"Shelly, you know you supposed to pick up my dry cleanin' every Wednesday. Now, what I'm gone wear for bible study tonight? Huh?"

"Well, David you can wear your other black suit. That one is…"

"You don't tell me what I can wear. I already had in mind what I wanted to wear, and you done messed that up. Darn it! Sometimes, I don't even know what I need you round here for."

"David, I'm sorry. I…It's just been so much going on with the church and everything and it must've slipped my mind. I'm sorry. It won't happen again."

"Oh, it bet not happen again," he snapped.

After standing around in the kitchen for what couldn't have been more than 5 minutes, he was still going on and on. Katina looked at me and smacked her teeth and asked, "Can you walk to the store with me?"

I nodded, completely understanding her frustration.

Katina and I walked to a little corner store down the street from her house. We went there sometimes when we wanted to get some snacks. She said she just wanted to get out of the house. I could tell she was still mad about Mr. David.

"Man, I can't stand him. And my momma just sit there and don't say nothin' to defend herself. She just let him run over her. He so stupid."

Katina folded her arms, smacking her teeth. I didn't know what to say. I mean, he was who he was. Living in that house meant I had to put up with him from time to time, but Lord knows, if I had a better alternative, I wouldn't have been there.

"Oooh, there go Jontae."

I looked in the direction of Katina's stare. Two, teenage boys stood on the side of the convenient store. They were both brown-skinned, one a little lighter than the other, and slim and tall. I noticed Katina straightening the blue sundress she had on, while fluffing her hair out. She did it quickly, as if trying not to make it seem obvious that she was doing it for him.

As we got closer, she said, "Hey, Jontae."

He looked up and smiled. They hugged each other. I remember0ed him from the time we went to the movies.

She hit the other guy playfully, saying, "Hey, James."

James, with a low haircut, looked up from his phone and said, "Hey," before looking back down.

She turned to me and said, "Oh, and this my friend, Rodeo. You remember her Jontae, right?"

He nodded.

"Hey," they said.

"Hi."

I hardly knew what to do in situations like this. Situations where I'm around Katina and some boy she knows. It was always like, I was the one standing around looking stupid, trying to act like I wasn't listening to whatever conversation they were having. Like now.

"Tina, what's up," Jontae asked.

"Nothin'. Just had to get out of the house, away from my dumb step-daddy."

"Aw, well, you think you gonna make it to Kyree birthday party next month?"

Katina grinned and said, "Will you be there?"

He smirked.

"Come on boo, that's my brother. You know I'll be there."

I noticed her rub his chest with her finger, in a flirty way.

"Then, I'll be there. And my friend comin' too."

He smirked and said, "Cool. So, I'll just get with you later, baby girl."

"Ok."

Katina was smiling like a little girl as the two of them strolled off.

"Girl, I love when he call me baby girl. Come on, let's go and get some snacks."

I don't know why I woke up, but I did. I gasped, quickly sitting up in bed. My back was pressed against the back of the sofa. Thanks to the light, seeping in through the blinds, from the street lights, I was able to make out the black figure standing beside my bed. Mr. David. He was just standing there, staring at me. All he had on was some gray boxers.

I looked at the red numbers on the clock. 3:12. I glanced at Katina. She was still asleep. Then, he just…walked out.

What in the world was that about?

I watched the door for a moment. I wondered what, if anything was going to happen next. That really freaked me out.

Finally, after the beating of my heart slowed down from the adrenaline of shock, I sank back into bed.

I started to put the covers over my head, but I decided against it.

No way am I going back to sleep tonight.

That was sad. I shouldn't have to live in fear, no matter where I am. I closed my eyes and did the only thing I knew to do.

"Father God. I really don't know what all that was about, but you know. I also know that I shouldn't have to feel afraid and uncomfortable in a place where I'm living. I don't know. I just…" I sighed. "Okay, God. I trust you. I…trust…you. I know that you will not let any harm come to me and I know that you will never leave me. Please give me the peace I need right now because I don't know what to do. In Jesus Christ name I pray. Amen."

I lay there for a moment, staring at the ceiling. Then, I slowly drifted off to sleep.

Chapter 14

Today was a Friday. All that day Katina had been

begging me to go to some church function with her. She said
all the girls who were in our church group would be there. It
wasn't that I didn't want to go, well, I really didn't want to go.

I mean, all those girls ever did was gossip and talk
about boys. Jesus was usually the last thing on their minds. Yet
and still, after asking me for the hundredth time, I'm
exaggerating, but it was a lot, I'd decided to go with her.

Now, she was being grilled with questions by Mr.
David, as we sat around the dinner table.

"And where y'all gone be at," he asked, stuffing his
mouth with spaghetti.

Katina let out a frustrated sigh.

"I told you we gone be at Tiffany's house, but her
momma gone take us to the movies."

"And who is her momma," he asked.

"Ms. Tracy," she quickly replied.

He sat back, wiping the spaghetti stain off his white T-shirt, which only smudged it in even more. He shook his head.

"I ain't heard of neither one of them."

He looked towards Mrs. Daniels and asked, "Shelly, you heard of them?"

"Hmm," she said, thinking for a moment. "No. Those names don't ring a bell."

Katina smacked her teeth and said, "Well, of course, y'all don't know them. They only been there for about a month and when do y'all ever make time to meet anybody in the church anyway?"

I could tell she must have hit a guilty nerve by the way Mrs. Daniels paused as she put the fork full of food up to her mouth. As for Mr. David, he scowled at her like he wanted to slap her. He glanced at me. I looked away, but I noticed the look he gave me. One of those, I-don't-like-you looks.

He sighed, rolling his eyes and said, "Shelly, it's up to you. I'm goin' to watch TV."

He got up from the table and guzzled down the rest of his root beer. Then, he let out a loud burp and put his glass back down on the table, before walking out.

Katina looked at her mom and said, "Please momma."

"Well, I guess it would be okay."

"Yes," Katina exclaimed.

She got up and planted a kiss on her mother's cheek.

"Thank you, momma. Come on, Rodeo. Let's go get ready."

We put up our plates and I dragged myself up the stairs to get ready for this church thing.

Is it wrong that I secretly wanted her mom to say no?

Katina and I stood in the long driveway of Tiffany's house, waving goodbye to her mom, after she dropped us off. We began walking up the driveway, but as soon as Katina's mom was out of sight, she grabbed my arm to stop me from walking any further.

"Rodeo. I gotta tell you somethin'."

"Okay," I said, unsure and a little uneasy about whatever she had to say.

"Well," she began with a slight shrug of her shoulders.

Well?

Starting a statement off like that is hardly ever good. It's like asking your teacher if you aced the test and he says, "Well…"

I could tell she was reluctant to speak, but I forced her to continue.

"What is it?"

She rambled on saying, "We're not really going to the movies. Jontae's brother is having a party tonight and that's where we're going. So, come on. It's just over on the next street."

She grabbed my hand and tried to pull me along.

"Wait…what?" I pulled away confused.

I shook my head and motioned towards the huge, brick house behind me. "Whose house is this?"

She threw her hand. "Girl, I don't even know. I just told my momma this was it cause the lights in the house was on and it was cars parked in the driveway."

I was still confused.

"Wait? Okay, so, who's Tiffany…and Ms. Tracy?"

~ 173 ~

"Oh, girl," she laughed. "That's just somebody I made up."

She stood there with her hands on her hips, smiling, like this had been such a great master plan.

"Now, come on, Rodeo."

She went to grab my hand again, but I took a step back. I shook my head and let out a sigh of frustration. I knew she could tell I was mad.

"Rodeo, it's not like they gone find out. They don't know half the people in the church."

"Katina that's not the point," I snapped. "You know I don't like to lie. Especially, to adults."

She smacked her teeth.

"I know Rodeo, that's why I didn't tell you where we was really goin'."

My mouth dropped open.

"So, it's better to lie to me than let me make my own decisions?"

"Come on, Rodeo, you know it's not like that. I'm sorry. Look, technically you not lyin' because you didn't even know what was goin' on."

"Yeah, but now I know and that makes me a part of it."

I turned to walk towards the house.

"Rodeo. Where you goin'," she whispered.

I glanced over my shoulder saying, "I'm going to ask these *strangers* if I can use their phone, to get a ride back home."

"Rodeo."

She ran to catch up with me, blocking me from going any further. She put her hands up in front of her, pleading with me.

"Rodeo, please wait. Just hear me out okay?"

"You know Katina, I should've known this wasn't some church function by how excited you got when your mom said we could go."

She started to say something, but then, she thought for a minute and laughed. She knew I was right. I stood there with my arms crossed in front of me, tapping my foot, waiting to hear what she had to say.

"Rodeo, look. I'm so, so sorry that I lied to you, but I knew you wouldn't come."

"No," I interrupt, "You used me because you knew your parents wouldn't have let you come because they don't believe a word you say. And for good reason."

Guilt covered her face. She looked towards the ground. I stepped around her, heading towards the house, but she grabbed my arm again.

"Rodeo, please listen."

I smacked my teeth and stared at the ground as she spoke.

"I have used you, sometimes, to go places. I hate to say it that way, but it's true. I honestly never looked at it that way and I'm sorry. It won't happen again. I promise. But, just for tonight, could you come with me? Please."

I let out an irritable groan, shifting from one leg to the other.

"Please Rodeo. I really like this guy. I mean, we're already out. We might as well stay."

I glanced at her, letting her know that was not a good reason to stay.

"Please," she begged. "No more than two hours. I promise. Rodeo, you're the only true friend I've ever had, and

I promise I won't lie to you again. I like havin' you as a friend."

I shook my head. I didn't know if she'd truly meant what she said or if she was just playing with my emotions. After a few seconds, I finally gave in. I held up two fingers and said, "Two hours, Katina. That's it."

"I promise. Two hours."

She smiled like a little girl, bouncing up and down.

"Thank you," she said, hugging me. "Now, come on. I gotta find a house to hide behind so I can change my clothes."

I was wondering why she brought along that little, book bag purse. I rolled my eyes as she tugged me along.

It wasn't that cold at all for September, but the fall wind was still making its way through the jeans and thin, white, glittery shirt I had on. I was glad it was long sleeved because it was still sort of cool.

That's why I didn't understand how Katina wasn't cold in the black mini dress and black flip flops she'd changed into. It was so tight, it looked like it was painted on her. To make matters worse, it was a halter dress. Not to mention, the wind was blowing. I was so glad I'd put my hair in a ponytail. Katina had to run her fingers through hers, in an effort to straighten it, every time the wind knocked it out of place.

There were cars, which stretched at least 200 feet, parked on both sides of the street. It wasn't hard to tell where the party house was. It was the brick house with about 15 people standing around, talking, drinking and playing their own music from the cars parked in the driveway.

As we made our way up the driveway, Katina spoke to a few people she knew. I didn't know anyone, but I remembered seeing at least two familiar faces.

"You gotta go around back. The party's in the basement," some guy she knew told us.

We made our way around the nice-sized house and eventually found the only brown door, which I'm positive, led to the basement. I could hear bumping from the loud music before Katina even turned the knob. As soon as she pulled the door open, red light and music filled my senses.

Some people looked our way to see who'd come in. Others kept dancing or talking as if they hadn't noticed anything. We walked in the wide room, carefully scooping out the place, to see where our destination would be from there. Even though, the area was lit by four, floor lamps, placed in each corner of the room, it was still kind of hard to see.

Katina nudged me, "Come on. Let's go over there and grab those seats before somebody else does."

She was referring to the nice, black bar in the corner that had two, free bar stools in front of it. Thanks to the little desk lamp, sitting on the bar, the bartender was able to mix drinks with no problem.

"You ladies want a drink?"

"Yes..."

"No, thank you," I interrupted. "We're under aged," I added, giving her a stern look.

She reluctantly said, "No," in a whiny voice.

He shrugged his shoulders and went on to fix a drink for some other under aged person.

"Have you spotted Jontae?"

"Katina, I can hardly make out anything in here."

"Well, wait right here for a minute. I'm gonna go see if I can find him. Hold this for me, please."

She gave me her book bag purse.

"My cell phone is in there if you wanna play some games."

I really didn't want to sit there by myself, but I didn't want to be the party pooper I'm sure Katina thought I was. So, I just nodded my head and soon after, she got lost in the crowd. I looked around at all the people dancing to some fast song I'd never heard before. I was shocked at the way some of the boys and girls were dancing with each other. Now I could see why Mr. David called it "dry humping."

I didn't want to stare, and I didn't want to sit around looking stupid either, so I pulled out Katina's cell phone, to play some games. I'd been wrapped up in my game of Solitaire, when I heard Katina say, "Rodeo."

I quickly looked up to see her standing next to the person she'd come for.

"Hey," Jontae said, with a quick smile. Then, his attention turned to the guy behind the bar.

"Hey, Uncle Lewis, hook me up with some cranberry and vodka."

"I got you, nephew," he said as he began mixing the drink.

Katina tugged on Jontae's white T-Shirt as he took a sip of his drink.

"Come on baby, dance with me."

"Okay. James, hold my drink for me."

I did a double take as I looked to the left of me, to see who he was talking to. That was the guy I'd seen when Katina and I ran into Jontae at the store.

"I'll be back, Rodeo. You remember Jontae's cousin, James, right?"

I glanced at him and gave an awkward, half smile when he briefly made eye contact.

"Yeah, I remember."

She smiled while backing away into the crowd. I just shook my head and smirked. I looked down at the phone to check the time.

Only 7:20? One hour and 40 minutes to go.

"So," James said out of nowhere, "Your name is Rodeo, right?"

Without looking up from the phone, I nodded my head, "Yep."

I really didn't feel like making small talk.

~ 181 ~

"Rodeo, like…"

"Yeah," I quickly cut him off, "Like Rodeo Drive. Like the street in California."

He didn't say anything. I glanced at him out of the corner of my eye. He stared straight ahead, sipping on something dark in his clear cup. I closed my eyes and took a deep breath.

Forgive me, God. That was mean. Why am I being so snappy tonight? Maybe because I really don't want to be here. Still, that doesn't cause for me to be mean.

I sat up and leaned into him a little, so he could hear me over the loud music.

"I apologize. I wasn't trying to be mean."

He shrugged.

"It's okay."

He took a sip of his drink. I don't know why I expected him to say more than that. Maybe because he originally initiated the conversation? I figured I'd say something to keep it going. Not because I expected anything from him. I just didn't want him thinking I was stuck up, like I know some people thought. At least, those were some of the rumors I'd heard about me at school.

~ 182 ~

I looked at his clothes. White T-Shirt, dark blue jeans and some red and black, Jordan sneakers. I looked around the room.

What is it with all these guys wearing white T-Shirts?

I looked at him as he took another sip of his drink.

"Are you drinking alcohol?"

That's the only question that came to my mind in order to strike up a conversation again. He smirked.

"No, mom. It's just coke."

I giggled a little.

Loosen up, Rodeo. Stop acting like you're the police.

"So, you came here with Katina?"

"Huh?"

I leaned into him a little closer, in order to hear him better because it seemed as if the music had gotten even louder. I caught a whiff of his cologne.

He said, "I asked if you came here with Katina?"

"Oh, yeah, I did. Who'd you come with?"

"Well, I'm family so, you know," he shrugged.

"Oh, yeah. I forgot that."

~ 183 ~

We were still making small talk with each other when Katina resurfaced.

"I see y'all gettin' to know each other," she said, giggling.

"We're just talking, Katina."

I blushed a little from her putting me on the spot like that.

"Hey, Uncle Lewis. I know I need another drink," Jontae yelled across the bar. "I bet this one is all watered down."

"Hey, make me another on too Unc," some other guy yelled.

Is that who I think it is?

I caught a glimpse of "the other guy" when he got closer to James. What do you know, it was Mr. Pretty Boy/Mr. Arrogant. The one I'd gone to the movies with.

What was his name again? Oh yeah, K-Y-R-E-E.

I completely forgot he was Jontae's brother. Of course, he'd be at the party.

He slapped James on the leg and yelled, "Aye, what up Jimmy James."

James casually shook his head.

"Uh oh. I know you not drinkin'. You know you the designated driver. What you got in that cup…"

Even though, I wasn't looking at him, I saw the way he turned his nose up when he noticed me sitting next to James.

"Man, please tell me you not with her?"

He was talking to James, but I said, "No he's not, but do you have something to say to me?"

I didn't try to roll my neck or eyes, but that's what happened anyway.

He frowned and said, "Girl, I wasn't even talkin' to you. And who invited yo' uppity self to my party anyway?"

Uppity? Okay, do I really act stuck up? Rodeo, you have to work on that. But for now…

"First of all, you were talking about *me* and trust me, if I knew this was your party, I wouldn't have come."

He smacked his teeth and started to say something, but Jontae intervened just as his Uncle was passing them their drinks.

"Hey, hey, hey. Come on, Kyree. This your birthday party, so chill. Grab your drink and let's step outside for a minute."

He turned to walk away, but not before giving me an ugly look. Katina followed behind them.

Oh, he gets on my nerves.

I looked at the time on the phone. I sighed.

A whole darn hour to go.

I was lost in thought when I heard James say, "Um, I take it you two know each other?"

I looked at him. He had a smirk on his face. I knew he was talking about Kyree. My face softened and I giggled a little. I hadn't even realized I'd been frowning.

"Yeah, we...well, Katina hooked us up at the movies one night."

"Oh, so, y'all went on a date?"

"No."

I answered that quicker than I meant to.

"No," I repeated, calmly. "It was no date. Katina just wanted me to come along so she could go out with Jontae. I had no idea he would be there."

"Ooh," he replied, understanding the situation.

Honestly, he sounded sort of relieved.

"How old are you," he asked.

"15, but my birthday is actually three days from now, on the 27ᵗʰ. And you?"

"17. I just had a birthday last month."

He smiled. Then, I smiled.

"And if I don't get to see you again, happy…"

I'm almost certain he was about to say, "happy birthday," but he never got the chance because some girl ran in the house yelling, "Hey y'all, they out here fighting."

That made everyone who was anyone jump up to run outside. Even James and I got up, but we held back until it wasn't so crowded around the door. I knew Katina was outside which is why I was sort of curious to see what was going on.

Sure enough, when I get outside, Katina and some girl were rolling around on the ground. They were pulling hair, throwing punches and calling each other all sorts of names.

I yelled, "Oh my goodness, Katina."

I knew it was never a good idea to jump in a fight, even if you're only trying to break it up. I looked around to see

Jontae standing amongst the crowd, watching like everyone else, with his drink in his hand.

"Jontae, stop them."

He looked at me like he didn't have a care in the world.

"Man, these girls crazy," was all he said.

He finally passed his drink to Kyree. Then, he pulled the girls apart. Katina kept trying to get to the girl, but Jontae kept holding her back, saying, "Katina chill. Ain't nothing goin' on with me and that girl."

"You chill," she yelled. "You must be doin' somethin' or she wouldn't be actin' like this."

Oh Lord, I thought. I knew it had to be over something stupid like this. Hour or no hour, it was time to go.

Their Uncle Lewis finally came outside.

"Alright y'all, ain't nothin' to see out here. Gone and get back inside and cut all this craziness out."

Slowly, some people started making their way back into the house, while others hung around outside. Katina had walked around to the side of the house to fix her hair and clothes.

"Katina," I said as I approached her, "It's time to go."

Her mouth dropped open.

"Rodeo, we still got some time left. And I still got some words for that stupid boy."

She walked away, heading towards the basement door. I was getting mad. All of this nonsense for no reason. There was no way I was staying.

"Well, I'm leaving."

I started towards the front of the house.

"Rodeo, darn it!"

I turned to face her. She was standing there looking angry, holding her shoes in her hand.

"You know I can't stay…"

"Yeah, yeah, yeah," I cut her off. "I know you can't stay if I leave, but you know what, that's your problem."

I turned to walk away, but she grabbed me.

"Dang, Rodeo why you gotta be so mean?"

I glared at her. "Mean? How in the world am I being mean?"

"I'm sayin'," she smacked her teeth. "You don't never wanna do nothin' fun."

"Fun? You call this having fun? Fighting a girl over some boy who obviously enjoyed watching you fight, just as much as everybody else did. Darn Katina. Didn't anyone ever teach you about books before boys?"

That made her even angrier. With every word she said, her neck rolled, and she drew closer until she was only inches away from my face.

"Well, I'm sorry Ms. Goody-Two-Shoes, but my daddy didn't tell about that lil' book crap you talkin' bout. I didn't get the lucky life like you had, finding some rich, white man to take me as a daughter."

"Lucky?"

I took a step back because I wanted to slap her. I really tried to be grateful in life, but the last word I think of when it came to my life, was "lucky."

"Lucky?" I repeated.

I was hurt. Hurt by all the memories that started to fill my mind. Hurt by the things I'd gone through as a child. Hurt by the way my daddy was taken from me, after I felt like he was my Godsend. And hurt by how angry I got, the more I looked at that stupid look Katina had on her face, like she'd just told me a thing or two.

"Katina," I began.

I had to take a breath before continuing. "You call my life lucky? The only thing lucky about my life is that I had someone who cared enough to take me in, after my mother was killed and I was found sleeping on his train. Thank God he had enough sense to pay off my tuition before he died, otherwise, I probably wouldn't even be in school. Now, here I am," I threw my hands up, "Pretty much homeless."

I felt that lump in my throat, which meant tears would soon follow and that's what I did not want.

"I could go on and on about why I don't feel so lucky, but I'm not."

I looked around. I'd honestly forgotten that there were still people outside. Only a few of them were staring at us. Some wore looks of pity, including James. I quickly looked away and said, "I'm going back to where your mom dropped us off and I'm leaving."

I walked away, avoiding eye contact with everyone. As I walked down the street, I only looked back once to see Katina dragging behind me.

The ride home had been a quiet one. Mrs. Daniels asked a few questions but stopped after realizing she wasn't getting much conversation. I didn't answer any of them. I mean, it was Katina's lie.

When we got home, Katina went into the house first and headed up the stairs. As I started up the steps, I heard the door to her bedroom slam. I stopped in mid stride and turned around. Luckily, I had some of my belongings already downstairs in the basement, since I'd slept there a few times. So, that is where I slept.

Chapter 15

I woke up when I heard loud music coming from next door. I was hoping that by sleeping downstairs, I'd get me some extra sleep on this Saturday morning. Boy was I wrong. It seemed like I heard the bass from the neighbors' speakers even better than when I'd be sleeping upstairs.

I laid on the sofa for a while, thinking about what happened last night. Sometimes, I don't know how Katina and I were even friends because we were just so different. I could hear voices and shuffling from everyone upstairs. I didn't get up. If I hadn't already had two bags of chips and a bottle of water in my book bag, I would've had to go upstairs to eat, but I was glad I didn't have too. I didn't feel like being around anyone. I stayed downstairs almost all day, watching movies on TV and reading. Before I realized it, nightfall was coming, and my stomach was growling.

I finally got up, pulled my robe over my pajamas and slipped on my house shoes. Then, I went in the kitchen to fix me a sandwich. As I was spreading the mayonnaise on my bread, I got the feeling someone was in the room with me. I turned around to see Mr. David, standing there looking crazy, like he always does. All he had on was some Khaki slacks and house shoes. He didn't have a shirt on. I hated looking at his ugly chest with all that nappy hair on it. I didn't say anything. I just turned around and kept fixing my sandwich.

"Don't think I don't know you and Tina was out being some lil' fast gals last night. Y'all always chasin' after them boys and stuff like you ain't got no sense."

Was this fool talking to me? I really don't feel like dealing with him right now.

I didn't even turn around to look at him, I just said, "I wasn't doing anything."

"So, what you sayin'? You sayin' Tina was out there doing somethin'? Is that what you sayin'?"

I was trying my best to be cool, but I was getting irritated because I could tell he was just trying to mess with me for no reason.

"Mr. David, I'm not saying Katina was doing something, I just said *I* wasn't doing anything."

"Don't think you gonna come in my house and disrespect me lil' gal."

Disrespect him?

Now, I know he was just trying to pick with me, so I didn't reply. I went to the refrigerator to get some sandwich meat and a slice of cheese, but when I opened the door, he pushed it shut.

"You go buy your own darn food."

I had never raised my voice at him, but he made me so mad. I yelled, "What did you do that for?"

"You think you gone disrespect me in my house and eat my food? You gotta another darn thang comin'."

"I didn't do anything to you. You're just trying to mess with me for no reason."

He started walking towards me. Then, he pointed his finger in my face and said, "You know what? I ain't gotta deal with a lil' fast tail gal like you, who don't know how to respect her elders. You get outta my darn house."

I didn't wanna deal with him, so I yelled for Mrs. Daniels.

"Mrs. Daniels! Mrs. Daniels could you please come get your husband!"

He took a step back and said, "Come get your husband? What the heck she gone do? I pay the darn bills in this house. I'll put her butt out too. She ain't got no darn say in here. You should want to thank me for lettin' you stay here. I could of let you stay out in the streets with ya…"

"I would rather be living on the streets than to be anywhere near a snake like you!"

As soon as the last word left my mouth, he slapped me. I was so surprised. I stood there with my hand over my cheek. All of a sudden, I started laughing. I couldn't help it.

"What the heck you laughin' at?"

"You," I quickly replied.

I straightened up and looked him straight in the eyes. "I'm laughing at you. My daddy told me about people exactly like you. Acting like you this righteous, upright person."

The thought of Richie crossed my mind and I added, "I probably would have respected you more if you'd shown your true colors, but you're nothing but a wolf in sheep's clothing."

Now, he was speechless. He was looking at me like, "I know this girl is not talking to me."

"You're always trying to find some reason to mess with me. I bet you're just mad because I won't give in to your advances, but I would never, ever lay in the same bed with you."

Before I knew what was happening, his hand was around my neck. He pushed me up against the refrigerator, groping me all over. He was breathing heavily in my ear as he spoke. He sounded so evil.

"You think I'm mad cause you won't give me none? Huh? I'll take it from you if I want to. You in my house gal and I'll do what I want with you."

I screamed, "Get off me!"

I started swinging my fists everywhere until I got him off me. I ran over to the counter and grabbed the knife. He rubbed his face and saw blood on his hand from where I'd scratched him.

He looked up at me and said, "You scratched my darn face."

I still couldn't believe all this was happening. I didn't know what he might try to do. I held the knife up and said, "Mr. David. I promise, if you think about touching me, your head is coming off."

Before either of us could say anything, we heard someone unlocking the door. Katina appeared in the doorway. She stared at us, then yelled, "Momma."

Just then, Mrs. Daniels appeared. I was glad. For his sake and mine because I meant every word I said.

"What's going on in here?"

She looked at us both, concern all over her face.

Mr. David started yelling, "Shelly that darn gal got to go. She…"

I cut him off.

"Mrs. Daniels, your husband was in here trying to take advantage of me!"

I didn't try to yell or cry as I spoke, but I couldn't control my emotions.

"That gal is a lie. She just a lil' fast tail gal and I don't want her in here. She got to go!"

"Mrs. Daniels, your husband has been trying to mess with me for a long time now."

Katina shook her head and ran upstairs. I guess she didn't want to deal with everything that was going on. Mrs. Daniels was still standing there looking at me and Mr. David.

"David, why are you walking around with your shirt off?"

It looked like he wanted to slap her. He said, "Woman, don't tell me how to dress in my own darn house. I said I want this gal gone. Now get her out!"

As I watched him walk out of the kitchen, I realized I was still standing there holding the knife up. I put it down on the counter and looked at Mrs. Daniels. She was staring at the floor.

I said, "Mrs. Daniels, I wasn't trying to disrespect you or your house, but your husband started all of this. I was in the kitchen and..."

"Rodeo," she said in a dry voice, "I think you better just leave. But...wait, let me get my purse and at least give you some money."

Did I hear her right? Leave?

She started digging through her purse, when Mr. David yelled into the kitchen, "She don't get no darn money! She can leave with the same thang she came with! Nothin'!"

It was almost as if I hadn't heard anything other than, *leave.* I said, "But Mrs. Daniels...I-I don't have anywhere else to go. I didn't do anything. I mean, I would never disrespect..."

"I'm sorry, Rodeo." She shook her head, "I'm so sorry."

I looked at her with what I knew was a pitiful look. She looked at me like she'd been defeated. Then, she walked out of the kitchen and went upstairs. I stood there for a second, taking in everything that had just happened. I knew I couldn't do anything to change the situation. I ran upstairs to get my things together. I quickly threw on some navy, blue sweats and a long sleeved, black shirt. After I stuffed my book bag and duffel bag with the few items I had, I left without saying a word to anyone.

I stopped at the corner store Katina and I always walked to. I had to catch my breath. I walked to the side of the store and dropped my things beside me, as I sat on a wooden crate. I couldn't believe what had just happened. I was so mad. Mad at Mr. David, Mrs. Daniels and Katina. I know I shouldn't have been mad at Katina, but I guess I was just mad.

To be honest, I guess I shouldn't have been mad at Mrs. Daniels either. I knew she had no power or control in that house. Still, I couldn't help but cry. I didn't know what to do. As I sat there, feeling sorry for myself, I looked at all of the apartments and abandoned buildings around me. I was trying to see what I could do next or where I should go. Minutes must have passed as the tears continued to fall. With my face buried in my hands, I heard a soft voice say, "Rodeo?"

I quickly looked up through a blur of tears. All I saw was a dark figure, wearing all black. At first, I couldn't tell who it was. In fact, I was a little scared, but as the slim figure got closer, the dim streetlight revealed who it was. I cried out, "James!"

I jumped up and wrapped my arms around his neck. I know I'd caught him off guard, but I guess I was just so happy to see someone I recognized. I couldn't help crying harder than I had before. I could feel his hesitation as he slowly began to pat me on the back.

"Wha-what's the matter, Rodeo?"

I started to say something, but my constant crying wouldn't let me. I just continued to hug him with my face resting on his shoulder. I knew he was only, what I considered, a boy, but for some reason, I felt so safe at that moment.

After a few seconds, I'd finally calmed down enough to talk. I pulled away from him, only to see concern written all over his face. It was hard to tell, but it looked like he was a little teary eyed.

"I'm so sorry, James. I-I guess I'm just happy to see someone I know."

"Umm," he began, obviously not knowing what to say, "Are you hungry?"

I lowered my head because I was sort of embarrassed and ashamed to admit anything about my current situation. I could hear the nervousness in his voice as he spoke, slow and steady.

"I was about to go to Wendy's. It's right down the street. You wanna come?"

Wendy's. My Dave.

I could feel that annoying lump forming in my throat. I quickly took a deep breath and exhaled, "Yes."

James carried my duffel bag and I carried my book bag, as we walked in silence the whole 10 minutes it took to get there. I sat in the far back at a table for two, while James ordered our food. I watched him sit the tray down which had two cheeseburgers, two orders of fries and two drinks on it. I knew he was wondering what was wrong with me, but he hadn't asked any questions.

"Thank you, James."

He looked at me like I'd surprised him. He sat down, smiling shyly, "Oh, it's no problem."

I picked up a fry, thinking, maybe I was being sort of selfish. James had been super nice to me and he hadn't bothered asking any questions. Not that he had to know my business, but I wanted to tell him. Plus, I really needed someone to talk to.

"Katina's parents put me out," I blurted out.

We barely made eye contact with one another as he asked, "Why?"

I didn't know where to start, but I had to start somewhere. I took a deep breath and told him all about it. Wow. Even though, he wasn't someone who could take all my troubles away, it was just like therapy. After we'd gotten full

and had a few laughs, I felt so much better. I hadn't realized
how much I'd been holding in. I not only told him what had
happened, but I told him about my daddy and a little about my
momma too. Not too much though, I didn't want to overload
him with my bad memories.

We must have sat there talking for almost 3 hours.
Through it all, James followed my lead. He laughed when I
laughed. He smiled when I smiled. He even showed sympathy
when I was sad. He was so laid back and easy to talk to. I liked
that about him. I couldn't help but wonder what he thought
about me. So, I asked, "You probably think I'm weird, huh?"

"No," he laughed. "Actually, I think you're very
interesting. I'm sorry you had to go through all of that."

Although, he didn't describe me in one definite word, I
took the word "interesting" to mean something good. That
made me blush. I thought fast so I could change the subject.

"So, what were you doing before you ran into to me?"

He took a sip of his drink and said, "Oh, I had just left
work and I was about to grab something to eat before I went
home."

"Oh. What kind of job do you have?"

"A friend of my dad owns a barbershop by that store. He lets me clean it."

I waited for him to say something else. I don't know why. I could tell he was just as private as I was.

"Oh, well," I said, "I know you're glad you have a job. At least you get to have your own money."

"Yeah, well, it's not really by choice. My dad made me get it so I could help out with bills, but I like it because then I'm not home so much. Anyway," he hurried on as if he didn't want to get into all of that, "What you bout to do?"

I put my head down and sighed.

"You know...that's a good question."

I thought about blowing the question off like, "Oh, don't worry about me, I'll be okay," but I didn't know what I was going to do. So, I replied, "I really don't know what I'm going to do."

That's all I could say. He stared out of the window for a minute. I'm sure he wasn't staring at anything in particular. It looked more like he was thinking.

Finally, he said, "Maybe you could stay at my house."

I looked up at him. I couldn't tell whether that was a statement or a question.

"I mean, only if you want to," he added.

I had to think for a second. Not because I didn't want to take the offer, but because I never thought I'd have to make a decision like this. A guy, who I really didn't know, but trusted more than anyone else I knew, was offering to let me stay with him. Plus, this wasn't just his house, so I knew he probably wasn't the sole decision maker in this.

"Wouldn't your parents mind if you had a girl staying with you?"

As if he were talking to himself, he smirked and said, "Probably wouldn't even notice."

What was that supposed to mean?

"But, umm, no." He cleared his throat. "It's just me and my dad."

I didn't dare ask about his mother. I gathered that he probably didn't want to talk about it anyway. I really don't know why I was thinking, as if I had a lot of options. I didn't even have two pennies to rub together. I had to laugh to myself when I thought about that. Momma used to say that a lot.

Every time I asked her if she could buy me some candy, she would go off on me because I was asking her to spend some money. Then, she'd say, "You ain't even got two pennies to rub together."

One time, I asked her what that meant because I was always finding pennies on the floor. So, technically, I knew I had more than two pennies. She said, "That mean you ain't got $#@!," or, nothing, in my words.

"Sooo?"

I snapped out of my trance.

"Umm," I cleared my throat, "Sorry. I just...I hate to seem desperate, but I really do need a place to stay."

I put my head down and before I knew what was happening, he'd leaned forward and raised my chin up.

"Rodeo. It's okay if you need help. I don't mind. Come on. Let's go."

Wow. I could see the care in his eyes, and we hadn't even known each other that long. *Perhaps*, I thought, *he's just a caring person*. Either way, I thanked God for him.

Chapter 16

"*I* apologize. I know it's not what you're used to."

I glanced at James as we walked down the long, infested hallway of his apartment building. I kept telling myself that this must have been something I had to go through to get to wherever or whatever God had planned for me. I didn't want to get to the point where I thought I was too good for anything. So, I said, "James, I just thank you for helping me out like this. A lot of people wouldn't have done something like this and not ask for something in return."

Besides, he had no idea that the look and smell of this building was all too familiar to me. I had become immune to the smell of old urine and various drugs from having to sit out in the hallway so much. I'd seen plenty of those same urine stains and burnt spots in this rough, gray carpet.

"Sorry about the noise."

I looked at James. He was referring to the loud music, the yelling and the sound of a baby crying which could be heard through the thin, stained, white walls.

"Oh, I didn't even notice it."

He smiled shyly. I was glad. I tried to make light of the situation because I could tell he was embarrassed by the rundown, high-rise apartments he lived in and I didn't want him to feel that way.

After passing about 10, dark green doors on either side of the hallway, I began to wonder when we would get to his. All of them were decorated with writing and some type of art which was obviously done by the people who lived there over the years. Finally, we stopped at the last door on the right.

As he unlocked his door, using a single key, the door across from his flew open. Some shirtless, dark-skinned guy stormed out of the apartment, zipping up his denim jeans. Seconds later, a tall, bony, high-yellow woman stepped out into the hallway.

She yelled after the man, "You better bring my darn money back!"

"That crap ain't even worth my money," he yelled back as he casually strolled down the hallway.

~ 209 ~

The woman's long, tangled, blonde wig didn't move an inch as her head moved from side to side while she yelled explicitly to him. She had on a short, black, silk robe which hardly concealed her body because it was so loosely tied.

"Come on."

James stood in the doorway, waiting for me to enter. I quickly stepped in, not wanting to make eye contact with the lady. As he was about to close the door, I heard the lady call his name.

"Yes ma'am," he replied so respectfully.

"Yo' daddy at home?"

"No ma'am."

"Oh. Well, when he get there tell 'em I want my cigarettes and my money. I heard he got a new lil' girlfriend, but my stuff ain't free."

"Yes ma'am."

He slowly closed the door, locked it and took a long, deep breath.

There was a hint of annoyance in his voice as he said, "Come on. You can have my room."

I followed him, carefully stepping over beer cans, cigarette butts and stains on the, what probably used to be nice, beige carpet.

"I'm sorry about the way the place looks. I've been gone since 6 o'clock this morning. My dad must have been here today."

"Oh, it's okay," I say.

There wasn't much furniture. Just one TV on the floor, a brown, worn-out sofa and a card table with two folding chairs next to the small kitchen area.

James unlocked the door to his room and sat my bag down on his bed. I scooped the room out quickly, not wanting to stare so much. It was a room fit for a guy, but it was cleaner than I expected. His full-sized bed sat on the floor, covered with a black comforter. He had a four drawer, brown dresser that had a small TV sitting on top of it and a black, floor lamp in the corner of the room. Nothing to extravagant, but it looked comfortable enough.

He stood in the doorway and said, "There are some towels and rags in the hallway closet if you need a shower. Make yourself at home."

I looked at him. He was casually leaning against the door frame.

"I bet you say that to all the girls," I said playfully.

He chuckled, "Umm, as a matter of fact, I don't."

I caught myself staring. He had such a nice smile. I guess I never noticed it because he hardly smiled. I knew he wasn't some innocent 17-year old, but for now, I trusted him, and he made me feel comfortable. I was glad God had put him in my path.

"Thanks again, James. For everything."

"You're welcome. Let me know if you need anything."

When he closed the door, I gathered my things to take a shower and shortly thereafter, I laid down, thinking about how my 16th birthday was in two more days. I was too drained, mentally, to even think about it. I sighed. Then, I went to sleep.

Chapter 17

*E*very day, for the next two months, I left in the
morning when James did, and I returned home when he did. I
still hadn't seen his dad or anyone else in the apartment, but I
only felt comfortable being there when he was. Most days, I
spent my time at the library or park, unless it was cold, which
was happening now that December had approached. Usually,
I'd just wait around and read or do school work, while I waited
for him.

James would walk me to school in the morning. Then,
he walked the five blocks it took to get to his. After school,
we'd walk home together, unless he had to go to the
barbershop.

Of course, I still thought about my daddy. Pretty much
every day. I mean, it was kind of hard not to. Especially, since
I passed our old neighborhood all the time. I hadn't cried in a
while, though. That was a good thing. I even passed by
Katina's neighborhood on the way to school as well. I hadn't
seen her in a while, though. When I used to see her, walking

through the halls or at lunch, we didn't speak. After a while, I didn't see her at all. I figured maybe she didn't go to the school anymore.

Most evenings, or whatever time we got home, we were both too tired to stay up, unless it was the weekend. Then, we'd watch movies, talk and eat junk food. Being that I was in 10th grade, meant that the work got a little harder and my study time got a little longer, but I was still doing great in school and everything was going smoothly.

It was Saturday night. I sat on the couch in my pajamas and purple robe, while James, who wore black jogging pants and a white T-Shirt, made tacos for us. When he finished, we both ate while watching the movie *Dumb and Dumber*. We'd already watched it three times together over a two week stretch. I'd never seen the movie before, until he showed it to me. He said he'd watched it a numerous amount of times. This had become our favorite comedy to watch together.

"Is there some Ketchup?"

"Yeah, I'll get it," he replied as he sat his plate down on the couch.

He handed me the Ketchup while laughing at a funny part in the movie.

"What the..."

When I looked up to see what James was so taken aback by, he was looking at me.

"Rodeo? Ketchup? On Tacos?"

"Yes," I replied. "I like Ketchup. What's wrong with that?"

"Um, everything."

He took a bite of his Taco.

I shook my head, "Anyway."

"That's just nasty."

I put my Taco down.

"What? Is there a law that says you can only eat Taco's with Taco sauce?"

He made a funny, disgusted face and said, "It's just weird."

"Good. I like being weird. Weird is different. That's a good thing."

"It's still nasty."

I smacked my teeth, "Says who?"

He smirked and said, "Sir Isaac Newton."

I knew he was being silly, so I played along.

"So," I said as I shrugged my shoulders. "Who is he to me? He not my daddy."

We both burst out laughing. I always had so much fun just hanging out with him. I stuck my tongue out at him. He nudged me playfully and I giggled. Before long, I noticed he'd stopped laughing, but I still was. He had a smirk on his face, but there was something in his eyes. Something…different.

Before I knew what was happening, James leaned over and kissed me quickly on the cheek. Then, he proceeded to eat his Taco and watch the movie, laughing as if nothing had happened.

I, on the other hand, hadn't realized I was still staring at him. I quickly looked at the movie. Only, I wasn't really looking at the movie.

What was that? And why is he able to act so normal?

I laughed a little at a scene in the movie and took a bite of my Taco. I wasn't paying much attention to the movie. I was only trying to hide the fact that I was still thinking about James.

Did he...like me? Did I...like him?

It was hard to tell. Maybe because "boy stuff" wasn't something I thought much about. When I think about it, it was probably only because I was always thinking about so much other stuff. Like my daddy, school, my life and a place to call home. After a moment, I realized, I did like him. Of course, I wasn't thinking about anything too serious right now, but I did like him. I'm glad he was who he was. Not too pushy, but he obviously wanted me to know that he liked me.

Our night went on, filled with junk food, movies, talks and laughter. At around 2 in the morning, I finally told him I was going to lay down. I said a prayer, thanked God for my friend and went to sleep.

When I got up that next Sunday morning, I went into the living room to wake James up, who was asleep on the sofa.

That had become his new bed since I'd been there. I gently tapped his shoulder. He let out a low, sleepy moan.

"James," I whispered.

"Hmm."

"Where is the nearest church around here?"

He looked up at me, rubbing the sleep from his eyes.

"Church?"

I know he wasn't expecting me to say that, but I had to go. I had begun feeling like I was getting into a routine and in that routine, I was forgetting to give God more of my time. I had come to realize it was easy to sort of "slip away" and I did not want that to happen.

"Yes. Is there one close by?"

I'd already taken my shower and gotten dressed. I had on my black slacks with a long-sleeved, pink and black flower shirt. I was in the process of curling my hair which fell from my ponytail, when I heard a knock at the bathroom door. I knew it could only be James. I'd been in the bathroom for a while, so I figured he needed to use it.

"I'm sorry, James," I yelled. "I know you have to use the bathroom. I'm coming out now."

As I gathered my things, he laughed a little and said, "Well, yeah, I do need to use it, but I was wondering if I could go with you?"

I'm glad he couldn't see the look on my face because that really surprised me. Not that he couldn't go, I just didn't know how he felt about church and all that. I pulled open the door.

"Of course, you..."

Well surprise, surprise. I was completely caught off guard. James was already dressed in some blue, khaki pants, a short-sleeved, black, polo shirt and some black dress shoes. He smiled. I knew it was because he knew I hadn't expected to see him up and dressed already.

I smiled back and said, "You look nice."

"Thank you. You do too."

"Thanks."

I found myself blushing. I quickly finished gathering my stuff so he could come in.

It felt good to go to church. It felt even better to have James there with me too. Through the whole service I noticed people watching us. I'm not sure what they were thinking, but I assumed they were constantly glancing at us because we were two new faces. It was a small church that sat next to a convenient store on gravel ground. It held about 40 people. I could tell everyone was familiar with each other.

As the music played, James and I watched from the back pew, as some of the people danced and ran around the church. I laughed to myself as I thought about how I used to fall asleep in daddy's church. There was no way I'd be falling asleep here. We clapped along to the upbeat tempo of the music, as the short, gray haired preacher yelled, "I can feel the Holy Spirit in this place."

"Yeeeessss," the congregation yelled.

After the service ended, the preacher said a prayer and offered for anyone who wanted to be saved or join the church, to come forth. I thought about it. I could tell James did too from the questioning look he gave me. I was all for Jesus, but I didn't want to join the church. Plus, I had already been saved and daddy said you don't have to do again if you understand what you did the first time. So, I decided against it. After that, the preacher dismissed the congregation.

As we walked towards the wooden, doubled doors, there was a heavy-set woman, wearing a beige, two-piece suit, walking towards us. I'd noticed her staring at us, or me, from time to time, throughout the service. She, along with most of the women, had a fancy hat on that went with her outfit. She smiled and waved her hand to get our attention.

"Hey baby, how y'all doin'?"

"Good," we replied in unison, smiling.

I could tell she was probably one of those grandmothers who kissed all over her grand-kids and drowned them with cookies.

"That's good. Well," she started as she put her hand on my shoulder, "I'm glad to have y'all in church today."

"Thank you," we replied again.

We glanced at each other and laughed by our simultaneous responses. She just smiled, looking at us both.

"Well, I would love to have the two of you come back and visit us again, but just in case I don't see you no more, I wanted to give you something before you leave."

We watched as she dug in her oversized, black purse and pulled out a small, white, hand-held bible.

"Now, I only have one, but you can just share it with your brother."

"Oh, we..." I began to correct her on James being my brother, but she kept speaking so, I let her continue.

"I want you to stay in the word of the Lord and read your bible baby cause the devil sure is busy, you hear me?"

"Yes ma'am," I replied.

I smiled as a quick thought flashed across my mind about my daddy. I was glad she'd given me that bible because I'd lost the one daddy gave me. I think I left it at daddy's house when I moved to Katina's.

"Thank you so much," I said as she hugged us both before leaving.

❁

"Thanks for the food James…again."

He shrugged and said, "You know it's no problem."

After we left church, we'd come to Wendy's to have our usual bacon cheeseburgers and fries. I couldn't help but smile as I glanced at James sitting across from me. He'd been so nice to me since I'd been staying with him. I was greatly thankful for him, but I hated feeling as though I was a huge burden on him. It really seemed like he didn't mind, but I wished there was more I could do for him.

After we finished eating, he asked if I wanted to go see a movie. I knew movies were half price on Sundays, but for some reason, I was so tired. Besides, I had to finish reading a book for my English class before tomorrow, so I told him we could definitely do it next Sunday.

When we got to James' home, he plopped down on the sofa to watch some movie he'd put in. I went into the room and changed into a white t-shirt and some pink sweats, before grabbing my book. Although, *A Tale of Two Cities* was a good book, I'm not sure I got past the first page I was on before drifting off to sleep.

Chapter 18

"**W**hat the..."

I jumped out of bed and stumbled over to the light switch. I thought I felt something touching me, but I didn't know for sure. Once I flipped on the light switch, I had to blink a few times just to make sure I was really awake.

"What are you doing," I asked. "Who are you?" I was frantic.

Some shirtless, sweaty man, who only had on some dirty, white boxers and white socks was laying in the bed. The strong smell of alcohol seeped through his pores so much so, that the smell filled the room. He scratched his rough, black hair and folded his hands behind his head as he grinned.

"Who are you," I demanded.

He sat up in the bed and pointed a finger at himself.

"Who am *I*?"

He said that like I should have known.

Barely able to speak each word correctly, he said, "Baby gul, you in my house. James know he can't brang no women in this house that I can't have first. So, come on back over here."

He grinned again, showing a mouth full of missing teeth.

This is James' dad? Oh my.

I almost threw up as I stood there, motionless, staring at a chest and beer belly covered in nappy hairs. I hadn't realized I'd been staring until he patted the spot next to him, inviting me to join him on the bed. I went for the door as he yelled, "Where you goin'?"

"James."

I shook him. At first, he moaned. Then, he immediately sat up when he heard his dad yelling. He squinted through sleepy eyes asking, "What's goin' on?"

"James, your dad is trying to mess with me."

"What? My dad...what?"

"He's trying to..."

We both looked towards the direction of his dad. He was leaned up against the wall by the kitchen. He drank from a can of beer that came out of nowhere, scratching his belly. He let out a burp and said, "Ain't no woman gone be up in here if she ain't puttin' out."

"What? Dad, no."

James tried to explain as he sat up on the couch.

"This-this is just my friend. She just needed a place to stay. Why you go in my room anyway?"

His dad looked at him as serious as he could and said, "Punk, don't forget I'm yo' daddy. Talk to me like you crazy and I'm gone beat you down in front of this lil' (female dog)."

Only, he didn't say female dog. I gasped.

Did he really just call me that?

"Dad," James said calmly, "I was just askin' why you was in there to begin with?"

"Cause," his dad stumbled while walking towards him, "Yo' butt was sleepin' on the sofa, so I was gone sleep in yo' bed. Then, I saw it was a lil' treat in it, so I was gone help myself to some."

"Dad, she only 16. Just leave her alone."

James glanced at me as if to say, "I'm sorry." I could tell he was disgusted. Embarrassed? Maybe, both.

"You don't tell me what to do punk. She a woman ain't she? Now," he crept closer, staring at me with those yellow eyes. "If she gone stay, she gotta pay."

He started to reach for me, but James quickly blocked his way. His dad angrily looked at him. Then, he tried to shove James out of the way with his elbow, but he didn't budge. I could tell James was getting more frustrated by the second.

"Dad," he said in a calm voice, "Please just, just go to bed. I don't feel like dealin' with this right now."

That statement let me know his dad was usually like this. It also let me know why he didn't mind being away from home so much. His dad squinted his eyes at him, looking as if he was sizing him up. Before either of us knew it, he'd slapped James across the face, with the back side of his hand.

"James!"

I don't know why I said his name. I was in shock. I looked at him. He held his hand up to his face. I'm almost certain that since James' dad was already sloppy drunk, it was easy for him to lose his footing and fall, as James pushed him with all his might. His dad looked at his spilled beer on the floor. Then, he narrowed his eyes at James.

He said, "Oh, boy. You bout to get it now."

His dad struggled to get up, but before he could, James charged at him and began pounding him with his fists. I didn't know what to do. I wanted to yell "stop." Then again, I wanted to yell "Bout is not a word"....at least, not the way he used it.

I stood frozen, watching James punch his dad over constant yells of, "I'm sick of you" and "I hate you." He'd lost control. It was as if something in him had snapped. I started to feel sorry for his dad. I wanted to help him, but I didn't want to get in the middle of it. I didn't want to *be* in the middle of it at all and in my mind, I was the reason for all of this. I couldn't stay. I had to go.

I ran into the room and stuffed anything that was mine into my bags. I threw my black, pull-over on and slipped on my sneakers. Then, I grabbed my duffel and book bag. It probably didn't take three whole minutes for me to do that, but even in that short time, James was still going at it. He didn't even notice me run past him to go out the door.

Chapter 19

*I*f it were warmer, I would have walked around

outside, but instead, I sat at a back table in the Wendy's James and I always went to. I stared out of the window, watching cars go by. I guess I was in a daze.

I was so tired of thinking. All I knew was, here I was again. Homeless. I was homeless. I might as well call it what it really was. I'd been homeless ever since my momma was killed. I mean, even living with my daddy was only temporary. If it weren't, I wouldn't be here now.

I wanted to scream out loud so badly, but I just settled for screaming in my mind. Gosh. I was so frustrated. It was after 9 pm and I didn't have anywhere to go.

What now, God? Huh? What am I supposed to do now?

I threw my hands up and exhaled heavily. I slowly turned my head to look towards the front of the restaurant, scanning the room. Not many people were there. It was getting late and I didn't know how long I'd be able to sit in there. There was a young, Mexican couple eating together. Talking. Laughing. Looking so happy. Not a care in the world. There was also a little girl eating with, who I assumed, was her momma. I'd guessed they decided to come at the last minute because the little girl still had on her pink, Dora the Explorer pajamas.

She looked up from her chicken nuggets as if she knew I was looking at her. She smiled. Then, she waved. I smiled and waved back. Then, she went back to eating her food. She looked like she was at least 7 years old. Her hair was in two ponytails, hanging on either side of her head. I didn't know if her daddy was around. Either way, she looked happy.

I imagined my momma and I, sitting there. Doing simple things like that. I think momma always thought we had to have a lot of money to do things. The truth is, it would have made me happy just to watch a movie with her sometimes. My smile faded as real, bitter memories took over my make believe, happy ones. I quickly turned my head and let the music from the intercom fill my mind.

Since it was so close to Christmas, every song that played was a Christmas song. There was no snow on the ground. In fact, it seemed like most parts of Georgia hardly ever produced a white Christmas. Still, anyone could tell it was here because almost every store on the street was decorated with lights and different sorts of ornaments.

It's sad, but I couldn't remember a Christmas with momma. I don't know why she was the way she was. Of course, my best memories of Christmas were with my daddy. All of them. I looked at the jewelry I had on. Daddy always drowned me with gifts. He also drowned me with, what I knew was, love.

Oh, how I wish I could be with him right now. I wish...

I turned around when I felt someone tapping my arm. It was the little girl. I looked around to see her momma throwing their trash away. I figured she must have snuck away quickly, to come over to where I was, before they left. She smiled, revealing two, missing, front teeth. I couldn't help but smile. She handed me a small, peppermint, candy cane and said, "Merry Christmas."

"Thank you so much. Merry Christmas."

Just like a talkative little girl would do, she went on to say, "I like your rings and bracelets. I bet you can get a lot of money for those. I like..."

"Tabitha. Get over here so we can go."

I looked towards her momma, who was standing in the door of the restaurant. The little girl, now known as Tabitha, ran towards her. She looked back once to smile, before they left.

I smiled. Tabitha. She was so cute. I looked at my jewelry again. I probably would have said the same thing to someone. I probably could get a lot of money for them too. I stared at them for a while as the words she'd said sank deeper into my mind.

Wait a minute. I probably could get a lot of money for them.

I studied the jewelry for a moment. I felt sentiment for all of it because it had come from my daddy. Still, I knew what I had to do. I mean, it was all material stuff anyway. Sometimes daddy would say, "You can't take any of this stuff with you when you're dead." Besides, I could always get other things.

I stood up and gathered my things. If I didn't know anything else, I knew what a pawn shop was. Momma made many trips there. That's how we went from having some things, to having no things at all. James and I passed one not far from here every time we came to Wendy's.

But darn it! They're not going to be opened at this time of night.

I looked around the restaurant. I was the only customer there. Two female employees had been cleaning up the lobby area. They tried not to make it obvious, but from their constant glances, I knew they were probably wondering when I was going to leave. I slumped back down on the chair. I tried not to panic after getting my hopes up so high.

Ok, Rodeo. You only have to find somewhere to sleep tonight. Even if you can find a place to hide out just for tonight, that...would be...great. Think. Think. Think.

I noticed the manager looking at me from behind the counter. She was standing at the register, counting some money. I knew it was time to go. I looked out of the window. It only took a few seconds for me to realize that the answer had been there from the start. I knew what I had to do. I mean, at this time of night, it was the only thing I could do. I pulled the hood to my black pullover over my head and left, making my way across the street.

❀

I stood in front of a black tent that was big enough for two people. It was one of the three tents on display, just barely out of camera view. Since it was so late, there weren't many people in the store that night. But still, even I knew there were always people at Walmart. Especially, a 24-hour one.

After I made sure there was no one around, I quickly tossed my bags into the tent. Next, I strolled around the store to the food isle, making sure I didn't look suspicious. I grabbed a small, fruit punch drink and a turkey sandwich from the deli. Then, I walked back to where the tent was. After looking around, I quickly got in and zipped it up.

As I prepared to eat the sandwich, I looked up and whispered, "You know I wouldn't have stolen this if I didn't believe I had to. Please forgive me."

I blessed my food and ate it. After I finished, I hid the stolen evidence in my book bag. Then, I laid down. There was no need in staying up. It's not like I had a TV to watch. I kept on my clothes, so it would be easy to get up and go. I decided I'd just sleep until morning and then, go to the pawn shop.

"Attention Walmart shoppers..."

I woke up when I heard someone talking over the intercom. I wasn't sure what time it was, but I figured I'd find out soon enough. I grabbed my bags and zipped the front of the tent down just a little. I peered out to see if there was anyone around. Then, I slowly zipped it down just enough to stick my head out. After I saw that the coast was clear, I stepped out.

I could see that it was daylight outside, but first, I made my way to the bathroom. I at least had to wash my face and brush my teeth. Afterwards, I left, making my way back across the street, to the pawn shop.

"You got to be 18 years or older. You got ID?"

I stared back at the black man. Knowing he knew I didn't have ID. Even more, I knew he knew I was not 18.

Why in the world hadn't I thought of that?

I looked at the gray-haired, 60 something, looking man and slightly shrugged my shoulders. He shrugged his back and said "Sorry."

He didn't sound sorry at all. He went on to ask another customer if they needed help with anything. I slowly walked towards the door, wondering what my next move would be. This had been my only hope to get some money. I knew if I went to another one, they'd probably say the same thing. I started to open the door, but I stopped. After he was finished with the other customer, I walked back up to the counter.

"Sir, please," I begged. "I don't have anywhere to go. I'm homeless. I just spent the night in a tent, at the Walmart across the street, before I came here. I mean, I'm only 16 and I don't have ID, but I do have this jewelry and it is mine. My daddy gave it to me before he died."

I watched as he lowered his eyes in a sorrowful way.

"I'm very sorry to hear that."

Now, he actually sounded sympathetic.

"But, it's against store policy..."

"Please, Sir," I cut him off to further prove my case. "All I'm trying to do is get some money to get a hotel room. Please. I don't have anyone or anywhere else to go."

He let out a deep breath as if he really didn't feel like dealing with this today.

Finally, he said, "Let me see what you got?"

I carefully removed my jewelry. First, the four bracelets. Then, the two rings and placed them in the palm of his hand.

"What about that?"

He pointed to my locket.

"Oh, no."

I covered it with my hand as if I were protecting it.

"Not this. It's a picture of my daddy and me."

He nodded his head, letting me know he understood. I watched him examine every piece one by one. Then, he cleared his throat and said, "I'll give you $500 for all of it."

Whoa. I didn't know if he was cheating me out of anything, but that was more than I expected to get so, I took it. Now, I thought, as I stood in front of the Pawn Shop, if I could just find someone as sympathetic or maybe, greedy enough, to let me stay in their hotel without ID.

Since this was a busy street, there were plenty of shops and businesses on it. I spotted three motels across the street from me. I looked at each of the billboards which displayed the motel rates. $189.00 weekly...$150.00 weekly...$90.00 weekly. $90.00 weekly it is. I didn't have the money or the time to be picky.

As I neared the motel, I began to realize why this one was probably a lot cheaper than the others. I mean, the others weren't anything compared to the Hilton. Still, this one, The Dream Inn, according to the white, brick wall, bearing those bold letters in green paint, was anything but a dream. It was all one level. The building was pink with eight different color doors for each room. There was nothing spectacular about it. Just a building whose paint was chipping away with windows and different color doors.

It wasn't hard to find the office. There was a black, screen door located in the center of the building. Someone had used white spray paint to write the word "Office" on it. I passed by two guys, a black guy and a Mexican one. Both were shirtless, wearing jeans and holding beers. They were leaned up against the back of a long, blue, old school looking car. Both doors were opened as the music from the car played loud over the speakers.

"Hola Chica," said the Mexican guy. "You lookin' real sweet today mami."

I glanced towards the two guys and gave them a half smile before making bigger strides towards the office door. I didn't know whether they were men or boys, but that's the last thing I felt like dealing with today.

When I walked into the office, I was greeted by the sound of snores. As I neared the counter, I saw a heavy set, well...a huge, Mexican man laying back in a brown, worn out, office chair. *Poor chair*, I thought. There was a bell sitting on the counter, but I wasn't sure if I wanted to disturb his sleep. He looked and sounded like he was sleeping extremely well.

Even though, he was in an awkward position, he looked comfortable. His khaki shorts were unbuckled, his muscle shirt was rolled up over his big belly and his bare feet were resting on a foot stool in front of him.

Ding.

I hit the bell on the counter lightly. He didn't budge.

Ding.

I hit it a tad bit harder. Still, not even a twitch.

Ding. Ding.

I hit it hard. He jumped up so quickly, he almost fell over.

I watched him rub his face and wildly scratch his curly, black hair, before finally looking up.

"Yeah?"

"Oh, umm."

I had to gather my thoughts.

"Hello. I, I was wondering if I could get a room?"

He eyed me suspiciously. *Here we go*, I thought, *time to beg again.* I opened my mouth to say something, but before I could speak, he said, "How much you got?"

"Oh, um, I," I stammered over my words, "I have $400."

I'm not going to give him everything I have.

He reached into a drawer attached to the desk and pulled out a key with the number 5 written on it. He laid it on the counter and said, "I'll give you one month and a week. If you need any clean towels or anything, you'll have to get it from here."

Then, he held out his hand. I pulled out $400 and put it in his hand. He took it and put it in his pocket. Then, he kicked his feet back up, lay back in his chair and closed his eyes. I didn't know how a motel transaction worked, but I was sure that wasn't it.

"I'm sorry, sir, but is that all you need from me?"

He tilted his head, glancing at me through one eye, "You gotta be 18 or older to get a room. You wanna show me some I.D.?"

I bit my bottom lip.

"Didn't think so," he said.

He gave a fake smile and added sarcastically, "Have a wonderful stay at The Dream Inn."

I said nothing else but "Thank you," as I left to go to the room.

Room number 5 wasn't a dream, but it was reality and it was somewhere to stay. I glanced around the room, trying to remain grateful that God had given me a place to stay. I knew this was only temporary. Of course, I didn't know where I'd be going next, but I was trying to remain faithful.

Of course, there was a bed and a bathroom with a sink, toilet and shower. I placed my bags on the dark green, wooden table I was standing next to. It had two, hot pink, folding chairs around it and a white microwave sitting on top of it. There was a small, old fashioned TV sitting on a tall, blue, four-drawer dresser. As I walked over to the bed, I looked around at the pink carpet.

Okay...what's with all the colors? Someone sure tried to make this place look like a dream. More like a colorful nightmare.

I took a deep breath and held up my hands, like I was being held hostage.

"I'm sorry, God. I'm sorry. I won't complain. Could be worse. But," I said as I looked down at the ugly, flower print bedspread, "I will be washing this stuff before I lay on it."

I grabbed my Lysol and went to work.

Chapter 20

*E*very day, after school, I'd come…home. Take a shower, eat, and do any homework I had. Sometimes, I'd grab a burger, at least, once a week, but for the most part, I ate what I had. Noodles, snacks, peanut butter and jelly sandwiches, among other cheap and nonperishable items. I know that was a bad diet, but I had to make it work with only a microwave and $38 left in my pocket.

It had been almost five weeks since I'd been staying at the motel and the only reason I had that much left is because I opted out of riding the bus to school every day. I mean, I'd been walking to school before and even though, being at the motel added an extra 15 minutes to what used to be a simple 15-minute walk, I had to do what I had to do.

The only time I went out was when I needed more toothpaste, soap, tissue or towels from the front office. That was creepy enough. I never had to go out to see what was going on because I could hear more than I needed to, through the thin walls of the room.

Different arguments every time someone stayed there. All kinds of loud music. Different...noises from the never-ending amount of people that came to use it for only minutes at a time. I tried to read most times, but that hardly ever worked. Sometimes, I'd plug my ears up with my earphones and listen to music on my tablet or play games. When I watched TV, I'd turn the volume up as loud as it could go, in an effort to drown out the surrounding noises.

One day, I decided to watch one of the ministry channels, since I hadn't been to church in a while. I was still trying to read my bible every now and then, but it was so hard to stay consistent with it. I came across some guy from Singapore named Joseph Prince. I was instantly drawn to what he was saying about God's love and grace for us.

He always says, "When you believe right, you will live right," which makes perfect sense. Not to mention, he was extremely funny! Even though, he kept me laughing, I knew my spirit was being fed, which was exactly what I needed.

One day, he was talking about how he prayed to God to restore his youth. He said you have to be specific when you pray about things because the next morning, he woke up with a big pimple on his nose. I laughed so loud. I know my motel neighbors must have heard me. I know God has to have a sense of humor. I mean…He did make us.

In his message, he talked about the scripture in 1Corinthians 10:13. For some reason, even after the program had finished, that scripture stuck with me. I took out my bible and read it aloud to myself.

"There hath no temptation taken you but such as is common to man: but God is faithful, who will not allow you to be tempted above that you are able; but will with the temptation also make a way to escape, that you may be able to bear it."

I sat on the bed, reading it a few more times and pondering on it at the same time.

"So," I said aloud, looking up, "The temptations I or anyone else faces, is nothing new in life? It may seem like you're the only one dealing with that situation, but others have faced and probably will face something similar at some point in their lives?"

I nodded to myself.

"But You," I smiled, "You will never put more on us than we can handle because You know how much we can take.

You will always provide a way out…because You are faithful."

I giggled a little at realizing that I fully understood what God what saying. I looked up again saying, "You are so awesome. So smart."

As I lay in bed that night, I thought about that scripture. It even stayed with me every day thereafter. Little did I know, I would have to apply it, sooner than I expected.

Chapter 21

I'd just gotten home from the library. It was a little after 7 and nightfall was approaching. When I got in, I put my book bag down and prepared to take a shower. Then, there was a quick knock at the door. It made me jump. I wasn't used to visitors.

"Yes," I called out.

"Office manager."

I exhaled slowly, realizing I'd tensed up from the unexpected knock.

"Here I come," I yelled.

I quickly slipped on a white T-Shirt and some black jogging pants. I jogged over to open the door. When I opened it, the first thing I saw was an exposed, hairy chest, partly covered by an unbuttoned, khaki shirt. Then, I saw the manager's face. He propped his hand against the frame of the door and said, "Your time here is up."

"My…what?"

There's that "what" again. What. When you know you heard right the first time, but for some reason, you want to make sure that's what you heard.

"Your time here. It's up."

"Oh, I…"

I laughed uneasily. I was stumped. Time had completely caught me off guard.

I know that was so irresponsible of me, but I'd been busying myself with school so much, I'd honestly lost track of time. It seemed like it came so fast.

"I'm so sorry. I, I mean, I had no idea. Time had slipped by so fast."

I stood there, staring at him as he stared at me. I don't know, I guess I thought maybe he'd say something like, "Oh, it's ok. Feel free to stay until morning." Something. He didn't say anything except, "Yeah. I started to sit your stuff outside, but I didn't want nobody to take it, so I thought I better let you get your own stuff together."

"Well, can I at least have until morning?"

"Sorry, little lady. I got somebody need a room right now."

I sighed heavily. I could tell there was no way he was going to show any empathy. So, I asked if he'd give me a minute to get my things together. Thankfully, he agreed, but he didn't leave, he stood right there in the doorway.

I hurried around the room gathering my school things to put in my book bag. Then, I started stuffing everything else into my duffel bag. As I finished gathering my things, he said, "You got somewhere to go?"

I shook my head, "No, sir."

"Well, I mean, I am the manager. I can always let you stay."

I quickly looked up, smiling.

"Really?"

"Yeah. But um," he stepped in and pushed the door closed, "How bad do you wanna to stay?"

I opened my mouth to speak, but nothing came out.

Wait a minute, Rodeo. He's not talking about letting you stay for free. Is he really talking about what I think he's talking about?

He licked his lips and tilted his head to the side, giving me a once over from head to toe.

Yes. He most certainly is.

I quickly gathered my bags.

"That's alright. I'll be fine," I say, almost in a whisper.

I slowly walked towards the door, hoping he'd have it open before I reached it. I stopped a few feet away from him. I raised my eyes to meet his. He smiled. He then moved to the side and held out his hand, inviting me to pass by. When I got within inches from the door, he put his hand on the doorknob.

"You know baby girl, I know you got no place to go. Right?"

I didn't answer. My eyes were fixed on the floor.

"Right," he repeated.

I nodded slowly.

"Well, listen. I promise I'll take it easy with you."

I shook my head.

"No. No, that's okay. I'll be alright."

I reached for the door.

"Hey."

He gently placed his hand on my back, the other still on the doorknob.

"I know I'm asking a lot, but listen, you got nowhere to go. It's night now. Where you gonna go? You can stay here for as long as you need to. I promise. Okay?"

I didn't answer.

"Okay," he repeated.

He's right. I don't have anywhere to go. What am I going to do? I mean, I don't have any money. I don't...

"I know you don't have no money. I can give you all the money you need. I own this place. I can do things how I want. Okay?"

I didn't answer yes, but I didn't answer no either. He slowly took my bags, placing them on the floor. Then, I let him guide me towards the bed. He put his hands on my shoulders and lowered me down onto the bed. I sat there, stuck. It's like I wasn't thinking anything. Like, I'd forced myself to go numb as to what was happening.

"Lay back," he said.

After seconds of staring into space, he gently pushed me back onto the bed. I could tell he was trying to be cautious in the way he did things. Maybe he feared that if he seemed too forceful, I'd snap out of it and realize what I was giving into.

I heard the zipper to his shorts unzip. He pulled down his shorts, revealing a dingy pair of white boxers. I hadn't made eye contact with him at all, but as he reached for my jogging pants, I looked at him. He licked his lips, smirking. I felt disgusted as sweat beads formed on his hairy, rough face. I quickly looked away and closed my eyes. Over the next few seconds of him trying to wiggle my pants down, I began having a conversation with myself.

Are you really this desperate, Rodeo?

I mean, I don't have anywhere else to go. I know I could probably stay here for a long time if I just...just.

No. Rodeo, no. Is this how you want to lose your virginity? Didn't God say, He would never leave you nor forsake you?

Well, yes, but I only have $38 and...

Rodeo. You're letting him tempt you.

I opened my eyes. My pants were pulled down to my ankles, exposing my pink, cotton panties. He was about to slide down his boxers. I closed my eyes. Suddenly, I heard the scripture.

"There has no temptation...God is faithful...but will with the temptation, make a way to escape..."

Escape.

I opened my eyes as he was lowering himself on top of me. I put my hands on his fat, sweaty, hairy chest to stop him. He hardly budged.

When did he take his shirt off?

"Stop, please. I'm sorry, I can't. I-I just can't do this."

He spoke with, what I knew was him trying to act as if he were being understanding.

"It's ok, mami. I'll take care of you."

He rubbed my thighs.

"No, that's okay. I'll be fine on my own."

I gently pushed him away from me. As I started to sit up, he grabbed my wrists. I could feel his hands tighten as he lowered them down beside me. I looked at him. He narrowed his eyes at me. Now, his voice sounded cold and harsh.

"You nothin' but a lil' tease ain't you."

I could tell that was more of a statement than a question.

"What? No. I just, I can't do this. I'm sorry that I led you to believe that I would do…"

"Oh, you gonna do it. And then, you still gonna get out just for thinkin' you can play with me like that."

"No, I won't do it," I yelled as I struggled to push him off of me.

My struggle was no match for his weight.

"Stop," I screamed.

He placed his hand over my mouth as he tried to pry away my panties. I felt them starting to rip.

Oh, God. I'm sorry I was even considering this. What am I going to do?

I put up a good fight, trying to keep him from accomplishing what he wanted to. I had to think fast because it didn't take much for him to overpower me. Suddenly, I did the only I knew would hurt him in some kind of way. With all I had in me, I dug my thumbs into his eyes and kneed him in his special no-no place.

He went to the floor, screaming in agony. He was calling me all kinds of names. Things I'd never even heard of. I knew I didn't have much time before he regained some type of strength. I quickly pulled up my pants, grabbed my bags, and ran far away from The Nightmare Inn.

Chapter 22

I stood in the bathroom of a small, seafood restaurant, staring at myself in the mirror. I looked tired. I *was* tired. Tired of running. Tired of not knowing how things would turn out or where I might end up the next day. Instantly, my eyes were blurred with tears. I clutched the counter top as I cried.

"Now what do you want me to do," I yelled, looking up towards the ceiling.

"I'm 16 years old. What am I supposed to do? You want me to go live in Walmart? No, wait, I know," I said sarcastically, "You want me to sleep with some nasty man in order to survive, right? Huh? Answer me!"

I fell to my knees and cried. God knew all I had was Him to depend on. What was all that stuff about Him never leaving nor forsaking me? How could He expect me to go through so much? I cried so much, my head began to hurt.

For a moment, it seemed like I'd forgotten where I was. I didn't know how long I'd cried, but I didn't snap out of it until I heard the bell to the restaurant sound. That let me know someone had come in.

I stood up and turned on the hot water. I threw water on my face a few times before drying it with a hand full of paper towels. I stared at myself again. I thought about drowning my face in the water once more, but I knew it wouldn't make my red, puffy eyes go away, so I just gathered my bags and went to sit down.

There were two women who'd come into the store. I stared out of the window at nothing in particular while they joked and laughed loudly with each other. I could tell they were a little drunk. One had gold and black hair and the other had red and black hair.

I got a little nervous because the one with the gold hair kept glancing me. Suddenly, her glance turned into a stare. She was a dark-skinned, slim lady, wearing a tight fitting, dark red dress which was somewhat covered by the long, black, leather jacket she had on. She took her time in her high heeled, black boots as she strolled over to my table.

She placed her hand on the table revealing some long, red, fingernails and said, "You look like somebody I know. Just a little darker. What's yo' name baby?"

"Rodeo," I replied.

She looked off into space like she was thinking. Then, she chuckled and said, "I can't believe she really named you that."

I started to ask her what she meant by that, but then, she asked, "What you doin', sittin' in here by yourself?"

I put my head down and sighed heavily. I didn't even know where to start. I looked up to see her staring at me, eyebrows raised, waiting for me to say something.

"It's just been hard. I-I don't have anywhere to go right now."

Normally, I wouldn't have confessed that to anyone, especially, a stranger, but it seemed like the words just fell out.

"Umph," she said. "How old you?"

"16."

"Well," she sighed, "You ain't old enough to work and help bring in no real good money, and plus you doing your schooling so, you gone have to keep the house clean if you wanna stay with me. Now come on and let me get you somethin' to eat so we can go."

I'm sorry...did I miss something? Was she saying I could stay with her? Who was she?

On que, she turned and laughed saying, "I bet you thinkin', who in the world is this lady? I'm sorry, baby. Just cause I know who you is don't mean you know who I am, right?"

I nodded, even though, I knew the question was rhetorical.

"Yo' momma TT ain't she? Teresa?"

She asked as if already knowing the answer. I nodded again.

"Me and yo' momma used to be best friends."

From the way she stared off into space, I could tell she must have been having a flash of memories about the two of them. Then, she intertwined two fingers, held them up in front of me and said, "Me and yo' momma used to be like this. You didn't see her without seein' me. I knew you was her daughter. You look just like her. Only darker. But come on baby, get yo' bags. Oh, I'm Gwendolyn, but just call me Gwen."

She went on to order more food. I smiled. Ms. Gwen, I thought to myself. As I gathered my things, I glanced up and whispered, "I'm so sorry...thank you."

❀

I watched Ms. Gwen fumble through her big, black purse for her keys.

"Sorry baby," she said, "I don't know why I don't ever find my keys before I get out the car. If a killer was after us, we would've been dead by now."

She laughed. I didn't. I glanced around the brick, apartment buildings, careful not to make eye contact with any of the people standing around outside. All of the apartments had two levels. Ms. Gwen lived on a top level. Even though, it was after 9 o'clock on this Thursday night, I could tell that people hanging out most nights was something that happened regularly.

When Ms. Gwen finally found her keys, she waved goodbye to her friend from the seafood restaurant, whose name was Lisa. Lisa blew the horn as she drove off. When we stepped into her home, Ms. Gwen removed her coat and her boots and slipped on some black slippers.

"You can put yo' bags down for now, baby. Let's go in the kitchen and eat our food."

"Okay," I replied.

As Ms. Gwen made her way into the kitchen, I quickly took in the contents of the living room.

Black and gold must be her favorite colors.

I sat my things down on one of the black, leather sofas. There was a big, flat screened TV sitting in the middle of a black entertainment center. It had glass doors attached to it, on both sides, which held black plates of all sizes, trimmed in gold. It was nice.

As I walked towards the kitchen, I passed by a statue of a gold lion. It looked like it was, at least, three feet tall. Above the sofa hung a nice, huge picture of a lion. The lion was trimmed in gold on black glass.

I guess you really can't judge a book by its cover. She had her place fixed up really nice.

While Ms. Gwen and I sat at her black kitchen table, eating the food we'd gotten from the restaurant, she made small talk. I nodded and smiled when she said certain things, but I was only half listening. I was thinking about how my life had made another unexpected turn. Wondering where I was going to end up next.

I'm not going to worry about it. I believe it was God who set this meeting up, so I'll just have to keep believing that He knows what He's doing.

Ms. Gwen was still talking. When I finally tuned back into the conversation, she was supposed to have been having with me, she was talking about a niece of hers who'd just moved out recently. Said she'd run off with some guy. I really couldn't think or receive much of what she was saying at the moment. I picked over my food, wondering if she knew about my momma.

"My momma was killed," I blurted out of nowhere. I didn't look up, just continued to pick over my fish.

"Oh, I know," she said, which caused me to look up. "I'm so sorry that happened."

"How-how did you know?"

"Baby, news travel real fast round here. They told me she was found dead behind a dumpster. But they didn't say nothin' bout a lil' girl."

I quickly looked down after noticing the empathy in her eyes. I had to look away. I felt like I was about to cry.

That's strange.

I hadn't had that feeling in a long time. I quickly cleared my throat, removing any lump that was trying to form, before I spoke.

"Back at the restaurant, you mentioned how you knew my momma was going to name me Rodeo. How?"

She got up and walked over to the counter, grabbing her gold, cigarette purse. She took out a cigarette, lit it and took a lengthy pull, like she was preparing herself to tell a long story.

"One day," she started as she blew out a puff of smoke, "Me and TT found our way out to California. Child, we thought we was gone go out there and end up like Julia Roberts in *Pretty Woman*."

She was laughing so hard, she had to grip onto the counter just to hold herself up.

"Child, that movie tricked the heck outta us!"

I couldn't help chuckling a little at the way she cracked herself up. After she calmed down and took another pull of her cigarette, she continued.

"Honey, me and yo' momma went out there to make us some good money, you hear me? We was right there on Rodeo Drive. Them darn men was pickin' us up left and right.

Sad part about it is half of 'em was married. These men ain't no darn good. I ain't met a good one yet."

"My daddy was a good man," I stated, as if trying to clear his name from that group of men.

"TT found out who yo' daddy was?"

She asked that question as if a "yes" was impossible. She continued saying, "Cause that night we was so high, drunk and stuck on makin' money, we could've slept with the president and we show wouldn't of knowed it!"

She laughed loudly.

I raised my eyebrows and shook my head. After I got the picture she so kindly painted for me out of my mind, I said, "No, not my real daddy. My adoptive daddy. I still don't know who my real daddy is."

"Umph. Well, you ain't the first and you show ain't gone be the last child who don't know they daddy. But that's why she named you that. Cause that's where we was and all she knew was that she got pregnant on that street. She had already said, if she really was pregnant, she was gone name you that. Whether you was a boy or a girl."

She looked at me and said, "Good thang you was a girl, huh?"

I watched her smoke her cigarette as she talked and giggled about memories of her and my momma. After almost 2 hours of Ms. Gwen's trip down memory lane, I followed her to a room located at the end of the hallway.

"You can use this room," she said as she opened the door to let me in. "It ain't much, but it'll do."

"Oh, no, this is more than enough," I said, letting her know I was grateful for it.

"Well, let me know if you need anythang. It's some clean towels, sheets, and covers in the hallway closet."

"I will. Thank you for everything, Ms. Gwen."

She said, "You welcome, baby."

After she closed the door to the room, I looked around, taking in the scenery, or lack thereof. I laughed a little thinking about how James had more stuff in his room. This one only had two, twin sized mattresses, stacked on top of each other, on the floor. Nothing else was in the room. I'm guessing she didn't use this one too much.

There was a closet, but it looked like it was only used for storage space. There were boxes, bags and whatnots in it. I didn't need much. Just a place to lay my head. I made up the bed. Then, I plopped down on it. I was exhausted.

It was cold outside, but it wasn't as cold in the house because Ms. Gwen had the heat blasting. I was glad there was a ceiling fan in the room. I lay back, watching it spin around, as I thought about James. Sometimes he made his way into my mind.

I wondered what he'd been doing since the last time I saw him. If he was still living with his dad? If they'd gotten into a fight again? I wondered if he'd even...killed him. I worried about him sometimes. But I'd always push it out of mind. Kind of like I did with anything that made me sad. Like, thinking about daddy. Of course, we had some great memories, but I'd always end up sad because I would eventually start to think...*I wish he was here.*

I closed my eyes and said a prayer. I began to feel myself drifting off to sleep, when suddenly, I opened my eyes and sat up in bed. I'd just had one of those moments where I'd realized something. My name was Rodeo Julia Turner. I laughed aloud to myself.

"Momma, I bet you would have given me the last name Roberts if you could have, huh?"

I laid back down, smiling to myself, as I drifted off to sleep.

Chapter 23

𝓔very day, I'd get up at 6:30 a.m. to get ready for

school. I had to catch the bus, therefore, I had to make sure I
was on time because if I had to wait for the next bus to come,
I'd be late for school. I didn't have any money, so Ms. Gwen
said that she would get me a bus card every month and try to
give me a little bit of money to keep in my pocket. So far,
she'd kept her word on that. She said that would be a part of
my earnings, in a way, for keeping the house clean.

For the first two Saturday nights, while I was staying
with Ms. Gwen, I'd stayed in the room because she'd had
friends over. If I had to come out the room, it was only to go to
the bathroom which was in the hallway, so I never had to go
pass the living room. She later told me she had card and
domino parties from time to time. Well, after a few months, I
began to see that this was something she did every Saturday.

I'd just left the library and nightfall was approaching.
By the time I reached the house, I could hear loud music
coming from the apartment. Before I turned the knob, someone

from the inside opened it. It was some old guy who, obviously thought he was still young. I really can't remember what he looked like because my eyes were too fixed on the small amount of gray hair he had. I'm sure someone must have had trouble gripping it because the braids in his head looked like they were about to pull his scalp up.

He eyed me as I brushed past him to go into the house. I never got in the way when Ms. Gwen had her parties. Usually, I was gone or in my room. That doesn't mean I didn't hear the parties. Sometimes, I'd put on my earphones and listen to music on the laptop daddy had given me for Christmas. Other times, I'd fall asleep to the sounds of drunk people talking, arguing, or singing along to the loud music that played.

There were card and domino tables on either side of me, as I made my way to the hallway. I paused when I heard Ms. Gwen yell, "Hey baby."

I looked up to see her standing in the kitchen entryway, sipping her drink, threw a straw. There were 5 card tables in between us. All of them had three to four people around them, playing either dominoes or cards. All the tables had money scattered on them. I waved and smiled a little. I thought to myself, *"She must be watching that money."*

I thought about the night I heard Ms. Gwen while she was talking to someone on the phone. She said, "Honey, I can't play. I have to stand and watch that money cause people sneaky."

I made my way through the hallway, to my room. When I got there, the door was locked. I knocked slowly, wondering why my door would be locked. I heard it unlock and out walks some guy, with a lady following behind him.

I could tell he was a young guy. He was brown skinned and his thick, black hair was pulled back in a ponytail. He was matching from head to toe. Red shirt, red cargo shorts with red and white sneakers to match. The lady looked a little older. She had on a tight, baby blue dress with some black slippers. She was so light, she was almost yellow. She glanced at me while straightening the black wig on her head.

I backed up into the door of the bathroom as they walked by me. He eyed me with a smirk on his face. I walked into the room and closed the door behind me.

Eew. What is that stinky smell?

The sheets and cover were scattered all over the bed. I put my book bag down and thought to myself for a moment.

Now, I just know they weren't doing what I think they were doing.

I sniffed the foul odor of the room again.

Why'd they have to be in here? And on the bed, I sleep on?

I went for the doorknob and opened the door.

I have to talk to Ms. Gwen about this.

I walked towards the kitchen and let Ms. Gwen know I needed to talk to her. She followed me back to my room. I noticed the concerned look on her face as she asked, "What is it, baby?"

"Ms. Gwen, some young guy and a lady were in my room. I think they were doing something in my room."

I gestured towards the bed as I said, "Look at the bed."

She inhaled and exhaled deeply. Then, she cocked her head to one side.

She looked at me and said, "Listen baby, I'm sorry they was in here on the bed you sleep on, but before you came I was making my money, the way I make my money. It's best that that's all you know. Now, you can stay here long as you like, but the way I make my money ain't gone change."

I tried not to give her an unbelievable look as she backed away saying, "Gone and change the sheets."

I watched her as she walked away, disappearing around the corner of the hallway.

Wow.

I stood there for a moment, shaking my head. I looked at the bed. Then, I sprayed the room with Lyson before going to get two comforters from the hall closet. I took a shower, laid one comforter down on the floor and the other on top. Then, I lay on them and read my bible for a moment, before saying a prayer and going to sleep.

Chapter 24

Today was Saturday, two days after my 17th birthday.

Ms. Gwen threw a somewhat, party for me. I say somewhat because I didn't know anyone there. It was all her friends. I could tell this was just another way for her to have a party. Yet and still, I was grateful for it.

This afternoon, I'd gotten myself ready to go to the movies since I didn't get a chance to do anything Thursday. Ms. Gwen had been sitting on the sofa, wearing an oversized, leopard print gown, talking on the phone. When she saw me leaving, she blew out a puff of smoke and asked, "Where you goin' lookin' all cute this early?"

"Oh," I'd smiled.

All I had on was some black, skinny jeans, an orange and gray, mermaid T-shirt and my black, Mary Jane shoes. I did curl my hair down and put on some pink lip gloss, which was something I hadn't done before. So, perhaps, I did look sort of cute.

"Well, since I didn't get to do anything Thursday, I'm just going to go to the movies today."

She blew out smoke and asked, "What was Thursday?"

"It was my birthday."

She'd quickly sat up on the sofa and said, "Girl why you ain't tell nobody it was yo' birthday?"

Before I had a chance to respond, she went on to say, "Gone and sit down, baby. We bout to have a bar-b-que and party."

I'd stood there watching her as she spoke to the person on the other end of the phone.

"Lisa, you and Johnny come on and take us to get some stuff for my niece birthday party."

I'd still been standing there, sort of confused. When she got off the phone she said, "I'm bout to get dressed baby. We gone go get some meat for the grill and some cake and ice cream. Gone and sit down 'till Lisa and Johnny get here."

I just shook my head and sat down as Ms. Gwen walked pass me to go to her room. She always had a nice, bossy way of telling people what to do. I didn't mind though. I figured I'd just go to the movies another time.

So, here I was, sitting at the kitchen table while a man named Johnny, bar-b-qued on the back porch. I played a game of Hearts on my laptop, as the music, laughter and chatter blasted through the apartment. I recognized some of the people there, but I didn't know their names.

Of course, Ms. Gwen had already introduced me to about 13 people and it only took a few minutes before I'd forgotten more than half of their names. It was hard to remember them all at once, but it was even harder to understand most of them over the music. I was beginning to think some of them were already drunk before they got there.

"You alright in here, baby?"

Ms. Gwen had come into the kitchen holding a cigarette in one hand and a plastic, red cup in the other. By now, she'd changed into a tight, black, spaghetti-strapped dress. She still had on her leopard-print, house shoes. If she was in the house, she had on her house shoes.

I glanced up and replied, "Yes ma'am."

"Okay, well, I'm bout to see how close Johnny is to finishin', so we can get ready to sing happy birthday."

After a few minutes, I sat at the table watching Ms. Gwen and her friends sing happy birthday to me. There was almost an equal amount of men and women there. Most of the men had on their causal jeans and t-shirt while the women had on dresses or mini-skirts with some type of blouse.

I watched them sway from side to side as they sang. Some were really off beat. They made sure they held on to their red cups though. The Johnny guy sang the loudest and messed up the song the most. I thought to myself, *How do you mess up the birthday song?* From behind me, Ms. Gwen put her hands on my shoulders and said, "Now make a wish and blow out the candles."

I looked down at the lit number 1 and 7 on the round cake, with white icing. The letters "Happy Birthday" were written on it in blue icing. I closed my eyes and wished that my daddy could have been there. I knew it wouldn't come true physically, but I liked to think he was there in spirit. I thanked God for this day. I mean, even though, only her friends were there, Ms. Gwen didn't have to do this for me. Therefore, I was grateful. I opened my eyes and I blew out the candles. Afterwards, we all ate ribs, hot dogs, hamburgers, cake and ice cream. While I sat eating some ice cream and cake, Ms. Gwen whispered in my ear, "I'm gone pin some money on you and everybody else gone follow suit. Watch."

She pinned $5 on my shirt with a safety pin.

"But you can't just sit here, sweetie. You gotta move around," she added.

Sure enough, as I maneuvered throughout the apartment, people pinned money on me, wishing me a happy birthday. After everyone left, there was only Johnny and Lisa left. They sat at one of the tables playing dominoes with Ms. Gwen. I'd been cleaning up the kitchen, even though, she'd told me I didn't have to clean up on my birthday.

"Bring me some more of them ribs, baby," Ms. Gwen yelled from the living room. "Then, won't you gone out somewhere for yo' birthday. Just be careful."

"Yes ma'am," I replied back.

It was only a little after 7, but I didn't plan on going anywhere. I put some ribs on a paper plate for Ms. Gwen.

"Here you go, Ms. Gwen," I said as I sat the plate down next to her.

"Thank you, baby."

"You're welcome."

I heard Ms. Gwen say, "She so sweet," as I went back into the kitchen. I know she said I didn't have to clean up, but I didn't have anything else to do. So, I did it anyway.

I heard Mr. Johnny say, "You say that's yo' niece, Gwen? Who lil' girl that is?"

"I just call her my niece cause me and her momma used to be best friends. You remember TT. That's her baby."

"TT," he repeated, unsure of who that was.

"Yeah TT," she replied as if he should have known who that was.

I heard Lisa jump in and say, "You remember TT, Johnny."

"Naw," he replied, "I don't remember no TT."

"TT," Ms. Gwen said. "Teresa Turner? Ms. Doris child?"

"Teresa Turner? Oooh," he said, as it finally dawned on him as to who they were talking about. "You talkin' bout that TT."

"Yeah," Ms. Gwen assertive.

"Who else you think I was talkin' bout? I didn't hang around no other TT but her."

"Well, it's been so long since I seen her. I had just seen her momma the other day when I passed by her house."

Wait. What? Did I just hear him right?

They were still talking about my momma, as well as, giving a clueless Johnny the news about her death, but my mind was elsewhere. I know I'd just heard him say he'd passed by her momma's house the other day.

That would be my grandmother.

I stood frozen at the sink. My hands were still holding onto a pot in the dish water. I felt nervous and excited all at the same time. I'm not sure why. I guess it was because of what I knew now.

I knew I had a grandmother out there somewhere. But, should I try to reach out to her? Would she want to see me? I mean, some grandparents could be like that, but I didn't see why she wouldn't want to see me.

After more questions than I could keep up with, went through my mind, I concluded that I had to find out more.

I stood in the walkway of the living room as Mr. Johnny slammed a domino down and yelled, "Domino!"

He laughed a good, hearty laugh as Ms. Gwen and Lisa regretfully tossed some money towards him.

"Honey, I'm bout to go home," Lisa said as she got up, straightening her gold, skinned tight, dress.

"I know that's right, Lisa," Ms. Gwen added. "He takin' all our darn money. I'm bout to..."

"Um, excuse me," I cut in.

They all looked towards me at the same time.

"What's the matter, baby?"

Ms. Gwen looked concerned. I know it was because I must have looked nervous, even though, I didn't try to. I noticed my hands were fidgety, all tangled up with each other. I slowly brought them to my side.

"Um, when I was in the kitchen, I heard you guys talking about my momma and I heard Mr. Johnny say he'd just passed by her momma's house."

"Yeah," he nodded.

They all waited for me to go on. My hands had somehow gotten intertwined with each other again. I couldn't stop them from playing with each other.

Why was I so nervous?

"Well, do you think you could tell me where she lives, please?"

Johnny looked towards Ms. Gwen. Then, back to me. He frowned and asked, "You never met yo' grandma?"

"No," I said quietly. I slowly let my head fall towards the floor.

"Gwen, why you ain't never take that girl to see her grandma?"

Ms. Gwen threw her hands up and said, "I swear I'm just findin' this out now. I didn't even know Ms. Doris was still alive. When me and TT ran off that last time, Ms. Doris told me I better not never set foot in her house again. I hadn't seen her since. I figured since she," Ms. Gwen motioned to me, "Wasn't with her, she couldn't have been alive."

She looked towards me and said, "You wanna meet her? We can take you over there right now."

Wow. I sure was nervous. Was I ready to see her? Did I want to see her? Yes. Yes, I did, but I wasn't quite sure if I was ready. Perhaps, tomorrow.

"Um," I began, "Maybe, tomorrow?"

Even though, they were drunk, they all made me believe they understood with a nod of their heads. Ms. Gwen took a bite of her ribs and said, "Johnny, just come back tomorrow round 3."

He nodded, "Alright."

I said, "Thank you," before heading to my room.

I closed the door behind me and lay faced down on the covers, on the floor.

Tomorrow, I'm meeting my grandmother. I wonder if I look like her. I wonder what she's like. Maybe, she's one of those sweet grandmothers, who loves her grand-kids and bakes pies. Or maybe, she's the type of grandmother who is a reflection of the way her own kids are.

I didn't know what to expect. Either way, I'd find out tomorrow. Even though, it was still early, I was ready for tomorrow to come. I took a shower and got ready for bed. Then, I laid down, closed my eyes and said a prayer before drifting off to sleep.

Chapter 25

I walked up the somewhat, long driveway as the black screen door inched closer to me. With every step, it seemed as if my heart beat a little faster. I took long, deep breaths. That didn't help.

I looked towards the sky. It was a cloudy and breezy day, but still, pretty warm for late September. It looked like it was going to rain. Now, I wished I would have put on some sneakers instead of my black, suede loafers. I just wanted to look nice. I only wore them because they were the only shoes I liked wearing with the black, one-piece, silk suit I had on.

I looked around, admiring how well kept her garden was. The flowers and roses were so beautiful. It looked like she had every color of the rainbow. The vinyl on her house was a nice, baby blue color. She even had a white swing on the porch. *How nice*, I thought.

With caution, I walked up the white, wooden steps. I stopped in front of the door. Smells of good, southern home cooking hit my nose hard. I didn't know what she was cooking, but it sure smelled delicious. I could see in the house, through the screen door, being that the front door was opened. I saw some light coming from the kitchen area. It was dark in the living room, but I knew the TV was on. I couldn't see it because it was facing away from me, but it was loud enough to where I could hear Steve Harvey's voice. I knew she was watching Family Feud.

Suddenly, I remembered Ms. Gwen and Mr. Johnny were still waiting for me. I held my hand up to knock. Then, I put it back down. I turned to see them both sitting there with a quizzical look on their faces. I smiled nervously. Then, quickly looked away.

"Get it together, Rodeo," I whispered to myself.

I raised my hand and knocked before I had time to think about anything. I heard a high-pitched voice yell from the direction of the kitchen, "Who knock?"

"Umm," I stammered, "Rodeo."

I had to raise my voice over the sounds of the TV.

"Who?"

Before I had time to reply, she appeared from the kitchen. From the outline of her silhouette, I could tell she was a heavy-set woman. Not too big, but big enough to where she probably wouldn't fit in an airplane seat comfortably.

"Hold on," she said as she grabbed the remote to turn the TV off.

As she walked towards the door, I could hear her slippers sliding across the floor. She had on a black house coat. Her hair was short. She had it combed straight back, revealing the full structure of her face. I stepped back as she opened the door asking, "Can I help you with something, sweetie?"

Her cheekbones were high. Small freckles and moles covered them. Her round, almond eyes went perfectly with her smooth, milk chocolate skin. I smiled at the way her cheeks plumped up from the smile she was giving me.

"Hi…I," I stuttered a little.

She cocked her head to the side, but she was still smiling, waiting for me to speak. I let out a heavy sigh and said, "Hi."

"Hi," she said…still smiling.

She was so welcoming. What was I afraid of?

"Hi, umm…"

Will you stop saying hi dumb dumb, goodness!

"Okay, umm, I'm…my name is Rodeo and I…I, umm…"

She squinted her eyes and wrinkled her forehead as she leaned in closer asking, "What you say your name is, baby?"

"Umm, Rodeo."

She stumbled backwards. She put her hand over her chest as her mouth fell open. The next words fell from her mouth as if she couldn't believe what she was saying.

"You my, you-my-grandbaby."

I slowly nodded my head.

She yelled, "Oh Lord," and fell to her knees.

"Thank you, Jesus," she cried, "Thank you, Jesus."

She was crying with her hands stretched above her head. She kept saying, "Jesus" and "Thank you, Lord."

I stood there watching her. I could feel tears welling up in my eyes. Using the sturdy, brown TV stand as a crutch, she finally struggled to stand up. She looked at me with tears in her eyes and said, "God has finally answered my prayers. Give me a hug baby."

She pulled me into her arms and embraced me tightly. I returned the hug, squeezing just a tight. She was crying and then, I started crying, but it was a happy cry. I was smiling so hard it was ridiculous.

I hadn't known what to expect from this meeting, but I was already happy with the way things were going. She finally pulled away. She stared at me, smiling. Then, she spoke, struggling to get her words out.

"Well, where, what, I mean, how you get here? How you find me?"

I motioned towards Mr. Johnny's blue, four door truck saying, "Ms. Gwen and her friend brought me over here. He knew where you lived."

She had a strange look on her face, like she was thinking. She whispered, "Gwen," as if trying to recollect who that was.

"Ooh, yeah, Gwen," she said.

"Okay. Well, can they come back later? I want you to stay for a lil' while."

I nodded my head and said, "I'm sure they can. Hold on."

I jogged to the car to let them know I'd be staying for a little while. They agreed they'd come back in a few hours.

"I'm sure y'all got a lot of catchin' up to do," Ms. Gwen said.

I waved goodbye to them and turned back towards my grandmother...*my grandmother*...who was standing in the doorway, smiling.

Only two hours in and so far, we'd talked, and she'd fed me good. She tried to make sure she catered to my every need. I finally had to assure her that I was just fine. I was more satisfied than she knew.

She plopped down on the black, leather sofa and asked, "So, how you like stayin' with Gwen?"

I gave a slight shrug and said, "It's alright."

"Well, I got two extra rooms in this house and ain't nobody here but me. So, you welcome to spend the night anytime you want."

"Okay. Thanks."

We were both quiet for a moment. Both lost in our own thoughts. Then, she said, "You know," she paused, "You welcome to live here too."

I looked at her and said, "I know grandma."

She smiled warmly. I smiled back.

Wow. I loved her already.

Chapter 26

I visited my grandmother almost every other day over the next few of months. I started going to church with her every Sunday. Sometimes, I even spent the night there. Not because I planned to, but just because it'd get late or I'd be too tired to leave.

When Christmas came, we stayed up listening to Christmas music, talking and eating snacks. She'd told me more than a few times that I could move in with her. I mean, I was glad she wanted me to live with her and I wanted to, but I thought about how Ms. Gwen would feel. Of course, I knew Ms. Gwen would get along well without me. I guess...I guess I felt like I owed her in some kind of way.

I know she probably doesn't feel that way, but I was grateful for her taking me in when I didn't have anyone. Not to mention, she hadn't asked for much in return. Perhaps, she would like having her place to herself again. I don't know. I just decided to pray about it.

Today was Wednesday and it had already been a tiresome day for me, mentally anyway. I'd taken two tests today. Thanks to God and my long nights of studying, I'd aced them both.

I'd been at the park for most of the evening. Before that, it was the library. I had an English paper due on Friday and I'd just finished it. Now, it was 7:30 and I was ready to shower and go to sleep.

As I passed by the bathroom, the door to my room opened and what do you know? Out walks that same guy who was in there the last time. This time, he was with a different woman. This one was dark-skinned.

Why do they always have to be in my room? I'm so sick of this.

The hallway wasn't that big, and it seemed like they didn't care that I had to get by. So, I politely placed my back up against the wall as they neared me.

The guy smacked his teeth and said, "What's up lil' mama?"

"Hey," I quickly replied.

Even though, I had my head turned away from them, looking at nothing in particular, I noticed the ugly look the woman gave me. I didn't know why she did that and I didn't care because Lord knows I did not want him. I slipped into my room and closed the door. I heard the woman say something smart to either him or me.

Anyway, I thought.

As I put my books down and turned on the lamp, I noticed that foul smell again. I went over to my suitcase and took out my Lysol. My belongings looked like they'd been tampered with. Good thing I kept everything that had any value with me. There's no telling what they were doing.

I sprayed all over the room. The door knob. The light switch. My bags. Even though, I hadn't been sleeping on it, I sprayed the...the bed?

"What in the world is that?"

I leaned in to get a closer look. I gasped but started coughing from inhaling the Lysol so quickly.

"Eew."

There was a used condom right by my pillow. My adrenaline started pumping almost immediately. I clinched my fists and stormed towards the door. I was prepared to go to Ms. Gwen and say…I don't know, something. I was mad. I mean, I know she has to so called, "make her money," but gosh. Where's the respect? Eew.

As I reached for the doorknob, I stopped. I let out a very, long, heavy sigh. I whispered to myself, "What am I doing?"

I looked around the room. I looked at my book bag, my duffle bag and the garbage bag which held my possessions in them. My life in them.

This isn't my room. I don't even pay rent here. I have no say so in this place whatsoever. I mean, she already made it clear that this is how she does things around here.

First, I changed into my white t-shirt and black sweatpants. Then, I grit my teeth, grabbed a huge amount of tissue and removed their leftovers from the bed, where I flushed it down the toilet. Then, I scrubbed my hands for ten hours. I'm exaggerating, but I did wash them for a good minute or two. After that, I laid the two comforters on the floor and lay down on top of them.

Before I fell asleep, I thanked God for this disgusting thing that had once again happened, because I knew what I had to do. I'd be moving with my grandmother.

Chapter 27

The next morning, I woke up a few minutes before my alarm clock was set to go off. I lay there for a moment, talking to God. I always tried to make sure I thanked Him for waking me up in the morning, amongst other things. Then, I got up and went to the bathroom to prepare for the start of another day. Even though, it was mid-March, it was still cold, so my matching red jogging pants and shirt was ideal for the weather I had to face this morning.

After I put my hair in a ponytail, it was only 6:30, so I still had some time to kill. I decided to fix a grilled cheese sandwich. While I sat at the table eating, I heard Ms. Gwen's house shoes sliding across the floor, from behind me. She scared me for a moment because I wasn't used to seeing her up this early.

"Good mornin', sweetie."

I turned to face her.

"Good morning, Ms. Gwen. What are you doing up so early?"

She laughed. Then, she lit a cigarette and said, "I know you ain't used to seein' me up this early. Heck, I ain't used to seein' myself you this early. But, um."

She paused to put some coffee on as she spoke.

"I gotta go down to this darn office to make sure these folks don't cut off my food stamps. Gotta go early. Otherwise, I'll be down there all darn day."

I nodded my head in understanding as she sat in the chair across from me. She took a pull of her cigarette and asked, "How school goin'?"

"It's going really well. I had a lot of work to do this week, but I got it all finished."

She nodded her head.

"That's good. Education is real important. And it's free. You better get it while you can."

She puffed on the cigarette again, before dumping the ashes in a black ashtray, on the table.

"I wish I had paid more attention in school. I was too busy chasin' boys and worried bout the wrong darn thangs. I wasn't smart enough to know that all this crazy mess that's goin' on in the world, was still gone be here every day, for the next thousand years."

I watched her smoke, in a daze. Maybe, contemplating about her life...the things she did...the choices she'd made.

Then, she said, "But you ain't nothin' like I was. Or your momma, to be honest. You a good girl. Keep yo' head in them books and not on them boys. Them boys gone be there, but that education ain't."

I said, "Okay," because I really did understand her, but I laughed a little on the inside because I thought about daddy and the 7 B's. I could hear him now. "Rodeo, books before boys because boys bring babies."

I was lost in thought until she said, "You and yo' grandma get along good, don't you?"

"Oh, yes," I nodded. "I really didn't know what to expect, but I love her. She's a sweet lady."

"Yeah," she agreed. "Ms. Doris was always nice to everybody."

She stared off into space again. There's no telling what she was thinking about this time. Then, she jumped up and went over to the counter to fix her coffee. After I finished eating, I went to the sink to wash my plate. Ms. Gwen put her cup down and turned towards me.

"Listen baby," she said in a calm voice.

"Yes," I turned to look at her.

"I know yo' grandma like havin' you round there and I know you like bein' there too. So, don't think you'll be hurtin' my feelin's if you go stay with her. Okay?"

I didn't want to seem too eager, so I gave a half smile and said, "Yes ma'am."

She went back to fixing her coffee. After a couple of minutes, she said, "She want you to move over there, don't she?"

"Yes, she does."

Instantly, the next question followed.

"And you wanna move over there too, don't you?"

I hesitated. Then, I nodded, "Yes."

"Then gone and stay with yo' grandma, baby. I'm not tryin' to put you out and I do like your company, but do what make you happy, sweetie. She'll be happy too."

She took a pull of her cigarette and added, "You don't owe Ms. Gwen nothin'. You hear me?"

I smiled.

"Yes. Thank you, Ms. Gwen."

"You welcome, sweetie. I'm still here for you if you need me."

"Okay. Thank you."

I watched her disappear into the darkness of the living room. Then, her door closed. I smiled a big smile. I didn't believe I needed any kind of approval from her, but I guess God knew I needed something. I looked up and said, "Thank you for working it out." Then, I gathered my things and left for school.

I'd been happy all day just thinking about moving with my grandmother. I'd been so ready to go, but I decided to wait until that following Friday, so I'd have the weekend to help my grandmother get the room together, that I'd be sleeping in. Now, after gathering all my things and saying my goodbyes, I'd just gotten out of Mr. Johnny's car and I was walking up the driveway to my grandmother's house.

Chapter 28

I loved going to church on a beautiful Sunday. I

looked out at the blue sky and inhaled the fresh, spring air,
before walking into the house. We freshened up. Then, we
baked some chocolate chip cookies. Now, we were sitting on
the porch eating those cookies with milk. We both had on our
comfortable, lounging clothes and slippers.

My grandmother was sitting in her brown rocking
chair and I was sitting on the swing. This had become one of
our normal routines. Especially, after church. We'd gotten so
close and I loved it. I was taking in the cool breeze blowing by,
when my grandmother asked, "What you think about service
today, baby?"

"Oh, it was good," I answered.

I thought about what the preacher was talking about
today. Trusting in God. No matter how the past was or how
things may look. It made me wonder what my grandmother
thought about the stuff my momma had done. I wondered if
she had any regrets about anything. I wondered a lot of things.

My grandmother and I had become so close over the time we'd spent together, and I knew I could talk to her about anything. I didn't want to hurt her feelings by bringing up certain things, but still, I was prompted to ask.

"Grandma?"

"Yeah baby?"

"How did you find out my momma had been killed?"

She cocked her head to one side, staring at the ground. I'm sure she probably wasn't expecting that question and by seeing the somewhat, painful look on her face, I sort of wished I hadn't brought it up. Still, she took her time, speaking in a careful, soft tone.

"For about three months, I went through this phase, I guess I could call it, where I was so mad. So mad at, at myself, at the people Teresa was around. Even the people in this world."

She looked at me, with hurt in her eyes and said, "I was just mad."

She shook her head and went on.

"I found out from a friend of mine. She read the paper every day and she always read the obituaries. Said she never knew if she would see somebody she knew in it. One day, she brought me the paper and Teresa name was in there."

I looked away for a moment, not really wanting to see the hurt on her face. After a few seconds, she muttered, "A crackhead."

She chuckled a little, but there was no joy in it.

"That's what they called her. A crackhead. A crackhead was found shot behind a dumpster. That's what it said in the paper. I was so mad."

She looked at me again, with those same hurtful eyes.

"They made it seem like my baby didn't have no family. Like she wasn't nobody's child. Like she was a…a nobody."

She looked away, but then, quickly turned her attention back to me saying, "And they didn't even say nothin' bout a lil' girl. I didn't know if they had took you or if somethin' had happened. I didn't know what to think."

She took a deep breath, then continued.

"When my friend brought me the paper, it had been a whole day since it'd happened because she was just comin' back in town. So, she didn't get to see her paper that same day. But honey, when I found out about it, I got her to run me over to where y'all stayed. When I got there, it was nothing worth lookin' for. They was already cleanin' it out for the next people to move in. When I asked them about her daughter, they acted like they didn't know what I was talkin' bout."

She shook her head. I could see some of the anger written all over her face from how she must have felt that day. I was stuck. In a daze. That was such a horrible way to find out your child was killed. I hated that she had to relive that moment. I hated to keep asking questions that would take her back down memory lane, but I couldn't stop. I had questions. And thankfully, it seemed like she didn't mind answering.

"Did you know how my momma and I was living?"

She sighed.

"I would hear some of the stuff people said Teresa was doin'." She shook her head and said, "After a while, I told people to stop tellin' me stuff. I just prayed for her. I had to let it go cause it was gone kill me to think about what y'all might of been goin' through."

She looked at me and smiled weakly.

"Don't ever think I didn't want y'all. Everything I found out, I found out from other people. Even when it came to you," she pointed at me and smiled.

I smiled back, but it quickly faded. I was glad we were having this conversation, but I felt so indifferent about everything. Like, why? Why couldn't I have met my grandmother as a little girl? Why did I have to go through so much? Why do people have to go through so much? I just didn't understand. I listened as she continued.

"I found out where y'all was stayin' and came to the apartment as soon as I could. I wanted y'all to come stay with me, but Teresa was still holdin' on to everything she was mad about. She cussed me out so bad and told me she didn't wanna see me. Boy, yo' momma could cuss a sailor out and make him run home cryin' to his momma."

She laughed and I chuckled a little because I could vouch for that.

"But sometimes I'd come by with food and clothes and lil' things here and there. I would leave it at the front door cause she wouldn't never open it. Ain't no tellin' what happened to it, but still," she looked at me, with a serious look on her face, "Don't think I didn't want y'all."

I nodded my head in understanding. Sometimes, I hated the fact that I remembered things better the older I got. Which meant, I understood and realized some of the things my momma was doing. Of course, I didn't understand why she did certain things, but I always wondered if anything bad had ever happened to her. I started not to ask, but again, I wanted to know.

"Did something bad ever happen to her?"

My grandmother stared off into the distance and said, "You mean, was she ever raped?"

She said it more like a factual statement rather than a question. I was a little hesitant. Then, I said, "Well, yes."

She sat her glass of milk and plate full of cookies on the small, white table next to her. Then, she inhaled very deeply, exhaling as she leaned back in her rocking chair. I could tell she was trying to gather her thoughts. Like she was trying to see where to begin with whatever truth she was about to reveal.

"You know, baby," she began, followed by another heavy sigh. "I used to have so many regrets in life. You know, like, what I should have done or what I could have done differently."

She looked at me and threw her hand as she said, "Honey, it was a whole bunch of mess that used to go through my mind."

She chuckled a little. Then, she pointed her finger towards me and said, "But you know what?"

I could tell she was about to give me some valuable information I needed to hear, to take with me throughout life.

"God showed me that, just like stress, regrets will kill you too. I mean, what can you do about the things you can't change? So, I just say, no regrets, only lessons learned. Always remember that, baby. And if you do make a mistake, which you will, learn from it and you won't keep making those same mistakes. Even better, learn from somebody else's mistakes so you won't do the same thang. But hey," she threw her hands up, "Sometimes, we gotta learn the hard way."

I nodded my head.

"But, um," she began as she stared off into space, "When Teresa was 10, her daddy left us for some other woman."

She shook her head.

"Anyway, he had been gone for bout, three years and in all that time, me and her had got real close. Then, her daddy decided he wanted to do right by us, so I let him come back."

She looked towards me, shaking her head, "He didn't wanna do right. I found out later that other woman had put his butt out cause he was messin' round on her with somebody else. He just needed a place to stay. But," she sighed and stared off into space again, "I let him come back and that's when thangs changed."

"I started puttin' more of my time in him and I kind of, I kind of forgot bout Teresa. Teresa started gettin' into all kinds of stuff. She was runnin' off and stayin' gone for two and three nights at a time."

She sat up and cleared her throat.

"She used to always say," she paused for a moment, "She used to always say her daddy would mess with her when I was gone or sleep. One night, when she was 15, I walked in on them..."

She let her voice trail off and her face fall towards the ground. She never finished the sentence. She looked at me with sadness in her eyes and said, "I blamed my child for what they was doin'. I blamed my own 15 year old child."

She looked towards the ground again. My heart hurt for her.

"I was so dumb. Thinkin' I needed him. Like, I had to keep him there or somethin'. When I could of been doing better by my darn self."

She leaned over and pointed her finger towards me again. I could tell more valuable information was coming.

"Listen baby, you know how people say, "I can do bad by myself?""

I nodded after realizing she was waiting for me to acknowledge, what I thought was a rhetorical question.

"Well, that's true. But I say, if the man ain't no good...you can do better by yourself. Cause a no good man sure can bring a good woman down."

"Anyway," she settled back into her chair, "That's when she ran off to California with that Gwen girl and ended up gettin' pregnant with you. I heard about it a few months after she came back."

Wow. Neither of us said anything. We sat in silence for a while. Like, everything that had just been said needed a moment to settle in. At least, for me it did. In my mind, I'd heard all the important things I needed to know about my momma's life. I didn't need to hear anything else. As far as, the other half of me...

"Grandma?"

"Hmm."

"Do you think...I mean...could my daddy be..."

"No," she quickly said. "No, baby. That ain't yo' daddy."

I sighed with relief. I was glad she knew what I was about to ask without asking.

She went on to say, "A few years after Teresa was born, Robert found out he couldn't have no mo' kids. He had got into some mess." She didn't explain anything. She just threw her hand like she does.

"But," she said in a perky way, "Like I said, no regrets, only lessons learned. Now, let's go get us so mo' milk and cookies and leave the past, in the past."

And that's exactly what I planned to do, but I had one more question and honestly, I really had her in mind more than myself.

"One more thing," I said.

She looked at me, giving me her full attention.

"So, you never got to see her at all before she died. I mean, you never got a chance to see her at least once, even without her knowing?"

She took a deep breath and looked towards the sky.

"The last time I went was four days before she was killed. I knocked. She didn't come to the door. She had a peep hole so, I'm sure she probably saw me out there sometimes. I hardly ever left stuff that needed to be refrigerated because I didn't know if she would get it before it spoiled or not. But I did leave a bag with some bread, chips and snack cakes in it."

I gasped on the inside.

I remember that.

"But no," I heard a slight crack in her voice, "I never got to see her."

I ate bread, chips and snack cakes all those days leading up to my momma's death, while she was either sleeping or gone.

She laughed out of nowhere, interrupting my thoughts. I was glad.

"What," I asked with a slight smile, wondering what could be so funny.

She chuckled a little more before saying, "That was the same day one of them darn knuckleheads snatched my purse from me."

"They did," I asked shockingly.

"Yep. But I know they was mad, though."

"Why you say that grandma?"

"Cause, it wasn't nothin' but bills in there and I know they didn't want those cause I didn't want 'em either."

We looked at each other. Then, we both burst out laughing. We sat on the porch for almost the whole day talking, eating, and laughing, until it was almost time to get ready for bed.

Chapter 29

During the summer, I mostly stayed around the house with my grandmother. I didn't go out much, thanks to the hot summer days. If I did, I'd wait until it was a nice, sunny day, but still cloudy and breezy, just like today. I was sitting on a bench at the park, reading a book I'd found on my grandmother's bookshelf. She had a big collection of books, ranging from history to romance. The one I was reading at the moment was called *The Chance*, by Karen Kingsbury. I was so deep into the story, it took me a minute to realize someone was calling my name.

"Rodeo?"

I got goose bumps. So much so, that I didn't want to turn around. Then again, I did, but I was hesitant to do so. I slowly turned, hoping the voice I thought I'd heard, was really the voice I thought I'd heard. As I glanced over my shoulders, that voice...that smile…came to life. It was James.

He stood there smiling. As if they were out of my control, my eyes slowly traveled from his face to his black tennis shoes. I took every bit of him in. He had on some blue, Nike, gym shorts. His sweaty white T-shirt revealed his newly formed muscles.

He didn't have those the last time I saw him.

I hadn't realized I'd been staring until he said, "Hey."

My eyes quickly went back up to his face. His smiled looked more like a grin now. He knew I was checking him out. I smiled, but I was more embarrassed than anything.

What in the world was that?

I had never looked at a boy, I mean, a man, like that before.

"Hey," I said with a nervous laugh. "How are you?"

"I'm good," he replied as he made his way over to the bench to sit down.

I turned away a little, trying to hide the fact that I was blushing. If I were lighter, I'm sure my face would have been red.

"It's been a long time."

"Yep," I nodded in agreement.

"I would give you a hug but," he pointed to his sweaty shirt.

I giggled a little and said, "Yeah, you're really sweating. What were you doing? Running?"

"Yeah."

He leaned back and rested his arms on the back of the bench. One of which was behind me.

"I go to the gym most of the time, but I like to run outside on nice days like this. So," he turned towards me and smiled, "What's up? How you been? How's everything been goin'?"

"I'm fine. Everything's good."

I was trying to avoid eye contact.

"Good."

He sighed. We both stared out into the park. Even though, there was sort of an awkward silence between us, I didn't know what to say to break it. Finally, I looked at the clouds that had mysteriously turned gray and said, "It looks like it's going to rain soon."

He looked up and agreed, "Yeah, it does. Did you drive?"

"No. I walked."

"I did too. You must live close?"

"Yep," I replied, "Over on Hester."

"Hester," he asked, almost in shock. "I stay on Border. That's just two streets over. Wow. How long you been there?"

My eyes widened because that *was* pretty close, and I'd never seen him before. I guess everything does happen when it's supposed too.

"Well, I moved with my grandmother and I've been there for a few months now."

"Wow. That's crazy. We been stayin' so close to each other and never knew it."

He was smiling like he'd just received some very good news. Him smiling, made me smile. Laugh, even.

"What," I asked, laughing.

"Nothin'. Just happy to see you, that's all."

We sort of had a "moment," where we looked at each other longer than I think we should have.

"Well, come on," he looked away. "Let me walk you home before the rain comes."

The walk home was nice. In the 15 to 20 minutes it took to get there, James and I had covered a lot of ground. He'd told me after high school, he joined the army, but he was still able to go to school because he only joined the reserve. Now, he was staying with his aunt. Even though, I wondered about what had happened with his dad, he didn't talk about it and I didn't dare ask. I briefly told him about my run in at the Nightmare Inn and I was just giving a little background on my stay with Ms. Gwen and how I'd found my grandmother, as we approached my house.

"This is where I stay."

"Okay. So, what do you most of the time?"

"Well, I mean, nothing really. Since I'm out of school for the summer, most of the time, I'm reading, going to church or talking and hanging around the house with my grandmother."

"You and your grandma best friends, huh?"

We both laughed.

"I'm laughing but, in a way, yeah," I added.

"Well, maybe I could go to church with you sometime?"

Wow. Wasn't expecting that one. But…

"Yeah. Maybe."

He looked at the house. Then, back to me. He smiled and nodded his head like he was waiting for me to say something.

"So," he started, "You think I could call you sometime?"

Boy, he sure isn't scared to ask for what he wants.

I was glad though, because I really did want to keep in touch with him. So, I gave him my number and we said our goodbyes.

Later that night, my grandmother and I were lounging around in our night clothes, watching one of our favorite TV shows, *House of Payne*. As soon as a commercial came on, my grandmother asked, "So, who was that handsome, young man you was out there talkin' to earlier?"

I couldn't help but blush. She'd completely caught me off guard and it seemed like she'd been waiting to ask me that.

I brushed it off like it was nothing, saying, "He's just a friend."

"Oh, so, you already know him?"

I shrugged, "Yeah."

"And?"

I looked at her and giggled.

"And what grandma?"

"Don't *and-what-grandma* me. I don't want none of them one, word answers. I saw the way y'all was talkin' with each other. You know, I *was* young once."

I sighed while blushing, yet again. Then, I went into the whole story of meeting James and how I'd stayed with him. I even told her what happened with his dad.

"Ooow child. Some of these men ain't got a bit of sense."

I nodded my head in agreement.

"But he beat the mess out of his butt over you."

Even though, it wasn't funny when it happened, she chuckled, which made me laugh.

"And ain't it somethin' how y'all ran back into each other after all this time?"

I nodded my head agreeing, "It is."

I couldn't deny that. I mean, I thought about him, but you never know if you'll see a person again, especially after you lose contact with them and so much time has passed.

"He wants to come to church with me."

She perked up.

"Really?"

"Yep."

"That's good. You don't find too many young men that actually wanna go to church. You should gone and tell him to come with us Sunday."

I thought about it for a moment. Maybe that's too soon. I don't know. It's not like we don't already know each other. Not to mention, we've already been to church together once before.

What's the problem, Rodeo?

I could tell I was a lot shyer around him than before. Maybe it's because we're older and emotions are a lot different now. More enhanced and noticed, maybe?

I glanced towards my grandmother. I hadn't realized she'd been staring at me, waiting for me to say something.

"You show is thinkin' mighty hard over there."

Finally, I said, "I guess it wouldn't hurt to ask."

"Uh huh," she said as she got up to go in the kitchen.

"You know you want him to come."

I just shook my head and smiled. I didn't have anything to say because truth be told, I really did want him to come.

Chapter 30

Of course, James said he'd be happy to go to church with us. So, on Sunday morning, we all piled into James' new, blue, Nissan Maxima and headed to church. Out of respect, James and I both tried to get my grandmother to sit in the front seat, but she insisted I sit there.

"I don't mind. I can see just as much from the back as I can in the front," she'd said. Then, she winked at me. I couldn't do anything but giggle.

The choir was already singing when we walked in the church. We walked towards our usual spot, somewhere around the middle pews. As we took our seats, I noticed two girls, who sat three rows behind us, eyeing James. They were giggling and whispering to one another. Being that I sat in the middle of James and my grandmother, she leaned towards me and whispered, "Alright now. You can act like you don't want him, but if you don't get him, somebody else will."

I didn't say anything, but honestly, I did feel a pinch of...jealousy? Maybe? I cut my eyes at James, to the right of me. He had on some nice, black, dress shoes. They looked like some type of snakeskins. He had on some black slacks and a tan, short-sleeved, Polo shirt.

I glanced at his face, in a way without him noticing. He always kept a nice haircut. I mean, why wouldn't he? He did work at a barbershop. He looked nice.

"Preach Pastor," my grandmother yelled as she waved her hand in the air.

I'd been so wrapped up in other things, I hadn't even noticed the sermon had begun. I focused my attention on Pastor Griffin, wearing a long, black robe. He wiped the perspiration away from his head, with a white handkerchief, before continuing.

"Listen y'all, some folks get so caught up in who they think God is that it makes them so religious. Then, they start judgin' others like somebody died and made them God. Christianity is not a religion. It's a personal relationship with God. God is not a religion. He is love. Having a true relationship with God doesn't make you religious it makes you spiritual because He is a spirit and His spirit lives in you. Don't let your Christianity make you religious."

He put emphasis on each word as he pounded on the podium saying, "God is not religion. God is love. He don't want you to condemn His people."

"Thank You, Jesus," someone shouted.

"Trust me," he said. "You don't have to condemn or judge nobody because once they realize the true love, grace and mercy of God, feeling convicted is automatic."

"Amen," a lady shouted from behind us.

As the sermon went on, more shouts came and soon the music followed. I looked at James and smiled. He was clapping and rocking to the music.

I yelled to him over the loud music, "Having fun?"

He threw his hands up and said, "Yep, thank you Jesus."

I laughed. I knew he was serious, but he always had a way of making me laugh.

On our way home from church, my grandmother asked, "So James, how you like church?"

"I really enjoyed it. I wouldn't mind goin' there again."

I noticed him glance towards me.

"Oh, that would be nice. I'm glad you enjoyed it. By the way, what you doin' after you drop us off? You got any plans?"

"No ma'am, I don't have any plans today?"

"Well, how bout you come over and eat dinner with us. I put some food in the slow cooker this mornin', so it won't be long before we eat."

"Oh, well," he stammered a little, "I mean, I would love to. Of course, if that's okay with Rodeo."

He quickly looked at me and then, back to the road as he turned on our street.

"Oh, she don't mind. Come on and get you a good meal."

How does she know I don't mind?

He pulled into our driveway and said, "Well, in that case," he looked at me. I smiled that awkward, shy, smile. "I'd love to."

❀

Before my grandmother and I fixed the plates, we changed into some comfortable sweats and t-shirts.

"Oooh Ms. Doris, you gone make me fall in love with you."

James took a long whiff of the food I'd just placed in front of him. It had some roast beef on it, macaroni and cheese, cornbread and black eyed peas. For desert, there was sweet potato pie. I loved my grandmother's sweet potato pie.

My grandmother chuckled, saying, "Boy you a mess."

"But yeah," she said after she finished saying grace, "I tell Rodeo all the time, good home cookin' is the way to a man's heart."

"You hear that, Rodeo," James said between bites. "She not talkin' bout noodles and weird stuff with ketchup on it either."

They both laughed.

"Ha-ha-ha," I said sarcastically, "Very funny. I can cook some stuff."

"Yeah," my grandmother chimed in, "She done learned how to cook a few things since she been here, and she gone learn how to cook a lot more."

James looked at me and smirked.

"Only time will tell," he said.

I shook my head and looked away. I think he noticed I was getting a little embarrassed. He turned his attention to my grandmother.

"So, Ms. Doris, who taught you how to cook?"

Although, I was a part of the discussion, my attention was focused on James and my grandmother, not the conversation they were having. He had her laughing so hard. I could tell they really liked each other.

"Ain't that right, baby?"

I looked at my grandmother, looking at me, with a big smile on her face. I had no idea what she was talking about, but I said, "Yep, that's right."

They both burst out laughing so, I'm guessing it wasn't anything serious. We sat there for at least two hours talking, laughing, and gaining pounds. Afterwards, James finally said his goodbyes and went home. After all was settled, my grandmother ended the night saying, "I really like him."

James started taking me to school and picking me up pretty much every day. He said it didn't interrupt his schedule because he went to school online. Honestly, the only time I didn't see him is when he had duty, which was only so many days out of the month.

He'd come over all the time and hang out with me and my grandmother. He'd even take us to run errands or to church. That was really good because we always had to ride the church bus to church or get rides from one of my grandmother's friends, who never failed to scare me with their driving. We'd gotten really close over the last few weeks. It was almost as if that time we'd been separated, had never happened. My grandmother and I both liked having him around. Most of all, I could tell he liked being around.

Chapter 31

As of today, Monday, August the 20th, 2012, I began my journey as a senior. Yaaay! Daddy would be so proud to know his money hadn't gone to waste. As for myself, I would have been a fool to let it go to waste. I'm sure he was happy for me.

Being that I only had a few classes to take before completing my credits for graduation, I was able to get out of school a little after 1pm. I'd finished any homework I had and now, James and I were sitting on the porch, enjoying the nice, fall weather. I sat on the swing while James sat on the top step of the porch. We were both eating some chocolate chip cookies my grandmother had baked.

"Your birthday comin' up soon, ain't it? September 27th, right?"

I looked at him. He sat there in some jeans and a black T-shirt. He was in the process of swatting a fly away, therefore, he didn't notice the puzzled look I had on my face.

I answered, "Yeah…that's right."

He went on to eat his cookie and say some other things, but I was only half listening. I was a bit shocked. Flattered, even. It surprised me that he'd remembered my birthday. I mean, I hadn't remembered his. I only found out it was August 29th when I heard my grandmother tell him happy birthday. I figured he must have mentioned it to her.

"So, if you want, we can do that."

"Huh? What? I'm sorry James, I was thinking about this test I have coming up."

Now, what was the purpose of that dumb lie? I'm sorry, God. Forgive me, but that's the first thing I thought of. I didn't want to tell him what I was really thinking.

"What were you saying again," I asked.

"I was just saying'" He continued, unbothered by the fact that I obviously wasn't listening, "Maybe we could go out to eat for your birthday."

"Oh, yeah, that'd be cool."

"Okay then," he said as he hopped up. "Well, I told my aunt I'll take her to run some errands. You know, she gotta go to five stores, stay in there forever and come out with three things."

I chuckled.

"What you bout to do," he asked.

"Nothing. I'll probably sit out here a little while longer and read this book I have. I've been studying to get my license. I'll be 18 soon so, I can take the computer test and the driving part on the same day."

"Oh, man. Rodeo is about to get behind the wheel of a car."

He turned to face the street and cupped his hands around his mouth, as if he was making an announcement and said, "Everybody watch out."

I laughed, "Honey hush. When I do get on the road, I'm sure I'll be just fine."

"Yeah, if you walkin' on it," he said, smirking.

I couldn't do anything but giggle. He got in his car and started backing out of the driveway.

"Hey," he yelled out of the window.

I looked up.

"We gone start driving lessons tomorrow."

And we did.

Today was Thursday, my 18th birthday. Besides a "Happy Birthday," being announced over the intercom at school, it had been a day like any other. After I got out of my last class, I, along with many others, waited around for my ride to pick me up.

I was in my favorite spot, sitting on a bench, on the grassy lawn, in front of the school. Marissa, a girl from my French class, sat next to me. She was someone I considered a school friend. Since the beginning of the school year, we'd gotten sort of close. Especially, since we were always paired with each other when doing assignments and projects in class. Being that both of us got out early, we usually sat next to each other until our rides came.

"So," she started, as she flipped her long, blonde hair out of her face, "What are you doing for your birthday?"

"Well, I'm supposed to be going out to eat tonight."

"Ooow," she said playfully, "With your boyfriend?"

I tried my best to avoid eye contact as I laughed uneasily and said, "No," while picking some "invisible lent" from my black, dress pants.

"Oh, so, that's not your boyfriend?"

I looked at her. Then, I followed her gaze to James standing outside of his car, waiting for me.

Well, I can see why she would assume he was my boyfriend.

There he was, standing there with a colorful "Happy Birthday" balloon in one hand and a bunch of purple and white flowers in the other.

I turned away quickly, blushing so hard.

OMG!

I quickly gathered my things as Marissa spoke sarcastically saying, "Well, have fun with the guy who's obviously *not* your boyfriend."

I giggled as I walked away.

"Au revoir," she yelled.

I turned and waved goodbye to her. As I approached James, he wore a grin on his face. He knew I was embarrassed. Not in a bad way. It was just so, unexpected.

"Look at Ms. Cutie," he joked. "You got your hair done and everything."

I giggled. I knew he was used to seeing me with a ponytail. Not with my hair down in loose curls. I stopped in front of him as he held out the balloon and flowers.

"Happy Birthday, mademoiselle."

I took the items. I couldn't help smiling.

"Thank you, James."

He then jogged around to the passenger side door and held it open for me.

"Come, my lady," he said in his best, Knight-and-shining-armor voice. "Your chariot awaits you."

I giggled, "Oh, stop it."

"What," he said as I got in the car. "I'm just tryin' to show a lady a good time on her birthday."

I rolled my eyes, embarrassed by the few students watching us, but still blushing as hard as ever. He got into the driver's seat, started the car and said, "So, you ready to go get your license?"

I quickly turned to face him, "What?

"You said you been studyin' and as your father," he stopped to smile really big, pointing to himself, "I was able to schedule both of your tests today. Hope you're ready."

My mouth must have hung open for almost a minute before I burst out laughing.

"Let's go," I said.

I glanced at him as he drove off.

He is something else.

My grandmother had been so proud when I ran in the house to show her my license. I'd been so nervous, but I knew I was prepared thanks to my studying and many driving lessons. James said he didn't want to risk getting pulled over on the rode with me not having a license, so we would always practice in a huge, vacant parking lot instead.

After James dropped me off, he'd gone home to get dressed while I freshened up and changed clothes. I put on a pair of midnight blue, spandex pants with a long, black, silk shirt that fell almost past my knees. It was short sleeved and loose fitting on purpose. I finished it off with a wide, blue waist belt and some cute, but comfortable, black, thong sandals.

When he pulled up, I told my grandmother I'd be home no later than 11pm.

"Y'all have a nice time," she yelled as we backed out of the driveway.

"You look nice," James said as he drove off.

"Thanks. So do you."

He did look rather handsome in his navy blue, Polo shirt and dark, blue jeans, with a pair of cream and navy blue, Polo shoes.

"So, where are we going?"

He smirked, "Just sit back and enjoy the ride."

I smiled thinking, there's no telling what he has on our agenda for tonight. I relaxed in my seat, looked out of the window at the clear, evening sky and enjoyed the ride.

❊

"Are you serious?"

My mouth hung open as I looked from James, to the Yacht, docked in front of us. It had to be at least 300 feet long. It was two stories, all white and the word, *Moonlight* was painted across it in big, sky blue letters.

"Oh, my goodness, James."

I playfully punched him on the arm.

"What," he asked, grinning, while holding his arm.

"This is beautiful, that's what."

He laughed, "Well, why'd you hit me?"

"Because," was all I could say. I was speechless.

"Come on, birthday girl. Let's go eat."

After we were seated at a table for two, along with about 30 other people and the waiter had taken our order, the boat slowly pulled away from the loading dock. I looked around, admiring the time the owner must have taken to dress the boat up.

Every table, was a table for two, covered with silk, white tablecloths. A small, crystal bowl sat on top of each table, with three, lit, floating candles in them. Besides the dimly lit, three, tier chandelier, hanging from the inside of the boat, the candles were our only light. Some of the tables were located inside and some were out. We sat at one on the outside. I was glad. It gave me more time to look at the night sky. So far, this had already turned out to be a great birthday.

"How'd you find out about this place?"

"Well," he cleared his throat, "One of the guys I serve with told me he brought his girl here once. I came to check it out one day and I thought you'd probably like it."

His girl?

I smiled.

"Well," I took a sip of my sweet tea, "I do like it. I would never have guessed that this is where you were bringing me."

"I just wanted you to enjoy your birthday."

"And I am. Thanks."

"You're welcome."

We both looked at each other, smiling, until the waiter appeared with our food, breaking our brief moment.

"Umm um," James said after the waiter left, "This looks delicious."

"Yeah," I agreed, "Mine does too."

I'd ordered a grilled Salmon with two of my favorite sides, mashed potatoes and broccoli with cheese. James, on the other hand, ordered a bacon cheeseburger with fries.

"Just can't seem to stay away from that ole Wendy's special, huh," I joked.

He laughed, "Hey, you can't compare a fast food burger to a nice, restaurant burger."

I nodded my head in agreement.

After dinner, we found a nice, quiet spot, away from everyone else, towards the back of the boat. Neither of us said anything. I'm guessing he was taking in the scenery, the same as me. The boat had stopped and we both stared at the night sky, accompanied by many stars. It was so beautiful. The light posts surrounding the lake, reflected off of the dark, still water. Huge mansions peeked through the many branches, from the trees encircling the water. I closed my eyes, inhaled the fresh air and let out a satisfied sigh.

"You look beautiful."

I opened my eyes. I'd almost forgotten he was standing next to me.

"Thank you. Thank you for," I paused, looking around, "For all of this."

"I know it's not much but…"

"No," I cut him off. "This is more than enough. This has been…everything about today has been great. I love it and I appreciate it. Thank you."

He smiled, nodding his head. I knew, he knew, I was sincere about what I'd just said. As we stood there in silence, I began to wonder how things would have turned out had I not ran away, after the incident with James and his father. Come to think of it, I never stopped to think about how James felt after I left. Or, if he felt anything at all.

"James?"

I could see out of the corner of my eye that he'd turned towards me, giving me his full attention. I kept my eyes fixed straight ahead.

"I'm sorry I left that night. That night when…"

"Rodeo," he cut in.

"No, James. Listen."

He exhaled, staring off into the night.

"I was just, I was so scared and mad at myself because I felt that if I hadn't been there, things wouldn't have gone the way they did."

I took a deep breath and continued.

"I was just so tired and frustrated at the way my life was going, but I didn't get a chance to say thank you. Thank you for taking so much time out of your life to help me. Thank you for putting your life on the line, *for me*. Neither did I stop to think about how you felt with everything going on. I'm sorry."

He waited to speak until he knew I was done talking for sure. Then, he said, "Rodeo."

Even though, he said my name in a gentle way, it almost sounded as if he was pleading with me. I made eye contact with his caring eyes.

"That wasn't the first time me and my dad had got into it. He's put his hands on me plenty of times. But," he paused, "That was the first time I went off on him like that. I don't know," he shook his head, taking a moment to gather himself.

"It was like…like I had just snapped."

That word made me think about the TV show *Snapped*. I could see that it was possible for people to snap. Especially, when they've been dealing with something bad for a long time. He leaned on the railing, staring into the water. I softly rubbed his back, in an effort to comfort him.

"It was only a matter of time until something like that happened. It was only a matter of time before I left. But," he looked at me, "Don't think any of it was your fault. If anything," he chuckled, "It was perfect timing. No tellin' where I would be or how I would've turned out if I had stayed."

I smiled, slightly. Somewhat relieved to know that perhaps, I'd helped the situation. Maybe?

"So, what did you do after that happened?"

He took a deep breath and once again, looked towards the night sky.

"Well, after I stopped seein' red, I stood there for a minute, lookin' at my hands. They was all bloody. My dad was bloody, beat up and moanin'. Then, I remembered you was there. I ran in the room and I didn't see none of your stuff. Then, I ran outside to see if you was out there but," he quickly glanced at me.

"Anyway," he cleared his throat, "I went for a walk, thinkin' bout everything and I decided I had to leave because," he paused, turned to me and said, "If it had happened again, I know I would've killed him."

Our stare lingered for a brief moment. Then, he hung his head low. After a few seconds, he rushed on to say, "I stayed with a few cousins, found my mom's sister, who I stay with now and then, I decided to go to the army."

I nodded my head slowly and said, "All in God's plan."

"Yep," he agreed.

"And then," he adds after a few seconds, "He brought you back into my life."

I looked at him. He looked at me. No words. There was no need. His eyes said a lot.

The sound of the boat starting up broke our concentration. I looked out into the water, watching the ripples form from the movements of the boat. A quick breeze passing through, gave me chills. I shivered a little and rubbed my arms.

"Cold," he asked.

I nodded.

"I got a little chilly, that's all."

He inched closer to me and slowly wrapped his arms around me. I tensed up, but just as quickly, relaxed. I stood there as he folded me in his arms, gently rubbing mines. It's funny. I felt so nervous, but yet, so calm. So comfortable. Nervous because I'd never felt these unexplainable emotions I was feeling right now. Relaxed because I knew I was in safe arms.

That following Saturday, my grandmother surprised me with cake, ice cream and two, happy birthday balloons. That evening she'd asked me if I could go to the store to get some bread. The store wasn't far, but she knew I'd have to walk being that James had duty this weekend, so it'd take me a little while to get back.

When I got back, she yelled, "Happy Birthday!" She said she'd waited a long time to give her grandbaby a birthday party. Even though, it wasn't much, and it was just the two of us, I loved it. After we'd stuffed ourselves with all we could, we settled down on the sofa, while I flipped through the channels, in search of something to watch.

"So, how was your birthday, baby?"

I smiled, thinking about last night.

"Oh grandma, it was so nice."

I started telling her everything, from the boat, to the dinner we had. Well, everything except the part about James cozying up to me.

I laughed a little at the thought of him remembering my birthday and added, "It's so funny. I didn't think he'd remember my birthday after all this time, but he did."

"Well, baby. That's how you know when a man like you. He remember the stuff you think he won't."

I looked at her for a brief moment. Then, I turned my attention back to the TV.

That makes perfect sense.

She chuckled and said, "That young man like you."

I slowly turned my face away from her, trying not to let her see me blush.

"But I'm sure you already know that, don't you?"

I nodded my head quickly.

Please don't ask me if I like him.

As if reading my mind, she said, "I'm not even gone ask if you like him. I can see the stars in your eyes when you talk about him."

I laughed uneasily, "Huh?"

"Uh huh. Don't *huh* me," she said. "Anyway, baby. I'm bout to gone and lay down. That cake and ice cream done got me sleepy."

She got up and headed to her room.

"Goodnight, baby. I love you," she yelled to me.

"Goodnight grandma. Love you too."

Chapter 32

Three more months and I'd be a high school graduate.
My how time flies. I'd just finished my art class and after
stopping by the restroom, I headed down the hallway, to the
lunchroom. As I passed by the hallway, leading to the front
office, I heard someone call my name.

I stopped in my tracks and looked to my right. There
was someone sitting on the black, leather couch that sat outside
of the office. I knew it was a girl's voice, but I couldn't tell
who it was because they had on a black hoodie which
concealed most of their face. I slowly inched closer and as I
got closer, I said, "Katina?"

I'm sure I sounded surprised, but I didn't try to. I just
hadn't expected to see her.

"Hey," I said, smiling as I sat down beside her.

"Hey," she replied, sounding sort of sad.

I could tell she was trying to avoid making eye contact. It was like she was trying to hide her face. I asked, "Is something the matter?"

She inhaled deeply. After about 10 seconds, which seemed like a very long time, she finally said, "I have a baby."

I wrinkled my forehead, confused. Then, I opened my mouth to say something, but all that came out was, "Oh."

She didn't say anything, and I didn't know what to say. It seemed like she wanted me to know or she wouldn't have told me. It also seemed like she was waiting for me to say something, so I said, "Well, did you have a boy or a girl?"

"A girl," she answered, still looking at anything but me. It was always hard to make small talk when the person you were talking to was giving close ended answers. Still, it was obvious something was bothering her and that was bugging me. I wanted to talk to her to at least try to lift her spirits. So, I asked another question.

"How old is she?"

I was prepared to hear her say, one month old...two months...maybe even five months, but then, she said, "She just turned one last week on February the 12th."

"Oh, wow. Well, congratulations, Katina," I said, honestly happy for her. Then, I got to thinking…

Wait a minute. It takes 9 months for a baby to be born. I was living there only over a year ago.

She finally looked at me, noting what I knew was a look of confusion on my face. She took a deep breath and finally let more than a few words fall out of her mouth.

"Before you left…I mean, before they made you leave, I was already four months. I just wasn't showing"

My mouth fell open, but I quickly closed it, not wanting to seem so shocked. I hadn't even noticed she was pregnant.

"Oh," was all I said.

She goes on to say, "I didn't start showing until I was about six months. Then, I just started wearing bigger clothes to hide it. When my parents found out, they started home schooling me."

Well, that explains why I didn't see her anymore.

I nodded my head in understanding. I didn't care to ask her how her parents had reacted to it. I could almost imagine. Neither did I want her to have to dwell on that too much because I knew she probably felt bad enough. So, I tried to change the subject to lighten the moment.

"So, are you going to come back to school now?"

She looked at me, then, quickly looked away.

"Rodeo? Do you know who the father is?'

Why would she ask me that? I said the only person I assumed was the daddy.

"Jontae…right?"

She still hadn't looked at me when she said, "My momma and Mr. David are in the office with the police. They came to talk to…to Mr. Demagio."

Why would they…ooooohhh. Good Lord.

This time, my mouth did hang open longer than I'd expected. I was shocked. I'd heard plenty of rumors and I could remember her always saying she stopped by the office to see him but, when, how…wow. Good thing she continued talking because I really didn't know how to respond to that.

"Everybody thought it was Jontae's, including him. It was Mr. David who kept questioning it. He kept sayin' she looked more like a mixed baby than just a really, light-skinned baby. He finally made me go get a test and…I mean, I had to tell them…"

Just then, the door to the office swung open. Mr. David had his back to us as Mrs. Daniels came out, followed by two policemen, who had Mr. Demagio in handcuffs. Nobody had noticed me sitting there with Katina.

Mr. David yelled things like, "You not gone get away with this" and "I don't care who yo' daddy supposed to be," amongst other things.

With a smirk on his face, Mr. Demagio yelled towards the assistant principal, Mr. Glenn, "Call my fatha and let him know what's goin' on."

Mr. Glenn nodded and went to do what he was told. As Mr. David yelled, Mrs. Daniels didn't say a word. She finally looked to where Katina was and said, "Come on Tina let's…," her words were cut short when she noticed me.

Shortly after, Mr. David followed her glance. With the look he'd given me, if looks could kill, I'd be dead. Katina got up to leave, but I quickly grabbed her and hugged her.

"It'll be okay," I whispered.

"Thanks Rodeo."

She pulled away and walked towards the door, with her mom in tow. Katina quickly glanced back towards me and smiled. Before Mr. David walked away, he had the audacity to say, "Y'all officers might wanna make sure you check her. She might've been sleepin' with him too."

He started walking towards the door and before I knew it, I'd said, "They might need to check you. You might've been sleeping with her too."

He turned and glared at me. Then, he forced the doors to the front of the building opened and walked out.

I stood there shaking my head. I didn't know how Katina felt exactly, but I sure felt empathy for her. I needed a moment. I went in the bathroom, asked for forgiveness for making that ugly remark and said a quick prayer for her, Mrs. Daniels and as hard as it was, Mr. David.

Later that day, after I'd gotten out of school, I went to sit at my usual spot on the bench, to wait for James. I was reading another book from my grandmother's random collection. It was called, *Casting the First Stone,* by Kimberla

Lawson Roby. All of a sudden, I caught a glimpse of a pair of long, pale legs, hardly covered by a denim skirt, standing in some bloody red, high heels.

"Hey Rodeo."

I looked up, avoiding the cleavage which is always busting out of some tight shirt she's wearing. Dallas. The school gossip girl. How she managed to where some of the things she did with such a strict school code was beyond me.

"Hey Dallas."

She flipped her long, black hair and smiled.

"Did you hear about Mr. Demagio and Katina?"

I looked back down at my book, annoyed a little, but I didn't show it.

"Yep."

"Oh, okay. I was just wondering because I knew you guys were good friends."

Oh, so, now you're concerned? Yeah, right.

I nodded my head slowly and continued reading my book. She stood there like she was waiting for me to go into details about it all. Maybe she was waiting for me to say more. I don't know. I didn't say a thing. Eventually, she walked away, mumbling something to herself. I rolled my eyes. I honestly didn't care what she was saying.

With all the talk going around about her and Mr. Demagio, she's probably just mad that she didn't have a baby by him. Oh, goodness. Let me stop being ugly. I'm sorry, Lord.

After the whole Katina thing, there were rumors that Mr. Demagio would remain the principal, because of who his dad was and all. We all thought that would be the case, but within just a few hours, the school board had received so many threats from angry parents, saying they'd remove their kids if Mr. Demagio wasn't fired. His father had no choice but to remove him. I mean, that's if he wanted to keep his money flowing.

It had been decided that the assistant principal, Mr. Glenn, would take over as the principal and they'd eventually find someone to fill his position. Mr. Glenn was no Mr. Demagio. He was short, stocky, wore small, thick, black glasses and had one of those haircuts where the only hair on his head, was around the sides of it.

He was a nice man, though. I honestly believe he genuinely cared about the students too. I'm positive, him being the new principal made all the dads very happy. I didn't care who was principal. As long as they didn't hinder me from coming to school and eventually finishing, I was alright.

❀

"He ain't nothin' but a old snake," my grandmother said after I told her about my run in with Katina.

I sat at the kitchen table, as my grandmother sashayed over to the stove to stir some sweet potatoes she was cooking.

"And that poor child. That darn principal ought to be ashamed of himself."

"Yep," I agreed, partly focused on the game I was playing on my laptop.

"Ain't no telling how many other girls he done messed with. That go for that *Mr. David* too."

She said his name as if it left a bad taste in her mouth.

"If he can do somethin' like that to you and claim to be a man of God, ain't no tellin' who else he done did it too."

I nodded my head saying, "You're right, grandma."

I heard her slippers slide across the floor as she made her way back to the table to sit down.

"So," she started, as she took a sip of her sweet tea, "You decide what school you want to go to yet?"

I finally looked up from the game.

"Hmm," I shrugged my shoulders, "Still undecided. Although, I have been thinking about Spelman College a lot."

"Ain't that the one where only girls go?"

"Yep."

"Well," she said as she got up to go over to the stove, "Not like you need to go to school with boys anyway cause you already got a boyfriend."

I'd been drinking my sweet tea and almost chocked on it when she said that.

"Grandma," I whined.

"Uh, huh. Whatever child."

I looked back down at my game. I hated when she put me on the spot like that. When she made, what seemed like the obvious…obvious.

"I got a new book I want you to read," she said out of nowhere, bringing me back to reality.

"Oh, yeah? What is it?"

I heard a low squeak from the door to the oven being opened. I knew she was checking on the chicken she was baking. After flipping the boneless chicken breasts around a little, she returned to her seat.

"It's called *Devine Alignment*, by this guy named SQuire Rushnell. He talk about how the things we see as coincidences, is really a part of God's divine alignment. He call 'em Godwinks. He have a lot of stories in there from real people, who talk about the things that happened to them and how God played a major role in linin' things up."

I cocked my head to the side as I listened to her. I sort of understood, but not really. She must have sensed this because she went on to clarify.

"Okay. Say it's somethin' as simple as, you planned to go to the store one day and for some reason, you had to wait until the next day. I don't know, maybe, your car wouldn't start. Then, you find out somebody robbed the store and killed somebody, the day you was supposed to go. Normally, we would probably see that as a coincidence or maybe it was just luck, but it was a Godwink. She smiled saying, "God set that up in a way to keep you out of harm's way."

"Ooooh," I said, finally getting it.

"Yep," she said as she went to check on the food.

"Think about how you here with me right now," she added.

She continued talking, but that had just triggered some thoughts in my mind. I thought about me being with Ms. Gwen and how I'd eventually been led to my grandmother. What I was really thinking about was what led me to Ms. Gwen. The incident at the motel. If that man hadn't tried to...rape me, I wouldn't have gone to the fish place that night.

I hadn't told my grandmother that part. I don't know why. I wanted to, though. I mean, I'd told her everything else. Why leave that part out? Why keep it trapped inside my heart where it bothered me?

"Grandma."

"Yeah, baby," she answered with her back turned to me.

"I need to talk to you about something."

She quickly turned around and made her way back to her seat.

"What is it?"

Her forehead had wrinkled up. I could see that she was really concerned with what I had to say. I tried to act as if it was nothing.

"I mean, it's not that serious, I just thought about something when you were telling me about the book."

It seemed like she only became more concerned.

"Well, what is it, baby?"

I took a deep breath and told her every detail about my stay at the motel. Before I finished the story about me breaking down in the fish restaurant, she was sitting next to me, holding me in her arms.

"And," I sniffled, wiping away a few tears that had fallen, "That's how I ran into Ms. Gwen."

"Aww, poor baby," she said, consoling me. "Jesus. You done been through more in your short life than any child should have too."

She kissed me on my forehead and said, "But you see how that scripture stuck with you? God always provide an escape and it truly is a fact that He will never leave you."

She held on to me until I assured her that I was alright.

"Um, um, um," she shook her head as she removed the baked chicken from the oven, placing it on the top of the stove. "I'm so sorry that happened to you."

"I still can't believe I was actually thinking about doing that. Just for a place to stay and food to eat. I even started talking to myself."

I quickly say, "In my head, of course."

She chuckled and said, "My momma used to always say it's alright to talk to yourself, just as long as you don't answer yourself. But I say, it's alright to answer yourself, as long as you don't argue with yourself."

We both laughed. I needed a laugh. I felt so much better confiding in her. After we finally stopped laughing and making jokes about arguing with yourself, my grandmother came to sit back down.

"But on a serious note. Sometimes people do things they believe is right when they desperate. Trust me when I tell you," she turned to me with an assuring look on her face, "I know. The devil love to play off your desperation. Some of these people out here, who think they success is a good thing, don't even realize how the devil will bless you, just to bind you. They think it's a blessin' until they life start goin' down.

But I thank God you didn't do it and I wouldn't of judged or looked at you no different if you had."

I smiled. I loved her. I loved that she listened. Even more, I loved that I could talk to her and not feel like less of a person.

Suddenly, the phone rang, ending our conversation. Since the cordless phone was closest to me, I grabbed it off of the receiver, hanging on the wall. I looked at the caller ID and giggled a little.

"I should have known."

"Who that," my grandmother asked.

I put the phone on speaker, so she could hear the caller.

"Hello?"

"What's for dinner," James asked.

I shook my head, smiling.

My grandmother chuckled, saying, "That boy a mess."

"I don't see why you even ask," I said. "You know you're going to eat whatever it is anyway."

He laughed, "Yeah, you right."

"Then again," I add, "I don't even see why you called. Just come on over Steve Urkel."

My grandmother and I burst out laughing.

"Hey, I'll be Steve Urkel if you be my Laura."

He snickered.

I smacked my teeth and said, "Boy, come on," as if I'm irritated and hung up the phone. Then, I snuck off to the bathroom, to make sure I looked alright before he came.

Chapter 33

I was standing at the podium, dressed in my maroon cap and gown. I could hardly believe it. Valedictorian of my school. I knew there would be a lot of people there, but I didn't expect it to be so many. I had already been told to prepare a speech of no less than 15 minutes. That was why I purposely wore my very short, black heels today.

Something other than trying to prevent my feet from hurting was bothering me. I'd prepared a speech, but, all of a sudden, I got a nervous feeling in my stomach and I wasn't so sure I wanted to use the opening introduction I'd already prepared.

I looked out into the huge crowd. I knew a lot of the people in attendance were probably shocked that a black girl like me, in such a prestigious school, where it's 98% white, was standing before them today. I also knew they were staring at my name on the program wondering if my momma had in fact, named me after a Jeep. Maybe they wrote it off as something typical for a black girl. I don't know. Either way, I was trying to think of what to say. Before I knew it, I started talking.

"Okay, so, my name is not pronounced Ro-dee-o, it's Ro-day-o. Like, Rodeo Drive. Unfortunately, that's the street my mother was prostituting on when she got pregnant with me."

I blurted it out without thinking of how the crowd would react. To my surprise, most, if not all of them, laughed. I didn't know whether they were laughing with me or at me, but the laughter helped my nervousness subside. I went on to give them a short visual of where I had been versus where I was now. Of course, I mentioned my daddy, Thomas Donovan. I wouldn't be the young lady I am today if it weren't for him.

I definitely planned on going to college and become something successful. Marry. Have kids. Live a comfortable life. Why not? My faith was so much stronger than it had been before. Daddy always said the trials you go through are just a test of your faith. Some things are meant to happen to make you stronger and depend on God even more.

Before ending my speech, I'd given my fellow classmates a few words of encouragement. Making sure to tell them to always seek direction from God, especially when you're going through tough times. I finished it with the scripture in Philippians 4:13, "I can do all things through Christ who strengthens me," because I wouldn't be where I am today without His mercy, His grace, and His love.

Wow. I was officially a graduate. After my speech, I'd surprisingly received a standing ovation. Honestly, I did not expect that. Then again, I hadn't expected a lot of things to happen in my life. After all the graduates were released, I went outside where I found my grandmother and James, waiting for me with cards and balloons.

"Ooooh, I'm so proud of my baby," my grandmother exclaimed as she hugged me tightly, rocking from side to side. I knew she wouldn't come here without wearing her Sunday best. She had on a colorful, flower print dress with a stylish, pink hat that almost knocked me in the head. Of course, her short heels were pink. Grandmother always made sure she was matching from head to toe.

"Ooooh, I'm so proud of my baby too."

We all burst out laughing as James imitated my grandmother.

"Hush boy," she said as she playfully waved him off.

"Thank you, Grandmother. James, I'm so glad you made it. I thought you had duty."

He looked at me as if saying, really?

"Now you know I couldn't miss my best friend's graduation."

I blushed a little as he hugged me.

"And check you out. Looking all spiffed up."

I took a step back and looked at him as he posed like he was modeling. Then, he popped the dark blue suspenders attached to his navy blue, dress pants. He wore a light blue and white, pin-striped shirt with some blue dress shoes to match.

He laughed and said, "Oh yeah, I can do it big when I want to. But wait a minute. Did you say that's the street yo' momma was prostituting on?"

He burst out laughing.

"I had to laugh at that one," he added.

I laughed at James as he talked about the way the old lady next to him reacted when I said that. He was so funny.

"Anyway," my grandmother cut in, "Y'all can flirt another time. I'm ready to go eat."

"Grandma," I whined from embarrassment.

"Whatever child. Let's go. I'm hungry."

I was explaining how nervous I'd been before giving my speech as we walked to James' car. Suddenly, I heard someone yell, "Ms. Rodeo Turner?"

We all turned to see some skinny, but professional looking white man, jogging towards us. He stopped within a few feet of us. Then, he held out his hand for me to shake it.

He smiled a friendly smile and said, "Hello Ms. Turner. My name is Brent Williamson."

I eyed his black, business suit. He looked really young. His haircut was short and blonde. He made me think of Zach Morris from *Saved by the Bell*. I didn't know who he was, but I thought maybe he was a college recruiter. So, I put a smile on my face and said, "Hello Mr. Williamson."

He eyed me for a moment in an admiring way. Then, he said, "My, Thomas always said you'd turn out to be an extraordinary young lady."

What? Was he talking about my daddy?

As if answering my unasked question, he said, "Yes, I'm referring to your father, Mr. Thomas Donovan."

I didn't know why, who or what questions to ask at that moment. I hadn't met anyone who knew my daddy and up until this point, I never thought I'd hear anyone else say his name besides me. He glanced at my grandmother and James, whom, for a moment, I'd forgotten was there.

"Rodeo, could I have a word with you, in private, please."

I don't know why, but I glanced toward my grandmother, as if seeking her approval.

"Go ahead and talk to the man, baby," she said. "We'll be in the car. Come on, James."

Mr. Williamson and I walked a few feet away from the car.

"Rodeo. My father had been your father's lawyer for many, many years. I met him numerous times over the years. Mainly, from working with my father in the business. You know, learning the ins and outs of...sorry," he laughed a little, "I'm rambling."

He quickly put on a serious face and said, "I've desperately been trying to get in touch with you for quite some time now. I don't mean to steal you away from everything, but I really need you to come back to the office with me. I have

some important things I'd like to discuss with you about Mr.
Donovan."

My grandmother checked out almost everything Mr.
Williamson had, making sure he was who he said he was.
Before she and James finally left, I gave her all of my
belongings to take home. I was glad I'd decided to put on my
black, pencil skirt with a nice, black, short-sleeved blouse. My
hair, which was pressed down on both sides, was now in my
famous ponytail. I always tried to make sure I had a hair tie
handy.

As Mr. Williamson and I pulled into the plaza of that
familiar mall, almost every memory I'd had there came back
all at once. I looked towards the Baskin and Robbins ice cream
shop. Still busy as ever. We stepped into the office I'd come to
with daddy all those years ago. It felt weird. I guess it was just
the point of being there now.

After we entered his office, I sat on a plush, green
chair, watching Mr. Williamson. He shuffled through some
papers on his messy, but polished, brown desk.

"I apologize. It's just been so much going on."

I sure was getting nervous. Not a scary nervous. Just ready to find out what was going on. I told myself to calm down and breathe.

"Aha."

He smiled, holding up a manila folder. I assumed that was what he was looking for. He walked around his desk, positioning himself next to me.

"Rodeo, what I have here are some documents I need to go over with you, and have you sign. I need to..."

I cut him off, "Wait. What documents?"

"Oh, my apologies. It's Thomas' will."

His will? Now, I'm really nervous.

He smiled and said, "I'm sorry. I know this is all out of nowhere but let me give you some background on everything that's happened since your father's death."

He got up and walked over to a mini bar, grabbed a small, clear glass and poured him a clear drink. I was sure that wasn't water. He lifted it to his mouth to drink, but then, he paused and said, "I'm sorry, do you mind?"

I shook my head, "No."

He took a few swallows of his drink. Then, he strolled over to a big window which went from the floor to the ceiling. He rested against the wall and stared out of the window before he spoke.

"My father had been handling Mr. Donovan's business, legal matters, you name it, since before I was born. In addition to that, they'd become friends, so I'm almost positive Mr. Donovan must have spoken to my father on a personal level as well."

He glanced at me over his shoulder and asked, "Do you remember Richie?"

At first, I frowned. I thought he must have been crazy to ask such a thing. But then, I had to remind myself that he didn't know Richie was someone I could never forget. I softened my face and nodded my head, "Yes."

He looked out of the window again.

"After Mr. Donovan passed away, it had been concluded that he'd died while sleeping, from a heart attack. Well," he took a drink, "Richie took his inheritance and moved out of the house. He didn't even bother to put it up for sale. He just…left. No one knew where he was, so the state took any property which was left behind."

He took a drink. Then, shifted from one leg to the other before he continued.

"About two years ago, someone bought your father's house. One day, the owner decides he wants to remodel the master bedroom and what do they find tucked away in a vent?"

He studied me like I was supposed to know the answer. Then, he squinted his eyes and said, "A video camera and a manila envelope."

I shook my head, confused.

A video camera? Why was it there? What...was on it?

He took a drink. The suspense of this story was killing me. I wish he would finish the darn drink already or at least put it down.

"Wha-what was on it," I asked reluctantly. Almost afraid to hear the answer.

Mr. Williamson looked down at his drink and bit his bottom lip. I could hear the sorrow in his voice as he said, "The envelope had his original will in it and the video..."

He didn't take a drink, but I saw his pointy Adam's apple move as he swallowed hard.

"The video showed Richie...it showed Richie holding a pillow over Mr. Donovan's face. In the will, he'd noted that he secretly installed it...just in case."

Just in case? Just in case? Did he know that Richie might try to do something to him?

I felt myself getting angry. Not at Mr. Williamson, but at the fact that my daddy let Richie stay there and it was obvious he feared for his life. I mean, that's what I get out of this.

I looked at Mr. Williamson. I could see the sympathy on his face.

"I'm sorry," he said. "I know you didn't know."

He placed his drink on the table as he sat down in his chair.

He ran his fingers through his hair and said, "I attended the funeral with my dad. I don't remember seeing you there, though."

"That's because I wasn't there," I said while staring at the cream carpet. "I didn't know where it was. I didn't know," my voice cracked, "Anything."

"Well," he sighed, "The information about where he was buried is in the will also. It's at Rosemont Cemetery. Not too far from here."

I didn't bother to look up. I didn't know where Rosemont Cemetery was but...

Rosemont...Rose...Ms. Rose.

My head snapped up.

"Ms. Rose," I said quickly. "Where is she?"

"Oh, yes. Ms. Rose. Well..."

I didn't like the way that "well" sounded.

He exhaled loudly.

"I'd been trying to locate Ms. Rose for just as long as I'd been trying to find you. I'd finally tracked down her sister in Ohio, about six months ago. She told me Rose had been living in a nursing home ever since Thomas had died. But," his voice went lower, "Her sister told me that she'd just passed away a month before. She said she was never the same after he died."

Poor Ms. Rose. I know she loved my daddy. I know he loved her. At least, it seemed like it. My heart hurt for them both. Especially for daddy.

"Rodeo."

I looked up.

"If there's one thing I knew for sure, it's that Mr. Donovan loved you."

I felt my face soften. I hadn't realized I'd been wearing a frown since he told me about the video.

Richie. That devil.

I know you're supposed to love and forgive one another, but boy, oh boy, it's so hard to do that with some people.

I hope they get him for this. Wait a minute.

"What happened to Richie?"

"Well," he smirked, "After everything had been taken to the police, they searched for Richie for a whole year. They finally found him in California. He was with Ms. Tiffany Logan."

I was confused.

"Who?"

"The secretary working for my dad at the time. The one who helped Richie alter the documents. She tampered with his will and altered it to make it seem as if Richie had gotten everything and you had gotten nothing. Altering those documents and attempting to pass them off as legitimate is a 1st degree felony offense. She received the maximum amount of 10 years in prison. She also has to pay a fine of $5,000. And Richie, he was sentenced to life without the possibility of parole."

He took a sip of his drink and added, "Good for him he wasn't in Texas or he would have been fried."

"Yes," I whispered. "He deserves to sit and think."

"Anyway," he clasped his hands together. "Everyone has gotten what they deserve except you. So," he grinned. "Let's get down to business."

When I closed the door to the office, I'd been smiling so hard my jaws were now hurting. I couldn't help it. I wanted to jump up and down for joy. I reached inside the manila envelope and pulled out the paper on top. I read it again just to make sure I'd seen it right. $1,000,000. I'd inherited 1 million dollars.

Wow. I was speechless when Mr. Williamson told me that. I looked over towards the blue BMW parked in the parking lot. The same car that helped me when I was learning my ABC's. Then, I looked at the keys in my hand and smiled. My daddy had left me his car too. My mind was racing with so much happiness and amazement. I wanted to thank my daddy. I wanted to tell him how much he meant to me. I knew there was one way I could do that.

I turned left at the rectangular shaped, stone sign Mr. Williamson told me to look for. I knew I was at the right place when I saw the bold, black letters on it, which read: **ROSEMONT CEMETERY**. I parked in the huge, empty lot. I sat there for a moment. It felt like thousands of butterflies were in the pit of my stomach, moving around, all at once. I took a deep breath and got out of the car.

I searched the area before walking through the cemetery. There was no one there at all. Well, at least, no one who was alive. The bright sun, blue sky, and green grass sort of helped to brighten the place, considering the circumstances.

Still, I was glad it was day time because this could have easily been a horror movie.

I scanned the tombstones carefully, reading the names of others who'd passed away. Some had fresh or old flowers, and some had nothing. Some even had little cars or action figures, letting me know there was a child there.

Finally, right in the middle of maybe, 300 graves, I saw his. I slowly sat down in front of it, with my legs crossed, as I read the tombstone.

THOMAS EARL DONOVAN

12/22/1938-01/12/2009

"Hi daddy. My Dave."

I smiled weakly.

"That's what I used to call you sometimes, but you didn't know it."

I picked at the grass while I tried to think of what to say.

"I wanted to thank you for the money and the car. Even though, I'd much rather have you."

I sighed. I really didn't know what to say. I studied his tombstone. Just a name and dates. I knew Richie must have handled everything. It angered me to see how much effort Richie put into everything. He was more than just a man who was born and died. Who was…killed.

Why Richie? Why did you...

I let out a frustrated moan and pounded my fists on the ground. No matter how hard I tried to hold back, the tears forced themselves out of my eyes.

"Daddy, why did you..."

My voice was louder than I'd intended it to be. I tried to lower it, but I couldn't.

"Why'd you let Richie stay? You *knew* he was up to no good. You *knew* you couldn't trust him. Why Daddy? Why'd you let him stay?"

I cried, staring at the tombstone like I was waiting for him to respond. Then, I buried my face in my hands and cried like a baby.

"You don't know what I've been through," I said through sniffles.

"I really needed you to be here with me daddy. I mean, why would God bring you in my life just to take you out of it? I don't understand. I just don't."

Suddenly, I thought about one of those Proverbs my daddy taught me.

Trust in the Lord with all your heart, and do not lean unto your own understanding. Proverbs 3:5.

But I wanted to understand. I mean, it wasn't fair. How come it seemed like the people you wanted to keep in your life, were always the ones taken away from you? I just wanted to know why?

"It's just not fair daddy. I didn't even get to come to your funeral."

After a few minutes, I finally began to calm down. I had to anyway. I'd developed a headache from all that crying. Not to mention, the mess I'd made on my clothes from snot and tears. Still, it was a much, needed cry. I looked at his tombstone as if I was talking to him directly.

"I know you don't want me to be sad daddy. I just miss you, that's all."

I smiled and added the fact that, "I know you miss me too daddy."

I stood up and kissed the top of his tombstone. Then, I dusted any leaves and grass from my skirt.

"Even though, I want you here, I'm going to try my best to stop crying and feeling bad because I know you wanted to be here just as much."

As I turned to leave, the last name on the tombstone next to his caught my eye. I knelt down to read it.

Marion Lee Donovan

05/23/1942-10/24/1990

Beloved wife and mother

We love you

I smiled warmly.

"It's nice to meet you Mrs. Donovan."

I leaned in and kissed the top of her tombstone. Before leaving, I glanced back towards my daddy's.

"I'm glad you're happy daddy. Thank you for everything. I love you."

When I got back to my car, I sat there for a moment. I smiled at the thought of that. *My car.* I couldn't wait to tell my grandmother and James about everything. I reached for the automatic start button, but quickly stopped myself. I began to think about how much my life had changed so much in the last two hours. Perhaps, I should say, how much it's changed over all the years of my life.

I'd been born to a mother who was in no shape to raise a child. She was killed, but then, a man named Thomas Donovan found me. Or should I say, I found him. Although, he was taken away from me and I had to survive the best way I could, it had all been a part of the broken road I had to travel. It had all been a part of God's plan. Not my plan or anyone else's. I'd gotten an inheritance that I surely wasn't expecting, as well as, a car. What a great graduation gift. Yes, it came from my daddy, but without God, I wouldn't have had any of it. Most of all, I wouldn't have had daddy.

I mean, God had always been there in every part of my life. The good and the bad. I would never have wished for my mother to get killed, but she did and if she hadn't, I wouldn't have stumbled upon my daddy's train. If he hadn't gotten killed, I wouldn't have moved with Katina. I wouldn't have met James. I wouldn't have met that little girl at Wendy's who gave me the idea of pawning my jewelry. I wouldn't have stayed in that hotel. I wouldn't have gone to that fish place where I met Ms. Gwen. And without Ms. Gwen, I wouldn't have found my grandmother. I had to thank Him.

I gazed out of the window towards the sky.

"God. I thank you. For everything. I mean, words can't express it, but I am truly thankful and grateful. I know there were times when, when I may have doubted you and I'm so sorry for that. Everything that has happened to me proves that you are real. I *know* You are. Not only can I feel it, but I can see it."

My eyes began to water, and a single tear fell from the corner of my eye. I wiped the right side of my face and cleared my throat.

"I know I'm not perfect and I know I won't always make the right decisions, but God, please, just keep me humbled. And don't let my heart be changed. I mean, help me to know what decisions to make with this money and everything in my life. Guide me in the way you want me to go and not the way I want to go. I trust you. I really do. Thank you for everything, but most of all, thank you for loving me so much. In Jesus name I pray. Amen."

Even though, I believe my daddy heard me talking to him, I really wished he could have talked back to me. I shook the thoughts forming in my head away and put on my seatbelt. As I did, the smell of the car hit me for the first time. I could smell my daddy. I swallowed hard. I didn't want to have another crying episode. So, just to keep my mind off things, I decided I'd turn on the radio for the ride back.

As I turned the car on, the tunes from the CD, which had already been playing, filled the car. I listened to Sam Cooke sing the words, "But I do know that I love you, and I know that if you love me too, what a wonderful world this would be." I knew it was daddy. Immediately, my heart was filled with joy. No tears. Just a calming peace.

"Thank you God, for the peace which surpasses all understanding."

I reclined my seat, laid back and listened to the rest of the song.

Prologue

My first two years of college went by so fast. I'd applied to over 15 schools and 13 out of those were ready to welcome me with open arms. After much consideration, I choose to go to Spelman College instead. Besides, really liking the school and everything that they stand for, I wanted to stay close to my grandmother and perhaps, James attending Morehouse College, which was just a short distance away, may have had a little to do with my decision.

He and I had gotten even closer over the summer after graduation. During our first year in college, we made it official, as far as, boyfriend and girlfriend goes. Things were going great. Grandmother was doing well. I wanted to buy her a new house, but she didn't want to move, so we fixed up her house just the way she wanted it. Thanks to Mr. Williamson, managing my finances, I made sure she didn't have to worry about money ever again.

I'd blossomed more and more into a person I never could have imagined I'd be. Life was good. I was happy. Of course, the inheritance helped make things better too. Still, I would not be where I am today if it weren't for God and for that, I give Him all the glory. Thank you.

A Word from The Author

Yes. *Rodeo* is a fictional story. And no. Not everyone stumbles upon a rich and caring person every day. Especially, one who is willing to adopt them, but blessings come in many forms. There are many Rodeo's, boys and girls, who are dealing with everyday issues, just like the ones presented in this book.

I'd like to point out that this book was not only intended for the young, but the old as well. It doesn't matter if you come from the richest family or the poorest, if a person feels as though no one loves them, there will always be an emptiness inside of them. That emptiness will affect their lives, as well as, the many relationships they will encounter in life. Just as Rodeo found out God had a plan for her life, He also has a plan for yours.

"For I know the plans I have for you," declares the Lord, "Plans to make you prosper and not to harm you, plans to give you hope and a future" –Jeremiah 29:11 NIV

About the Author

Jaketa A. McClure, originally born and raised in Atlanta, Georgia, currently lives in Benton, Arkansas with her three kids. She enjoys reading, writing, watching movies, and spending time with her family. Jaketa is available on Facebook and Instagram. Find out more news, information, and ways to contact Jaketa, by going to: www.gigpublishing.com.